MURDER

with Pictures

▲

MURDER
with Pictures

GEORGE HARMON COXE

PERENNIAL LIBRARY
Harper & Row, Publishers
New York, Cambridge, Hagerstown, Philadelphia, San Francisco
London, Mexico City, São Paulo, Sydney

MURDER WITH PICTURES. Copyright 1935 by George Harmon Coxe. All rights reserved. Printed in the United States of America. No part of this book may be used or reproduced in any manner whatsoever without written permission except in the case of brief quotations embodied in critical articles and reviews. For information address Harper & Row, Publishers, Inc., 10 East 53rd Street, New York, N.Y. 10022. Published simultaneously in Canada by Fitzhenry & Whiteside Limited, Toronto.

First PERENNIAL LIBRARY edition published 1981.

ISBN: 0-06-080527-7

81 82 83 84 10 9 8 7 6 5 4 3 2 1

TO
MY MOTHER

MURDER
with Pictures

▲

Chapter 1

$\mathcal{F}$OLEY, THE RED-FACED, uniformed deputy on duty in the hall, peeked through one of the glass ovals inset in the leather-covered courtroom doors and said:

"Hey, the jury's comin' out!"

A concentrated and irritable sigh from the group of news-photographers lounging in the hall greeted the announcement. There was an intangible flurry of movement, a casual shifting of stances.

Brant, of the *News,* sighed wearily. "Boy, it's about time."

Tobacco smoke, the residue of a four-hour harvest from an apparently inexhaustible supply of cigarettes, choked the air with a stale stuffy smell and hung suspended in a hazy, pale-blue blanket that shrouded the arched ceiling. Cigarette butts, matches, crumpled paper holders littered the ash-strewn floor. Cameras and bulky black plate-cases were stacked in a row along one wall.

3

Foley said: "It won't be long now," and kept his eye glued to the little glass window.

Brant sighed again.

Coughlin and Weinstock, who had been matching nickels for the past hour, continued, unimpressed.

"I'll bet he gets it," Kesler said. He looked around as though waiting for a challenge. "Who wants to bet Girard ain't guilty?"

"Girard's waiting to hear it," Foley announced.

Coughlin said: "That's four bits you're in me. A buck or nothing." Weinstock nodded silently and flipped his coin. Coughlin said: "Nuts!" and fished a crumpled bill from his pocket.

"It looks like an acquittal," Foley said. "Girard is—"

He broke off in sudden alarm and jumped aside. In the next instant the swinging doors slapped outward; Purdy, of the *Evening Standard,* bucked through the opening. Without breaking his stride, Purdy called: "Not Guilty!" and pounded down the marble floor in his race for a telephone.

Foley growled: "Hey, you! Quiet!" Then the rest of the reporters swarmed out of the courtroom and he was forgotten.

The photographers reached for their cameras and plate-cases and swung into action. In a body, they started down the hall. Some continued to the main entrance; others dropped out and, stationing themselves at strategic intervals along the walls, began to screw flash-bulbs into synchronized flash-guns. Kent Murdock of the *Courier-Herald* turned to Jorgens, who was covering with him.

"Stay here in the hall, Johnny. When you get one

come out. I'll be on the steps and you'll probably have to take my stuff in."

The courtroom crowd began to filter through the hall and down the wide stone steps of the main entrance. Most of them dispersed matter-of-factly when they reached the sidewalk. A few idled expectantly at the curb or on the steps, eventually collected in clusters of threes and fours and became separate forums of argumentation. A pair of ragged, smutty-nosed urchins strolled upon the scene. Deciding the occasion looked promising, they sat down on the bottom step.

A quartet of middle-aged women, apparently searching for any sort of thrill in lieu of housework, drew back against the wall of the recessed entrance, where they chattered in high, staccato voices and laughed with spasmodic abruptness. The burly, uniformed policeman stationed at the doorway stepped towards them and delivered an ultimatum. The quartet exchanged indignant glances. They went down the steps muttering and stood in front of the row of cigarette-smoking men who lined the curb.

A sleek black sedan, with some discreet chromium here and there, slid into the No Parking space opposite the entrance. Murdock, one of the five photographers flanking the steps, eyed the car and license number speculatively, his dark eyes narrowing. He looked back at the policeman in the doorway; then he stepped to the sidewalk, crossing to a Checker taxi, the first in a line of three cabs waiting at the curb.

"You're hired," he told the driver. "Wait for me."

The driver looked up from his newspaper, nodded indolently, and resumed his reading. Murdock went back

to his place on the steps. A few seconds later the policeman called:

"Okay, boys. Here they come."

Cameras swung up. Somebody cautioned: "Don't let
anybody spoil it now, Mac!"

The policeman winked and moved out on the broad
top step. Four of the photographers who had waited inside barged through the doorway in a mad dash. They
wheeled abruptly, lifted their cameras. An instant later
Mark Redfield and Nate Girard stepped from the gloom
of the hall into the flat, pale shadows of late afternoon.

A half-dozen of the more curious spectators—those with
the hem-of-your-garment complex—had remained in
waiting for their prey and now tagged closely behind.
Before they could surround Redfield and Girard the
policeman said: "Stand back, now!" and stepped in front
of them, arms outstretched, blocking them off.

"Hold it, Mark!"

Redfield, a big-bodied man with a florid face, a wing
collar and a made-to-order courtroom presence, searched
the faces of the photographers, trying to locate the voice.
Then he beamed and drew himself up in a definite pose.
Girard hesitated momentarily, smoldering dark eyes
sweeping the steps. He was a well-built man, tall and with
the heaviness of figure that comes with increasing matu-
rity rather than easy living. His rugged face was expressionless, his lips flat under his close-cropped mustache
during that instant he stood poised there. Then his brows
pulled into a frown and he started down the steps.
Redfield's pose dissolved and his jaw dropped. Discon-
certed, he had to hurry to catch Girard.

Murdock watched the scene through the metal rim of his finder, a faint sardonic smile wrinkling the corners of his eyes. Half-way down the steps Redfield drew even with Girard. Murdock pressed the shutter-release. Automatically reversing his plate-holder, he backed to the sidewalk, keeping pace with the two men as they crossed to the car which now stood with door open.

He took his second picture when Girard, again in the lead, put his foot on the running board and stooped to enter the tonneau. The rest of the photographers crowded around the sedan while Redfield slammed the door; one fellow thrust his camera through the lowered window and chanced a picture with a flash-bulb. Murdock was no longer interested. He pushed quickly through the crowd to where Jorgens stood at the foot of the steps.

Murdock held out his exposed plate-holder. "Take this in with yours. Take my plate-case too." He took a spare plate-holder from his coat pocket, slipped it into the back of his camera. "I want to follow this up before I go in."

Redfield's sedan was angling out from the curb when Murdock reached his waiting taxi. He piled into the back seat and said: "Follow the sedan."

The taxi-driver had a comparatively easy job. The sedan moved cross-town at a moderate pace, and from then on, it was just a question of keeping close enough to get the same break with the traffic lights. Twenty minutes later the two cars drew up in front of a modern brick apartment house that boasted a doorman, a marquee, and a rubber mat which said: *Embankment Arms.*

Murdock was out of the taxi a second after Redfield and Girard stepped to the sidewalk. As they started for the bronze-framed entrance without looking around, Murdock said: "Wait a minute, Nate."

Both men wheeled. The doorman, who had followed them from the sedan, continued discreetly to the revolving doors.

Murdock lifted the camera. "How about a picture? A nice one."

Redfield grinned and Girard said: "Hello, Kent. What's the matter? Miss out down below?"

Murdock shook his head. "No. But this is a different background, and I've got more time."

Girard's mustache spread in a wry grin.

Redfield said: "Where do you want us?"

"That'll do."

Murdock pressed the shutter-release. Then, before either man could move, he added: "One more. I want to be sure." He reversed his plate-holder, changed the stop-opening of the lens. He started to lift the camera again, then checked the movement, one eyebrow cocking.

"How would it be," he asked dryly, "if you sort of looked a little relieved, or pleased, or something, Nate? You know, like a man who's just had some good news."

Girard looked at Redfield, then back at Murdock. After a moment a slow smile relieved the set expression of his mouth and jaw.

Murdock snapped his picture. "That's swell," he said, and swung his camera down. "And now that the business part is over"—he stepped towards Girard and put out his hand—"congratulations."

"Thanks." Girard shook hands firmly, but he spoke without enthusiasm. He glanced over his shoulder at

Redfield, and his brows climbed slightly, framing an expression that asked a silent question. Apparently puzzled for a moment, Redfield frowned, then nodded.

"Oh, yes," he said, speaking to Murdock. "We're having a little show up at my place tonight. Why don't you drop in?"

"I'd like to." Murdock pursed his lips. "But I may be working and—"

"What of it?" Redfield spread his hands. "You live right here in the same building, don't you? You have to come home. We'll probably still be at it when you get through. Take a look in and see, anyway."

2

LEON'S PORTABLE BAR had been set up in the balconied dining-room. The party was far enough advanced so that there was no longer any rush for service, and when Kent Murdock put down his empty glass, Leon's left hand whisked it away and the right followed with the bar rag in an automatic polishing movement that was practiced, professional.

"Another, Mr. Murdock?"

"Later, Leon."

Murdock lit a cigarette and turned his back to the bar, hooking one elbow on the rounded edge. He glanced down across the drawing-room, saw that the girl in the blue dress who had attracted him from the instant he stepped into the room was still sitting alone. His eyes hesitated in a brief moment of study as they found her, then moved on to the grand piano.

The present entertainer, a tired-looking girl with nice legs and a fair voice, was just finishing her song. Because most hands were otherwise occupied, there was little applause; apparently none was expected. The blond youth at the piano transposed in a series of soft, full chords and continued idly on another chorus when the girl sat down beside him on the bench.

Nate Girard moved into the living-room from the terrace windows on the left. He held two champagne glasses in one hand, a cigarette in the other. As he walked diagonally across to the dining-room steps, he smiled and said something to the foursome on the modernistic sofa. He came straight to the bar and Leon said:

"Two more of the same, Mr. Girard?"

"If you please, Leon." Girard put down his glasses and shook hands with Murdock. "Glad you could make it."

"Hestor here?" Murdock asked casually.

"Yes. With me. Do you mind?"

"You don't have to be that polite, Nate." Murdock's tone was sardonic. "Where would I be, minding?"

"Well—" Girard's hands moved in a suggestion of a shrug. He glanced over his shoulder. Leon had not finished with the order and he looked back at Murdock. "Not drinking?"

"I've got to work in the morning." Murdock hesitated, his dark eyes speculative; then he took Girard by the elbow and drew him to one corner of the room, letting go of the elbow as he took another half-step to face him.

He said: "I like the party, but I don't know yet who's giving it. Are we celebrating your acquittal or Redfield's fifty-thousand fee?"

Girard smiled. "Call it a co-operative affair. I'm throwing it, and Mark and Rita are furnishing the apartment. Mine is too small."

"It's an idea." Murdock nodded in amused approval. "You've got something to celebrate. It must seem good to be out."

"You'll never know how good."

"A party tonight," mused Murdock, glancing down at the end of his cigarette, "and this afternoon—"

"A cold sweat," Girard cut in grimly, "while twelve good men and true argued for four hours and finally got the best of their natural sadistic impulses to send me to the chair." Girard's mouth dipped at the corners, pulling his mustache ends with it. His voice took on an undertone of cynicism. "It wouldn't have surprised me much. Most of the newspaper men, most of the wise money, thought I'd get it."

"A lot of them did," Murdock agreed.

"The police and the District Attorney"—Girard's lips flexed in a wry grin—"still think I killed Joe Cusick."

Murdock's brows lifted. "That's their job. Somebody did and—"

"You think so too, huh?" Girard's deep-set eyes were fixed, fathomless.

"I didn't follow the trial very closely." Murdock's glance touched some remote object, and his momentary frown was thoughtful. "But I've got plenty of gall and ill-mannered curiosity," he added dryly. "I have to have in my business, and I've known you quite a while. So when I pulled you over here, I had an idea—since you've had your acquittal and can never be tried again—I might ask you for the truth."

He dropped the cigarette in a pedestal ash-tray. "And now that I've gone this far, I think I would ask except that, as I think of it, it's sort of a stupid question. There's only one answer, isn't there?"

Nate Girard did not speak at once. Murdock met his gaze with steady eyes and they stood there like that, both waiting, each sizing up the other.

Murdock was nearly as tall as Girard, with a lean flat-muscled body that was loose, yet well knit. His brows were straight above brown eyes that were sometimes like copper—only harder, sometimes dark enough to be called black. Now shadows made them black. Girard was ten years older, a few pounds heavier. A close-up revealed the muscular leanness of a man who keeps fit and does not have to worry about his waistline. The ruggedness of his rectangular face, the close-cropped mustache, the black hair, gray-streaked at the sides, gave him a distinguished look that was both handsome and intelligent.

The intangible thing common to both, and as apparent as a physical characteristic, was that each had about him a certain hardness that varied only in type; apparent because there was no shifting of eyes, no fumbling with hands or nervous reactions as the tension grew. Murdock broke it without removing his gaze.

"It's okay. Tell me to go to hell."

"Why should I?" Girard's mustache twitched. His tone seemed rather grimly amused. "That question is so hackneyed I'm used to it. I've been asked it by experts—in the District Attorney's office."

Girard paused. Murdock seemed to relax, and his eyes narrowed with his smile.

"The answer is still the same," Girard added evenly. "And if I seem bitter about this trial it's because the answer happens to be the truth. I never killed a man in my life."

"But you know who did?"

Leon's anxious voice reached the corner of the room. "Ready, Mr. Girard."

Nate Girard glanced over Murdock's shoulder. "Don't be morbid," he counseled. "This is a celebration." He slapped the side of Murdock's shoulder smartly, stepped round him, adding: "What you need is another drink."

Kent Murdock moved to the bar and told Leon he thought it was time and ordered Scotch and soda. While he waited he leaned wide-spread elbows on the imitation mahogany edge and idly surveyed Leon's innovation, which was fast becoming an institution.

The whole rig was clever. The mirror on the wall directly behind the bar was plastered with a soapy scroll-work, and on the neat shelves that bordered this display was the usual motley assortment of bottles: whiskies, gins, liqueurs. There was a length of brass rail, portable like the bar, which was made in sections so that Leon could do a made-to-measure business, like a tailor, and satisfy the demands of all comers whether the occasion demanded a kitchenette bar or a dance-hall set-up.

It was all quite authentic—except Leon's name, which should have been Gus. He was bald, short, with a balloon-tire waist and fat dimpled hands that were red, like plums.

Mark Redfield joined Murdock as he finished his inspection.

"Making out all right?"

"Yeh." Murdock turned on one elbow. "And now I know why I see so many lawyers hanging around the courthouse. It's these fifty-thousand-dollar fees."

"Sounds good, huh?" Redfield grunted disparagingly. "Maybe I'm a second Clarence Darrow, or a Max Steuer."

"You do pretty well for a city like this."

Mark Redfield spread his hands, let them flop on the bar, palms down. With his florid, big-nosed face and pompous, well-fed figure he looked more like a successful politician than a criminal lawyer. His voice, carefully nurtured for courtroom use, had a booming, confident timbre regardless of pitch. Shrewd, spectacular, an artist at innuendo and repartee, he was a showman whose color, personality, and reputation were such that many a case was half won the moment he stepped into a courtroom.

Flushed with victory, stimulated by drink, his attitude towards Murdock became fraternal, confiding. The bars were down. He forgot his pose and spoke as one insider to another, his voice thick, a bit hoarse.

"I've worked for Girard for ten years; more'n that I guess. I've made a lot of money from routine stuff. But this is the first big fee. And why? Because Girard is smart. He never was a killer." Redfield shook his head. "It's funny. Ten years in the liquor racket and never mixed in a killing. For two years now he goes around minding his own business, legitimate. And then, blooie!" Redfield blew out his breath. "I damn near missed; the toughest case I ever drew. But fifty thousand sounds big, huh? Well, I can use it, and I earned it and—"

He broke off and pushed back from the bar. "What is this," he growled, "a lecture?" He made noises in his throat. "How do you like the party?"

Murdock said he liked it and, picking up the remainder of his drink, moved to the wrought-iron balcony railing.

The piano-player was talking to one of the other entertainers. The girl in the blue dress was still in the same chair, her position unchanged. Even her attitude seemed the same: aloof, superior. She acted as if she were sulking, yet did not look the type. And she was still alone.

For a moment Murdock watched her, noticing that her gaze was fixed upon Howard Archer, who stood in one of the open windows, his arm linked with Mrs. Redfield's; then he turned and went down five steps, carpeted in green, with an exaggerated thickness.

Most of the living-room furniture was modern, either sharp-cornered or flagrantly rounded. The chair the girl had chosen, in the corner behind the piano, was, however, more conventional and so deeply cushioned he could not tell how tall she was. As he approached he saw that he had been right about her hair. Ash-blond, it escaped being straight by the merest trace of a natural wave. It was pulled back, hiding two-thirds of the ears, so that he was not sure whether it was long or just a long bob. The pale-blue dress looked soft and heavy and shiny. There was a little jacket which reminded him of a vest without buttons.

In the artificial light her skin had an outdoor, an almost dusky tan. The cheek-bones were prominent and made shadow spots; the mouth was wide, full-lipped. In spite of the good clean jaw-bone he saw that the mouth was sulky, had about it a set expression that seemed to complement the fixed and smoldering stare. She did not seem to see the people or be conscious of the group. Certainly she did not see Murdock as he stopped beside the chair.

"Hello." He bowed slightly.

"Hello." The girl did not look up; her voice was flat, disinterested.

Murdock's brows lifted. He noticed that she had nice hands. Her nails were natural.

"Can I get you a drink?"

"No, thanks."

Still the girl did not look up. This time her voice was cold, a bit sharp. The tone irritated Murdock, and a frown started to work at the corners of his eyes.

"Are you alone by choice or—"

"By choice."

This time the voice held a definite undercurrent of annoyance. The eyes did not shift their gaze.

Murdock felt the flush that tinged his lean face. His eyes narrowed slightly. There it was. He asked for it and he got it. He did not mind the answer, the implication that he was intruding and unwelcome; but he resented the tone. The brief thought of trying to laugh off his admitted embarrassment fled before this resentment. He straightened up, found his voice stiff, sardonic, when he spoke.

"Sorry. I shouldn't have made the mistake. But, you see, I came late. I thought it was one of those parties where you can speak to anyone and at least be sure of a reasonable courtesy."

The girl's eyes, sullen, then uncertain, came up and caught his. He saw that they were darker than her dress, a smoky blue. And there was something sharp and clean and honest in her face which the make-up could not hide. Then he turned and moved towards the terrace windows.

Howard Archer spoke and stepped aside to let Murdock pass. Rita Redfield offered her hand. Murdock held it and said: "Mark did a swell job today."

"It's about time. What we need is bigger and better crime waves."

Archer, tall and blond above his gleaming shirt-front, looking like something out of a polite drawing-room movie, touched his pointed mustache with a thumb-nail and said: "It's the Shylock in her," in a languid drawl.

Rita Redfield was beautiful, dark, and society—or formerly so. Dressed in a brown velvet gown that molded a full, high-breasted figure and set off her well-modeled, if arrogant, neck and shoulders, she was a showy brunette, fifteen years younger than her husband. Beautiful in a superficial, jaded way, her make-up was the work of an expert and enhanced her beauty without making any pretense of naturalness or disguising the selfish mouth, the haughty lift of the trim brows.

Murdock smiled, turned his head. The girl in the blue dress had returned her stare to Archer, but as Murdock watched, the eyes shifted to meet his. The nod he gave her was like his smile: good-humored now, but with a touch of mockery. He let go of Rita Redfield's hand and moved out to the terrace.

The night was cool, yet soft. There was no moon, but countless stars combated the darkness and made it blue instead of black. Below, the river was wide and shiny black, splashed here and there with a sheen from the light-studded arcs of Harvard and Longfellow bridges, the huge electric clock on the other bank.

Murdock moved slowly down the length of the terrace, working his way through a confusion of wicker chairs and having a hard time identifying their temporary occupants. He found Nate Girard leaning against the railing at the far end. There was a woman at his side. They were both looking into the night so that, with her dark dress, the only discernible feature was her blond bobbed hair. Moving to the rail, Murdock leaned there beside her.

"Hello, Hestor."

"Oh, hello." There was no welcome or interest in the voice.

Girard turned. "I told Hestor you were here."

Murdock did not answer. He took out his cigarette-case, offered it to the woman, who refused. Girard was smoking a cigar. Murdock lit his cigarette, inhaled. An awkward silence closed in and he let his thoughts idle for a minute or so as he smoked; finally he jerked them back to the focusing-point he had decided upon.

He did not feel like arguing. Neither did he intend to drift like this indefinitely. His thoughts shot off on a tangent and touched briefly the girl in the blue dress. Something about her attracted him; he felt this in spite of his irritation at her manner, regretted somehow his stiff, churlish speech.

He forced himself to concentrate on Hestor again. She'd probably argue about going with him; before he got through she'd lose her temper. It would be difficult, he knew that. Seeing her here with Girard was what had made up his mind to try again. Perhaps she would be more inclined to agree this time. Anyway—

He said: "Could I borrow my wife for a while?"

Girard laughed softly. "Why—certainly."

"I'll bring her back," Murdock added dryly.

Hestor Murdock turned towards her husband, but he could not read the expression in her face, which in this light was just a flesh-colored oval. He thought she was going to speak, but she remained silent until Girard withdrew; then she said, indifferently: "Is it a game?" with an accent obviously cultivated.

Murdock took her by the arm. "I want to talk to you."

"All right." Then, as he drew her towards the nearest window, her voice showed pique. "Can't you talk here?"

"No."

"Well, where, then?"

"Downstairs. In my apartment."

Murdock kept the pressure on her elbow and they stepped into the living-room. She moved more readily there until they reached the entrance foyer. Here she stopped short, faced him.

"If you think I'm going down there to talk about divorce—"

"Listen." Murdock's lean face was sombre, his eyes humid. "I want to talk to you, and I'm not going to do it here." He glanced at his strap-watch. The hands showed two-twenty and he said: "This party is good for a couple hours. You won't miss anything. Fifteen minutes or so is not going to spoil your night, is it? Or am I unreasonable to suppose—"

"Oh, all right." Hestor Murdock flashed a look of impatient exasperation, whirled away from him. Murdock stepped in front of her and opened the door.

3

MURDOCK'S APARTMENT, AN inexpensive, two-room kitchenette-and-bath suite, was on the second floor, rear. Hestor stopped just inside the door as Murdock closed it, and it was apparent that her impatience had not lessened as she spoke.

"Well?"

Murdock achieved a grin, made an effort to be pleasant. "Relax," he said. "I can't talk to you this way. How about a drink?"

"I've been drinking champagne. I'll wait."

Murdock's brows lifted; then suddenly the grin broadened and it paid dividends in the form of a grudging smile from Hestor. She shrugged, moved across the room to the worn, comfortable-looking divan, and sat down.

"All right," she continued. "I'm relaxed—or I will be when you give me a cigarette."

Murdock held a light for her, blew out the flame, and bent the paper match between his thumb and first two fingers. He walked across the room, wheeled, returned to the divan, and stood there spread-legged, looking down at his wife.

Hestor Murdock, née Schultz, came from a coal-mining town in Pennsylvania. By virtue of a figure which would have done for a torso by Gaudier, by practice in dancing, plus a fair voice, she had worked herself up through burlesque to the front row of the chorus. It was there that Murdock had first seen her. He realized she had changed but little since then.

Thirty, he thought. Plump, but upon close inspection, plump in the right places. And the gown, black and of a material that was something like sequins only finer—a sort of metallic cloth—was typical, somehow. Showy. Like Rita Redfield. The difference was that Rita's showiness was on a higher plane because she was born that way and did not have to work her way up from small-town squalor.

Hestor's hair was yellow-blond, real yellow; and it had been waved so that it seemed to stick sleekly to her head. But it was frowsy in the morning; he remembered that. The rouge, the lipstick could not hide the sullen, sensuous character of her face, the droop of her lips. And she was smart, with the smartness of a woman who had been around in the world and had suffered somewhat from the contact. Yet it was her body that remained her chief asset. The tightness of the gown, and the way the light reflected from the metal cloth, accentuated the mounds of her breasts and reminded him that it was this body, dancing in the front row of a musical-comedy chorus, that had attracted him. He was aware of it now.

"Well?"

She broke in on his thoughts and he realized that she was watching him with a tolerant, half-amused gaze. He colored slightly, but spoke doggedly of the idea which was again foremost in his mind.

"Why not call it off? A divorce will—"

Hestor Murdock stiffened slightly. "I was enjoying myself," she said irritably and her eyes were sulky. "You pick a nice time to bring that up."

"Well—"

"I'm satisfied the way it is."

"You may not always be so well satisfied."

"It will be time enough then."

She started to get up. Murdock reached out and, without pushing, kept her from rising. He said: "Wait." She did not force the issue. Instead she settled herself again, puffed lazily at her cigarette, and watched him through the blue haze that hung between them.

To Hestor, Kent Murdock was a paradox. He was hard, yet mixed with this hardness was a certain refinement of feeling that she could not understand. He was intelligent, well educated; yet he was a newspaper photographer and he liked his job. She hated him, yet she liked him. Even now he was attractive to her. Good-looking, with a knack of wearing clothes well, he had a masculine vitality that had found a responsive chord in her from the first.

Their marriage had been a mistake. But she did not regret it. What she regretted, and she thought of this with irritation, was that she could not hold him. Not that it mattered. She was better off now, much better off. His weekly payments added to what she made with her radio program enabled her to live as she had dreamed of living in her burlesque days. And—she had told herself this before—this marriage was only an experiment; an expedient, rather.

She had known girls in the chorus who had married well, profitably. Such had been her intention—to wait until she could be sure of the financial success of such a venture. If she could have the thrill of it at the same time, so much the better. But given the security, she could find other outlets for a nature high-strung with passion. Circumstances changed her plans decisively.

When *Love Song* opened in Boston, an immediate marriage had no place in Hestor's thoughts. But when it closed on Saturday night after a week's try-out and the company disbanded, she had seized the only chance offered. Only—she smiled as she put her cigarette to her mouth—she did not seize it, she made that chance.

She had met Kent Murdock at a party after the opening performance on the preceding Monday. She liked him, and she encouraged him; during that week he had taken her out nearly every night after the performance. Yet she had no false ideas about his interest. He wanted a good time; he had sufficient money to spend. She made herself good company. But she had experienced that sort of thing before. When the show moved on, the affair would be forgotten. Only this time the show would not move on. And at the time she had her rent paid in New York for a month, and little else. The show business was in the doldrums. There were no angels, no suitable offers of marriage in sight.

She remembered that Saturday night the show closed. They'd had supper after the performance and gone on to a speak-easy. She had taken the reins from her affection, let her passion flow; she had even cried a little, she remembered. And it had been she who suggested they get married—after she was sure that the half-dozen drinks and her methods had made him forget any resolve or inhibition about her he may have had sober. . . .

His voice checked her thoughts abruptly. "I'm perfectly willing to keep on paying you—as alimony."

Hestor Murdock ground out her cigarette in an ashtray. "What," she drawled, "is the reason for the rush?"

"Rush?" Murdock scowled wrinkles into the bridge of his nose. "We've been separated over a year. I've asked you before."

"I know. But casually. Maybe you've lined up number two."

Murdock waited a moment before he answered. When he continued, his voice was level.

"There's no one else. The point is, I want to know where I stand. We made a mess of things. We both may want another chance some day."

Hestor frowned and looked away, her irritation rising again as she reflected how she could not hold him. The marriage was an expedient, yes; but with Murdock, because his virile hardness had attracted her, she had looked upon the venture with some excitement. It was to be a thrill. And into marriage she had brought a magnificent body, a well-sexed nature, and nothing at all of the give-and-take attitude. To her it was a physical, sexual thing; that and nothing more. Murdock had failed her there.

She knew that he looked with only partly concealed disdain upon her repeated demands, and she hated him for it. For the last month of their life together he had not slept with her. And there was no other woman at the time. Well—she tightened her lips and moved erect on the davenport—let him squirm. She was in no hurry. She could be free of him soon enough if it became necessary. Meanwhile she found that her married status helped her with other men. It seemed to furnish an enigmatic allure that made men more attentive.

Murdock knew he was losing his plea. He had long since accepted his part in the fiasco. He did not blame her for the failure. He had never been quite sure who had suggested the crazy idea of running off to get married in the first place. Probably he did. It did not matter now. In any case it had been an impulsive act. He regretted it and he expected to pay. But he saw no reason for continuing an arrangement that held no advantage, in his mind, for either of them. He held stubbornly to his plan.

"Why nurse it along?"

Hestor stood up, her expression bored, weary. "I've missed enough of the party already. I want to get back. Nate'll be looking for me."

Murdock did not move. He just stood there facing her, standing close to her now that she had risen. His lean face was sullen, his eyes brooding.

He said: "Out of my princely salary of ninety a week" —the voice was cynical—"you get thirty-five. That part is okay, but if you think I'm going to keep paying without getting anything for it—"

"You get your freedom, don't you?" Hestor's voice thinned out.

"No. I get the right to live alone, but—"

"That ought to be enough. It's what you wanted."

"Only partly. I've tried to be fair, to do the decent thing, to give you grounds and pay all expenses—and what does it get me? Spite."

Hestor's blue eyes blazed. "I'm entitled to something," she snapped, and her accent slipped back to the chorus.

"I don't want a compromise."

"All right." Hestor hesitated, measured him with her eyes, and one penciled brow arched as she studied him. "If you want to pay, I'll give you your divorce."

Murdock waited, silent, afraid to accept a solution so simple.

"You expect to pay, don't you?" Hestor pressed.

"Certainly. I told you I'd keep on—"

"You'll do better than that. Suppose you lose your job? I'm not taking any chances. But I'll sell you the divorce. For ten thousand in cash we'll forget about the alimony and—"

"I haven't got that much, and you know it."

"Get it, then. It ought to be a bargain."

"It is," Murdock said, and his voice was sharp with anger and exasperation. "But how—"

"Oh, it is?" Hestor smiled at him, but her eyes were bright and glaring. "Then either get it or let it ride, and you'll pay anyway. Mark Redfield drew the contract, and it ought to be good. I don't need the money, but I like getting it, because"—her voice rose—"it evens up for what you didn't give me when I married you."

Murdock's jaws went white at the corners, and his lips drew tight. "Don't be cheap."

"Cheap?" Hestor was white and shaking and her accent

was somewhere between the coal mines and burlesque. "You go to hell!" She seemed to choke on the sentence. Her hands drew into fists at her sides, and Murdock thought for a moment she was going to strike out at him.

He stared at her, incredulous.

"Who do you think you are?" she demanded, her white, rigid face thrust close to his. "I'm not good enough for you, is that it?"

Murdock said: "That isn't what I—"

"Oh, yes it is. I'm cheap. Because I gave you what I thought most men wanted—"

"Hestor!" Murdock's face was taut.

"What you need is a woman with the same narrow ideas as yours. Somebody prim and proper and cold and passive. Somebody who will make you sleep alone and let you come to her once a month to—"

Hestor's voice shrilled. The sort of voice which held all its nuances in the early stages, it had nothing left for emphasis but to talk louder and louder. And Murdock stood there rigidly, his face gray and stiff-lipped until Hestor ran out of breath.

Still shaking and infuriated, her outburst stopped as abruptly as it had begun. As she caught her breath, there was a silent instant when she seemed to relax from reaction; then she twisted, shouldered past him.

Murdock caught her at the door and got his hand on the knob. Those two or three seconds' respite were enough to tighten his grip on himself. He had failed again. He always failed—with her. No matter how he approached her, he was wrong. Regardless of his intentions to argue reasonably, he ended up saying the wrong things. Or would that make the difference? She held the whip hand. She could flaunt her power, and he could not take it. Perhaps because he had never, from the first week or so, respected her.

Wrongly or rightly, that was the case. And maybe she sensed this. Probably she did. Then there was nothing to be gained by mere talk. She held the advantage and she could continue to hold it until such a time as it pleased her to compromise for reasons of her own. He took a breath and stiffened there as he took his last chance.

"I'm going to get clear." His voice was a bit thick, but level enough to surprise himself as he heard it.

"Open the door!" Her stare was glaring, poisonous.

"So far," he went on slowly, ignoring her command, "I've sort of taken my medicine. I'm tired of the taste. If I can't give you grounds, maybe I can get them from you. You've gone about with no interference from me. How often I might not know if I didn't work for a newspaper. There were three or four before Girard. And during the trial it was Andrew Sprague. And now Girard is free, he's back. Well"—Murdock opened the door—"if I get evidence I'll use it. Watch yourself, Hestor!"

Hestor Murdock stopped in the hall, turned, and gave him a sweet, bitter smile that was as deliberate as the contempt in the voice, which had recaptured its accent. "Thanks for the advice—and the cigarette, darling."

Murdock stood in the open doorway for several seconds after Hestor left. His threat, born of no preconceived idea, stirred his imagination, and a thin little smile re-

lieved the grim cast of his lean, angular face. He knew
Hestor had been chasing around—would have known it
even if he had not seen her frequent companions, because
he knew Hestor. She still wanted a thrill, any kind of a
thrill.

For the past year she had become a minor fixture on
the radio. The fair voice of hers took on enchantment
through the microphone and the manipulations of the
radio engineer. He did not know what she earned—probably twice what he did. And she could always wear
clothes. Now she had the money to buy them. It was
absurd to think of her without the companionship of
men. Yet heretofore Murdock had not cared. He did
not care now. But the idea was worth considering; in
fact . . .

He stepped into the hall. Hestor was just disappearing
in one of the self-operating elevators. He watched it until
the door clanged shut. Then, as he stood there, groping
for the next step in his new-found idea, a man moved into
view at the far end of the hall.

The fellow was swinging round the newel post of the
front stairs. He was in view but a second, and in that
second his eyes caught Murdock's as he continued his
climb. The thin, scrawny figure, something about the
momentary glimpse of the white face, brought identifica-
tion to Murdock. Sam Cusick, brother of the man of
whose murder Nate Girard had just been acquitted.

Murdock pursed his lips, seemed undecided for a moment. There was nothing actually out of the way in
Cusick's being here, and Murdock was so selfishly wound
up in his own problem that he abruptly dismissed the

man from his thoughts. He stepped back into the room, crossed to the telephone stand near the doorway leading to the bedroom hall.

He found the number he wanted in the telephone book, asked for it abruptly. He had to wait two or three minutes before a sleepy voice answered. He said:

"Fenner? Kent Murdock—yeah. Listen, you busy?"

The voice muttered a curse, growled: "I'm in bed, you cluck."

Murdock grunted impatiently. "Sure, but are you busy?"

"How can I be busy when—"

"Skip it and listen. I've got a little job for you."

"For yourself?" This incredulously. "Now?"

"Hell yes, now! Get dressed and get over here—right away."

Fenner groaned, finally said: "All right, all right. Keep your pants on."

"Right away!" Murdock repeated sharply, then an undertone of grim amusement crept into his voice. "And listen. I'm expecting a cut rate."

4

JACK FENNER WAS a slim, wiry young man with a pale, wedge-shaped face and alert agate eyes. When Murdock let him into his apartment twenty minutes later, his new-looking blue suit showed no signs of hurried dressing; his red and blue striped tie sat neatly on a clean shirt, and his black oxfords were well polished. He pulled up the tails of a worn gray topcoat and dropped a somewhat battered felt hat in his lap as he sat down in the wing chair.

"What's the job?"

Murdock moved in front of the chair and looked down at Fenner for a moment without speaking. Then he took the cigarette from his mouth, studied the end.

"I want you to follow my wife."

"Oh." Fenner looked down at his hat, back at Murdock. "And what's the sweat? You know where she is tonight?"

"She's upstairs. Girard is throwing a little party at Redfield's place. She's with him."

Fenner pursed his lips thoughtfully. "I thought you were divorced."

"Just separated."

"Pay her anything?"

"Sure."

"And you want to get out from under."

"I don't mind paying, but I want the divorce."

"Why won't she give you one?"

"Damned if I know; maybe it's a complex." Murdock walked across the room, turned, and came back. He pulled a straight-backed chair around to face Fenner and sat down. "Maybe it's a lousy trick, putting a private dick on her, but—"

Fenner's lips twitched in a smile. "I resent that. You don't think much of my racket, huh?"

"I think you're a bunch of chiselers." Murdock smiled. "But you're the best of the bunch and—"

"All right, all right." Fenner returned the smile. "You want evidence." He cocked one eyebrow. "We don't have to frame anything?"

Murdock shook his head. "Framing is out. Straight or not at all."

Fenner looked relieved. "What did you marry her for in the first place?"

Murdock did not resent the question because he knew Fenner's interest was friendly rather than professional. They had known each other for a long time and each had helped the other at times in the past. He found himself unburdening some of the tangled thoughts that, pent up for so long, sought and accepted an outlet.

"I don't know. It was just one of those things where you do something and then wish to hell you hadn't the next day. A mistake, that's all, and probably my fault."

Murdock's eyes touched some remote object, fastened there. "She came here with the *Love Song*—it opened here. I happened to get in on the first night and there was a party afterwards. I met her, and I gave her a rush. It was just a good time—so I thought. And she, well—"

"I know," Fenner said dryly. "I saw the show. She was a looker and she was built."

"I had a good time, all right," Murdock went on, "but that's all I figured on. I knew the show was moving on to New York and I thought that would be the end of it. Understand, I never was serious about her. I had a date with her Saturday night. The show folded. She was sort of worked up, down. And I picked that time to go soft. We had a few drinks and somebody—probably me—said:

'Let's get married.' And there we were."

Murdock's tone grew amused in a grim sort of way. "We tried it for three months. But it just didn't work. She was a damn good-looking woman, and she was built. When you say that, you're through."

"You're kinda bitter about it," Fenner said.

"Not about that part. It was my mistake. I'm bitter about the rest of it. I told her I'd give her grounds. She didn't want it that way. So we got Redfield to draw up a little agreement—you can see what a sap I was in those days—and we separated."

"She won't sell out?"

"For ten thousand, and I don't think she's interested in the installment plan."

Fenner looked down at the polished tips of his oxfords, spoke without lifting his head.

"What've you been waiting for? You got another girl that—"

"No!" rapped Murdock. "But—" He broke off, scowled. "But to hell with all this! What's the matter, you guys got a new code of ethics or something? I give you a job and—"

"Okay!" Fenner grinned and stood up. "I've seen her around. She's been stepping some. We can do. Only I was just interested, Kent. For a photographer, you're not a bad guy, and I wondered how you tangled in the first place."

Murdock glanced at his strap-watch. "It's five of three. The party won't last much longer, so you'd better go downstairs and wait." He moved to the door with Fenner, and the detective said:

"I'll see what happens when she goes home and call you."

Murdock went back to the wing chair, picked up a copy of the *Courier* from the magazine stand. A four-column head said:

GIRARD ACQUITTED
JURY OUT 4 HOURS

He took out a cigarette, put it in his mouth, then removed it and, turning to a taboret table, dropped it in an ash-tray. He picked up a stubby brier with a scarred bowl and a mouthpiece nearly obliterated by tooth marks. Filling the pipe from a silk and rubber pouch, he struck a match, sucked slowly in deep puffs until he had an even light. Then, tamping the top with a match-box, he puffed gently, cuddling the smoke in his lips, and pushed down in the chair.

The shrill of the telephone woke Murdock some time later. He saw he had remembered to put aside his pipe, but he had no recollection of falling asleep. Pulling himself erect with a groan, he arched his neck to eliminate the kinks and crossed to the telephone.

When he growled: "Hello," Fenner said:

"They're over at her apartment." Murdock glanced at his watch, saw that it was nearly five o'clock. "They left Redfield's at three-thirty and came straight here."

Murdock said: "What's the rest of it?"

"They're still in there—at least Girard hasn't come out."

"Stick around another half-hour and then go on home."

"Okay," said Fenner. "It looks like we're making

some progress."

Murdock hung up, went back to the chair, and sat down. He did not feel the satisfaction he expected. To suspect Hestor was one thing, to have proof another. And he was uneasy in his mind now that he had taken the first step. There was something cheap and tawdry about the whole thing. That he was a party to the plot irritated him. He hoped he would not have to go through with it. Perhaps if he could build up a case-book of several such instances, Hestor would change her mind; they would not have to drag the evidence—his part of it—into court.

He leaned forward in the chair and ran lean fingers through his thick, straight, brown hair. It was tousled now, standing on end at the back. The black tie was askew, tucked up under one wing of his collar; his shirt-front was buckled and wrinkled.

For several minutes he sat there like that, immobile; then he stood up and went out to the kitchenette. From a pantry shelf he took a bottle of Scotch, nearly full, and a glass. He turned on the faucet in the sink, let it run while he poured an inch and a half of whisky into the glass. He tossed this down with a single movement, took a swallow of water, and then replaced the bottle.

He began to unbutton his waistcoat with one hand and pull at his tie with the other as he moved towards the bedroom. The whisky felt warm in his stomach. It erased the thick, sticky taste in his mouth, but his head was still fogged. As soon as he undressed he went into the bathroom, stood there for a moment like a man drugged and incapable of thought.

He brushed his teeth, then scowled at himself in the medicine-cabinet mirror. He finally took out his shaving accessories and set to work. He would not go to bed at all. He never got any rest that way; such a procedure always made him feel logy for the balance of the day. His thoughts stalled while he shaved, and then, with the remains of the lather still on his face, he turned on the shower, adjusted the spray to the proper warmth.

The shower bath was a combination arrangement, set in the tub, which was placed in one corner of the room. Murdock, facing the doorway, drew the circular-hung shower curtain just enough to keep the floor dry and stood there with his hands behind him, soaking up the warmth until he heard a sudden clicking noise, the sound of a door opening.

His first thought was that he had not locked the apartment door. His eyes darted to the full-length mirror which made one side of the bathroom door and which reflected, from its present angle, a narrow rectangle of the living-room.

He heard the door slam, and reached back to turn off the shower. Then the mirror reflected and framed the figure of a girl—a bareheaded girl with a blue evening dress and a loose wrap that was open and swirled around her as she stopped abruptly and stared about.

Sheer surprise robbed Murdock of logical thought. For a moment he just stood there and stared at the blond vision he had last seen in Redfield's apartment. Then the girl's eyes met his in the mirror. The eyes widened. She turned and ran out of his range of vision.

Murdock managed to turn off the shower. He heard

the soft thud of running feet and pulled the shower curtain about him just as she dashed through the bathroom door.

For a long moment they stared at each other, the girl white-faced, frightened, Murdock holding the shower curtain at his waist and peering incredulously at her through the V opening at his face. He had no warning at all for what happened next. He opened his mouth, started to speak. The mouth stayed open. The girl leaped directly towards him, stepped over the edge of the bathtub. With a quick, continuous movement that he made no effort to forestall, she yanked the wet curtain from his grasp, ducked in behind him, her body close to his; then she pulled the curtain around them both.

"Turn the water on!" she gasped. "Please!"

Murdock obeyed without conscious thought. The water came down in a deluge. He heard it pounding on the girl's wrap and she leaned close, her folded hands touching his back. In spite of the warmth of the shower the hands felt like ice and there was a tingle, a quick contraction of Murdock's skin all over his body before she said:

"The curtain!"

Murdock took a new hold on the gaping curtain and pulled it together just as the living-room door banged back against the wall. He heard a man's voice an instant before a tall, stiff-looking fellow in a loose-fitting topcoat dashed across the living-room and was mirrored briefly in the bathroom door. The man disappeared, came back a moment later to the visible rectangle. Then, like the girl, his glance touched Murdock, fastened upon him.

Seconds later Lieutenant Bacon of the Homicide Squad rushed into the bathroom, slid to a stop on the tile threshold.

"You seen a girl, Kent?" he lipped.

"When?" Murdock said, and with the recovery of his composure his tone was guileless.

"Now, damn it! She got off at this floor and—" Bacon broke off, dashed down the little hall. Murdock heard him barking profane commands to some unseen associates until the pounding of the water obliterated the voice. Murdock stood there rigidly and felt the chilled pressure of the girl's hand on his shoulders. Not until now did he feel any embarrassment. But it did not last and he finally managed to say:

"Well, what do we do now?"

"Wait," the girl whispered.

"What happened?"

"I don't know."

"You don't know?"

"No. I mean—" The girl broke off and Murdock felt her body tense against his as Bacon's voice cut in on them again.

The Lieutenant stopped in the doorway. "I'm gonna take a look around. She might've sneaked in while you were here. You wouldn't've heard her."

Murdock said: "Go ahead." But when Bacon disappeared he did not dare risk speaking again, so he waited until the Lieutenant returned.

"Well, she ain't here, that's a cinch." Bacon hesitated, pushed back his felt hat, and surveyed Murdock with eyes that were steady, and gray, like his hair. "You're one of those early risers, huh?" he said.

"I haven't been to bed."

"There was a party upstairs in Redfield's place." Bacon pushed aside his coat-tails and put balled fists on his hips. "Maybe you were in on it?"

"I was there for a while, yes."

"Hah." Bacon's lips parted in a thin smile, and one eyebrow cocked. "That's swell. I want to talk to you."

"And I want to talk to you," Murdock said, and made his voice flat. "What's this girl gag? Can't I take a bath without some cop busting in and—"

"Come on," Bacon cut in. "This ought to interest you, it's right down your alley."

Murdock nodded, unperturbed. "Okay."

The girl was all right now. He did not have any answers, but he found room amid the race of his disordered thoughts to remember his last conversational exchange with this girl upstairs. Now a sliver of grim humor knifed through his brain. "Okay. Wait'll I take a cold one."

He reached for the shower control as he spoke and turned it to COLD. The result was an icy torrent that stiffened him and pushed his breath through his teeth. He heard the girl gasp, felt her fingers contract. But she made no other sound and he turned off the water.

Bacon lingered in the doorway.

Murdock said: "There's some Scotch in the kitchen cupboard. Pour one if you like while I'm getting dressed."

Bacon grunted, and disappeared in the hall. Murdock pulled open the shower curtain, stepped out of the tub, and caught up a towel. The girl yanked the curtain around her as he turned and moved out of her sight to one side of the opening. When he had rubbed down, he wrapped the towel around his waist and went into the bedroom.

When Murdock stepped into the living-room a few minutes later, Bacon got up from the davenport. He waited silently, his eyes slightly narrowed as Murdock approached.

"So you were at the party? What time did you leave?"

"Around two-thirty—two-twenty, I guess it was. What about it?"

"But you haven't been to bed?" Bacon's tone was skeptical, but not unpleasant.

"I fell asleep in the chair," Murdock said. He scowled, then continued irritably: "And I don't like riddles."

"Neither do I, but—"

"Then why don't you speak your piece? Who's the girl? What—"

"I don't know yet," Bacon said slowly, "but I'll find out. You got a camera here?"

"I got one I can use in a pinch." Murdock's scowl remained fixed and he reached for a cigarette.

"Get it."

"Why?"

"Because I'm going to get big-hearted and give you the break you're all the time yelling for. Somebody knocked off Mark Redfield in his apartment."

"When?" Murdock's eyes widened as doubt and uncertainty surged through him.

"Tonight—this morning."

"Murdered." The word was more of a statement than

a question, and Bacon nodded, adding dryly: "Get the camera and come on."

5

SHE WAITED THERE in the shower for some minutes after she heard the door close. She was shivering now. The dress was a clammy, clinging mass weighed down by the pressure of the water-soaked wrap. And it was not alone this that made her shiver. The chill was mental, built squarely upon fear and panic and desperation. Under pressure the nerves held their necessary taut pitch. With the reaction they were frayed. She felt weak and more frightened than ever.

She finally pulled aside the shower curtain with a slow deliberate movement that was soundless. Water trickled from the soaked mass of her hair, oozed into her brows and down the back of her neck. She could hear the drip-drip of the drops in the residue in the tub, could feel them splash on her ankles.

There was no other sound but her own breathing, and her courage returned slowly, warming her and bringing assurance. She finally moved out from under the curtain and, still standing in the tub, peeled the sodden wrap from her shoulders. The little jacket stuck. She had to twist out of it; the dress dropped like a wet washcloth when she undid the shoulder-fastening. She stepped out of it, avoiding its touch as if it were the only wet thing about her.

Looking about the white, bare confines of the room, she saw there was a clean face-towel on a rack beside the washbowl, but no bath-towel. Doing the best she could with what she had, she began to rub her hair, continuing until the little towel was soaked. She shook her head then, neck arched back, until the hair settled to her satisfaction; then she sat down on the edge of the tub, pulled off her pumps, and peeled down her stockings.

Dressed now in a brassière and brief silken shorts that were as tight as her skin, she started to remove them, thought better of it, and stepped down to the bath-mat. She pattered into the hall, found a narrow closet between the bathroom and bedroom doors. Armed with a turkish towel of huge proportions, she went back to the bathroom and stripped off the shorts and brassière.

She went to work with a vengeance then, spending most of the time on her hair, rubbing it, massaging it until her arms were tired and she was out of breath. When she had finished she moved to the medicine-cabinet and peered into its glass.

Her face had a ruddy, freshly scrubbed look about it and she continued to study herself until she was able to smile. It was not much of a smile, but it helped. Even when she stepped back, traces of it remained at the corners of her eyes. She glanced into the tub, frowned, and, remembering the outer door, ran into the living-room holding the towel about her breasts with one hand. She opened the door a crack, pressed the locking button. When she closed it she gave a little sigh of relief and relaxed her hold on the towel.

Slowly she moved into the bedroom and opened the

closet door. On a hook on the inside of the panel was a dressing-gown of green flannel. Tossing the towel on the four-poster, she opened the robe, held it in front of her, measuring it. Poised there, her feet a few inches apart and her arms stiff and angling upwards, the even thoroughness of her tan was at once apparent. Only at the hips and for an inch or so at the small of her back, was the skin white. From a little distance she looked like an Indian with a brief white bathing-suit.

She turned quickly and slipped into the robe, knotting the wide strap tightly and turning up the sleeves until she found her hands. Then she faced the mirror on top of the maple chest of drawers and grinned at herself.

The grin died abruptly as her thoughts leaped from the moment to the reason for her being here. Her eyes widened. Trouble filmed them and settled over her. She had come back, but even now she did not know—

She spun quickly about, searched the room with a quick glance, and moved into the hall and living-room. Her eyes found the telephone just inside the door. She swept it up, gave a number in a low, jerky voice.

Fear, cold and gnawing, seeped into her brain. The operator said: "I'm ringing Charlesgate 8974."

"Keep ringing. There must be someone there."

She waited and tension gripped her until her muscles ached and her breath caught in her throat. She could hear the distant intermittent buzzing of the other telephone and began to count the rings. Then a sharp click knifed through one of those silent pauses. She said: "Hello, hello," breathlessly.

An interminable second or two later a man's voice,

which was low and sounded irritable and thick with
sleep, said: "Hello."

She gasped: "Howard?"

The voice said: "Hello. Yes—what—"

She clicked down the receiver arm with her index
finger and relaxed, propped there against the wall, low-
ering the two parts of the instrument until her arms were
straight down. For a moment or two she stood there while
the color surged back into the tanned cheeks and her
breathing became regular again. Then she lifted the instrument, replaced the receiver, and gently set it on the
stand.

Even then she remained standing and the sequence
of the drama unrolled before her mind quickly, but with
the clearness of a slow-motion film. The whole idea had
been silly, an impulsive course of action born of anger
and worry. It would have been better, she told herself, if
she had not come back. Luck—that and nothing else had
allowed her to escape.

She exhaled slowly and in relief, let her eyes drift
around the room. In spite of her keyed-up nerves she was
aware that she liked it, and this thought led her to Kent
Murdock. She had learned his name before she left Redfield's apartment; there was a touch of shame in her
memory that brought back the details of their first meeting. She had been a boor, an unmannerly little brat.

She walked to the windows at the end of the room.
Over the river the growing daylight was muddy, coating
the already drab factory buildings on the other bank with
a leaden, colorless brush; the Technology buildings
looked gray and cold and austere. Turning, she moved

back to the wing chair and switched off the floor lamp
beside it. From a jade box she took a cigarette, lit it, and
sank into the chair.

She drew her feet up under her and snuggled down in
the robe. She liked the way he reacted to the emergency.
He had been perfect, natural and at ease with the policeman. Even that cold shower.

She felt warm and safe enough now to look upon that
impish gesture with amusement, to understand the sense
of humor which prompted him to take advantage of her.

6

THE PLAIN-CLOTHESMAN at the door stood aside and
Murdock followed Lieutenant Bacon through the entrance foyer and into the living-room. Another plain-
clothesman, who was walking idly about, stopped idling
long enough to notice them, then he continued to the
terrace windows and looked out.

The place was otherwise deserted, its outstanding characteristic the smell of stale tobacco smoke. Leon's bar still
stood in the dining-room, its mirror and decorative bottles intact. Apparently no effort had been made to tidy
up: glasses of all shapes and sizes were everywhere, glasses
and overflowing ash-trays. Bacon continued on to a doorway on the right wall, and Murdock found himself in
a comfortably furnished pine-paneled and book-filled
room. He put his little camera-case and tripod just inside
the door.

Mark Redfield lay on his side, one arm doubled under

him and the other outstretched above him, pillowing his head. There was something horribly unfamiliar about the limp and boneless set of the limbs that spoke of death as surely as a coroner's verdict. His heavy face, curiously white now, was relaxed, peaceful. Upon the wrinkled shirt-front was a wide red stain reaching down towards the floor and disappearing in his waistcoat. At the upper edges of the stain was a gray-black smudge.

Murdock took in the picture of death at a glance and caught his lower lip between his teeth as he looked up. There were three other men in the room: a fingerprint man and a photographer from headquarters, Sergeant Keogh, and a thickset, sullen-looking fellow who sat on the window-seat between the bookcases, nursing a grudge and a somewhat battered face.

Keogh said, "Where'd you pick him up?" and nodded a greeting to Murdock.

"He lives here," grunted Bacon.

Murdock said: "Hello, Tom."

Keogh grinned, added: "That's swell, another suspect already, huh?"

Bacon took off his hat, wiped his forehead, put the hat on again, and pushed it back. He nodded to Keogh. "Take this down." Then, to Murdock: "Now, who was here?"

Keogh took out a little black notebook and a pencil. Murdock named those he knew at the party, and Bacon asked: "That all?"

Murdock shook his head. "Another half-dozen or so besides the entertainers, but I don't know their names."

Bacon grunted and fell silent.

Murdock voiced the question that had been bothering him; he was careful to speak casually, a bit lightly. "What's the girl trouble you were all steamed up about?"

"I wish I knew." Bacon shook his head. "The telephone operator on the desk downstairs saw her come in about four-thirty, maybe a little later. She had a blue dress and a dark cloak; a blonde and a looker. But we didn't know about it until it was too late. She was hiding in a closet in the foyer. Mahady, out in the other room, caught a glimpse of her sneaking past the door. She caught the elevator and went down to the lobby. I was down there and she must've figured me as a copper because she jumped right back in the car. It stopped at your floor. I think she's still in the building." Bacon grunted and his lips tightened. "If she is, she won't get out today."

Murdock's voice got sharp in spite of himself. "What time was he killed?"

"Between four and four-thirty, we think."

Murdock exhaled slowly, but it must have sounded something like a sigh of relief, because Bacon eyed him sharply and said: "That's all right with you, huh?"

Murdock avoided his gaze. "Where's the gun?"

"Haven't found it."

Murdock moved around the body and took out a cigarette as he stopped in front of the thickset man. "Been working you over, Spike?"

"Don't they always?" the fellow growled.

"He ran into a door," Keogh said. "Didn't you, Spike? We found him hiding in a closet in the outside hall." Keogh cocked one eyebrow at Murdock and spread his

hands, an expression of mock resignation on his broad
Irish face. "He tried to run and when we chased him he
goes smack into a door. He oughta know better."

A small man with pince-nez and a black bag bustled
through the doorway and greeted the room with a smile
and a cheery "Hello, boys, what's all this?" He put down
the bag and opened it, glancing at Redfield's body as he
did so.

Bacon and Keogh grunted acknowledgments. Murdock
nodded.

The examiner, sinking to one knee beside the body,
spoke as his fingers went through their practiced routine.

"Girard got out just in time. Anybody lined up for
this?"

"Naw," growled Bacon. "We just got here."

Keogh moved over to Murdock's side. "One thing," he
confided, "it's a break for the force. Without him to
defend 'em there's a lot of mugs around town that're
gonna end up in a cell. He sprung more guilty guys than
any three other lawyers in town."

Murdock smiled wryly. "A noble thought."

Keogh said: "Utsnay," hesitated, added: "Where's the
camera?"

Murdock moved to the door and picked up a small
metal tripod and a square leather case. Opening it, he
took out a flash-gun, a bulb, and a little camera in its
own case, about the size of a fifteen-cent can of tobacco.

Keogh, who had followed him, asked: "What the hell's
that? Can you take pictures with it?"

Murdock nodded. "My newspaper stuff is at the office.
This is some of my own rig. It'll take anything. You have

to enlarge 'em, but it's twice as fast and—"

"Then why don't you quit carrying that trunk around and use it all the time?"

"Because"—Murdock pulled out the tripod—"never mind. Will you take my word for it or do we have to argue it out?"

Keogh grinned and subsided. Murdock glanced at the examiner, then back at Keogh. He liked the stocky Sergeant, liked Bacon, too. They made a good pair, complementing each other, working well in double harness.

Bacon was tall, gray, stiff, with a dry, laconic manner. Keogh had a box-like face, a tough appearance; he was self-confident, loud, and suspicious of everyone. Neither man was brilliant, neither was spectacular, unduly imaginative, or blessed with more than average intelligence. But in their own line of work, which was often dull and almost always of a routine nature, both were hard, competent, and so honest they leaned over backwards.

"It looks like a contact wound," the examiner said as he straightened up. "I'll give you the bullet and a full report in the morning—today."

"When'd he get it?" asked Bacon.

"I'll guess for you. Between three-thirty and four-thirty; probably about four. It could be suicide except for one thing."

"We haven't got the gun yet," Keogh broke in.

"That isn't what I mean." The examiner snapped shut his bag and delivered his ultimatum with full consciousness of its import. "The index finger of his right hand is broken. Looks as if it had been snapped back. That's the trigger finger, isn't it?"

"Oh." Bacon scowled, then his eyebrows came up. "We figured there was a scuffle. That cinches it."

Murdock set up his tripod when the examiner left. Bacon cautioned: "Take a couple. The room is okay; I don't mind the body, but no close-ups or anything." He stepped back and his eyes fell on Spike Tripp.

"Move," he added dryly. "Get your picture and the first thing we know you'll be sayin' we beat you up."

"I'll say it anyway, and don't you forget it."

Murdock took three pictures of the room from various angles, got two more shots of the living-room and dining-balcony from the doorway. As he put away his paraphernalia he said:

"Well, I'm much obliged and—"

"That's only part of it," Bacon said. "You got your pictures and now I'm going to tell you what I know, and I'll tell you why." He hesitated, seemed to weigh his words.

"In the first place, you're the only button-pusher—the only newspaper guy I know, who don't clown around with the idea that he can outsmart the whole detective bureau; you can keep your mouth shut and sometimes you get an idea. In the second place, you were here; you know most of the people who were here, and you're already in this mess. But the main reason is that I know you've got the sort of luck that falls smack into the breaks. And it looks like we're going to need plenty of it. Come here."

He took Murdock by the arm, led him to the living-room. Keogh followed them, called to the plain-clothes-man and told him to watch Tripp. They moved across the living-room to a hallway to the left of the dining-balcony, but at the living-room level. Bacon opened the second door on the left.

It was a beautifully appointed bedroom done in cream and silver but Murdock was only vaguely aware of this. His eyes fastened on Rita Redfield, who lay fully dressed and sprawled across the modern, low-slung bed.

Murdock said: "What's the matter with her?" but his gaze did not shift. His lean dark face was somber.

"Passed out, if you ask me," Keogh said. "Do we get the breaks?"

Bacon blew out his breath in an impatient snort. "We couldn't wake her. The manager here called in for a doctor. He hasn't shown up yet. Come on." Again he took Murdock's arm, pulling him down the hall to an adjoining room.

The color scheme here was blue: hangings, furniture, walls. On a huge period bed lay another woman—a girl, rather. She lay face-down so that the back of a sleek bobbed head, and legs exposed to the thighs by a hitched-up dress, were the chief features of her appearance. Murdock recognized her at once as one of the entertainers, a singer, and he was immediately aware from the utterly relaxed position that her trouble was the same as Rita Redfield's.

"Two, huh?" he said absently, and when Bacon asked who she was, he told what he knew.

"Boy," Keogh breathed, "would I like to get in on a party like this some day."

"Sure," growled Bacon. "Who wouldn't?" He led Murdock back to the library and nodded at the plain-clothesman, who withdrew. "Here's what we got," he began. "I'll play ball with you. You'd better come clean with me."

He began to pace back and forth across the library, head down, chin on chest, talking as he walked.

"We get the call from the operator downstairs. He thinks the party broke up about three-thirty. After that he dozed off. He says he always does early mornings, that he's trained to wake up if anyone comes in or anything. Anyway, the first thing he noticed was the buzz of the switchboard. The light flashed from this apartment. That was about five after four. Now here's the funny part."

Bacon stopped pacing and faced Murdock, his gray eyes narrowed, thoughtful. "The operator was dozing, see? Leaning back in his chair. It took him maybe fifteen seconds or so to sit up and reach for the plug, but before he could make the connection the light went out."

Bacon hesitated. Murdock's gaze slid to the carved, Jacobean desk placed diagonally across one corner of the room, then to Redfield, who lay with his feet about a foot from the edge of the desk. The telephone was placed at this corner.

"The kid waited a bit," Bacon went on, "but the light didn't flash again. He wanted to show that he was there on the job, in case Redfield made a complaint that he couldn't get a connection, so he plugged in, gave the phone a quick ring. Nobody answered." Bacon moved his right hand in a resigned arc. "So the kid figured it was a mistake."

"You think," Murdock said slowly, eyes still on the desk, that the phone was knocked off in the scuffle—or maybe when Redfield was killed? That the killer picked it up as quick as he could?"

"That's what I think now."

Murdock nodded at the telephone, then stared at Bacon, who guessed immediately what he meant and shook his head. "No prints."

"How'd you learn about this? Who found him?"

"That," sighed Bacon, "is even funnier."

He doubled his right fist, looked at it, then swung his arm down and clasped both hands behind his back. His voice held an undertone of weary exasperation as he continued.

"About four-thirty, just after the girl came back in, some man called up, asked for Redfield's apartment. He said it was important, so the operator plugged in. He couldn't get an answer. The fellow on the wire was insistent. He kept after the kid to ring. And the kid did ring, for about five minutes. He says he could hear Redfield's phone buzzing. Well, this was only about thirty minutes after the other flash from the apartment. The kid got kind of worried. He finally argued himself into waking the manager. The manager went upstairs and couldn't get an answer to the door-buzzer; he tried the door. It was open and he took a look."

Murdock frowned. "He had a lot of nerve."

"Not so much. He knew that Redfield had let the servants go for the night, and the operator told him about this girl that come in. He was sure she had been at the party in the first place, and he thought she went back there. And don't forget Redfield and his wife were here, he knew that. But still no one answered the phone."

Murdock moved to the desk, slid one thigh over the corner, and took out his cigarettes. Keogh had knelt beside Redfield and was looking at the bluish, fractured index finger. Murdock offered him a cigarette, passed the pack to Bacon, who shook his head and kept scowling.

"Well, what else have you got?" Murdock wanted to know.

"Besides the girl," Bacon chafed, "besides the girl and Spike, here"—he nodded at the still glowering Tripp—"one other guy came back here. Your friend Howard Archer."

"My friend?" Murdock's brows came up.

"He came up here, or anyway he came through the downstairs lobby ahead of the girl—around four-fifteen. The kid downstairs just got one eye open in time to see him. And get this, *the Kid didn't see him go out and*—"

Bacon broke off as Mahady came to the door and ushered in two white-coated internes with a stretcher. The room was silent until the body had been removed. During that time Murdock thought briefly of Archer.

A typical man-about-town type, a play-boy, Archer was born to a position in society. His parents had been killed in an automobile accident six months previous, so that he had a small fortune and more freedom than ever to follow his own inclinations, which seemed to revolve about a penchant for first nights, floor tables, and night life in general. There had been at least one breach-of-promise suit. It was common knowledge that he had been unduly attentive to Rita Redfield for some time.

Belonging to the same social set, these two had, in a sense, grown up together. There had been an interim when Archer was in Europe, and during that time Rita had suddenly married Redfield. The fact that this marriage coincided quite closely with the acquittal of her father from a fraud charge in which he was brilliantly defended by Mark Redfield—this fact, plus the fact that Redfield rarely accepted cases of this kind, gave the gossips something to talk about. Now—

"So there we are," Bacon broke in on Murdock's thoughts. "We're gonna question everybody that was on this party. But Tripp and—"

"Where does he fit?" Murdock asked.

"Tell him, Spike," Bacon said.

"Nuts," gasped Tripp.

"See?" Keogh shook his head sadly. "That's the kind of co-operation we get."

Bacon said, "He's got a girl friend," and eyed Tripp sardonically. "He says he came to take her home. I don't know how he happened to come at four-forty-five, but—"

"Could you check on that?" Murdock cut in.

"Yeah."

"Then how can you hook him up with the job?"

"Plenty of ways, and it'll work for some of these others, maybe." Bacon's voice got thin, sharp, like his eyes. "There's a back door to this house, and fire stairs. And Spike's just dumb enough—if he did have something to do with this—to come back in the front way and try and pull it as an alibi or something."

Murdock grinned. "What did you run for?"

Tripp lifted sullen eyes. "Who wouldn't?" he snarled. "What's the take in being a punching-bag for a flock of dumb coppers? I'm waiting out in the hall when a load of 'em spill out of the elevator. What the hell? I'm right by the maid's closet and I duck. I want to know what it's about before I get tangled for a fall guy or something."

"Who was this girl you came for? What did she do?"

"She was a singer."

"What did she look like?"

"Look like?" For a moment it appeared that the question was beyond Tripp's powers of comprehension. "Why —well, she's kinda short, black hair and, hell, I—"

"What kind of a dress?"

"I don't know. I didn't bring her. I was just gonna take her home."

Murdock turned to Bacon. "Has he seen that girl out there?"

"No. You don't believe him, do you?"

"He could be right," Murdock said dryly. "Why don't you give him a look."

Mahady stuck his head in the door. "The doc's out here, the one for the dames."

"Take him out there. Tell him to see if he can't snap them out of it so we can talk to them." He turned to Tripp. "Go on out and take a look."

Bacon muttered a throaty curse, took off his hat again, and mopped his forehead.

"You birds," he fumed, looking at Murdock, "will eat this up. But for us it's a mess. Front-page stuff, huh? And"—he hesitated, slapped his hat back on—"say, whose party was this, anyway? I got the idea that Girard was so

tickled he missed the chair that he threw it for Redfield.
Or was Redfield all het up about the fifty-thousand fee
he tucked away?"

"It was Girard's party."

"Then what's it doing here?"

"Have you been through the place?" Murdock asked
flatly.

"Sure," interrupted Keogh. "And what a lay-out.
Eight rooms and three baths."

"Well," Murdock shrugged, "there's your answer.
Room. Girard's a bachelor and he's got a small place."

"Yeah." Bacon pulled at his straight nose. "And I
wish," he added thoughtfully, "I could tie Girard in with
this. I'll check him, all right, but it can't be figured. He
never spent fifty thousand any better in his life. He owed
Redfield plenty. Without him on the case, the D. A.'d
had his name on the chair just as sure as hell."

Then, and not until then, did Murdock remember.
The thought slashed into his brain and left chagrin in
its wake. He should have remembered it before and—

He took a breath, said: "There's one thing more." He
grinned a bit sheepishly, continued defensively: "And
don't tell me I've been holding out on you, because it
isn't that. I'm just dumb. Sam Cusick was here tonight."

"Sam—" Keogh went slack-jawed with amazement.
"Well, for—"

Bacon's face flushed. "Spill it!"

Murdock hurriedly told about the trip to his apartment with Hestor, of seeing Cusick in the hall. "I didn't
tie it up, that's all," he finished, and meant what he said.
"I was thinking about something else then and it didn't

register much. That's the truth, Bacon."

The Lieutenant moved to a chair upholstered in red leather, dropped into it, a weary and exasperated figure. He took off his hat again, turned it around, shaking his head sadly at it for a moment. Then he looked up at Murdock from under his brows.

"All right," he growled, and clapped the hat back on his head. "I guess I've got to believe you. And it makes a difference." He straightened in the chair, and his voice got crisp, decisive.

"It hooks up. Girard murders Joe Cusick—or, anyway, he got tried for it. And both Cusicks have been after him because he's the guy that put them away for four years on the extortion rap. And the main reason they got the four years is that Redfield would not take their case. So they hate him for that. They get out a couple of months ago. Girard kills Joe . . . in self-defense, we'll say. But Redfield is the one who gets Girard clear. Sam is nothing but a hood, never was anything else. So why not? It's Girard's first night out of jail. Sam figures to get Redfield for two things: not taking his case, and springing Girard. By gawd, he's liable to go gunning for Girard, too."

Bacon came out of the chair, strode to the telephone, and swept it from the desk. A moment later he was barking commands to someone at headquarters. When he hung up he spun about, his face flushed and holding a satisfied expression.

"What'd I tell you about that luck of yours?"

Keogh grunted: "If I had it I'd—" but Bacon ignored him and hurried on.

"Now we're getting some place. We'll pick him up,

and when we do—"

He broke off suddenly as Mahady appeared in the doorway. The detective jerked his head backward to indicate the presence of someone behind him and came into the room, stepping aside. A plump, bald man in a dark suit moved into the opening. Beside him, and leaning on one arm, was Rita Redfield.

Her face was worn and haggard—so deathly pale that the lips glared scarlet and the rouge stood out on her cheeks like fever spots. Her eyes were wide, but dull—the eyes of a woman struggling against extreme weariness or impending sickness. Yet for all of this her chin was up and, somehow, defiant.

Bacon moved towards her, took off his hat. "I'm sorry we—"

"What is it?" Her voice was flat, lifeless. "You're from the police?"

Bacon nodded.

She said: "But what's happened?" and her voice rose.

Bacon tightened his lips and took a breath. "It's your husband. He was shot—about an hour ago."

"Shot?" The word was a husky whisper, but the tone was still flat, indicating that she had not grasped the significance of Bacon's statement. "But—then, where is he?"

"The body's been removed."

"Body?" she echoed hollowly. And then her eyes went very wide, her voice shrilled hysterically. "He's dead!"

Bacon nodded and Rita Redfield stared at him, spoke just one word. She did not exactly speak it, she whispered it, faintly, almost inaudibly. But the room was so still

that both syllables were clear-cut, definite: *"Howard."*
Then her eyelids fluttered. She sighed and Mahady and
the doctor caught her as she swayed and slumped forward, unconscious.

7

*M*URDOCK LET HIMSELF into his apartment with his key.
The girl he had left in the shower was curled up in the
wing chair, and he saw her facial expression relax with
recognition. She waited, motionless, while he set down
his photographic gear. He walked over to her, said: "Do
you want a drink?"

"If I can have a very short one."

He went into the kitchen and mixed two drinks. He
came back, handed her the smaller one, offered her the
jade cigarette-box. She accepted and he held a light,
then moved the club chair by the windows and sat down.

She followed him with her eyes, finally spoke. "Have
they found out?" she said jerkily. "Do they know who
did it?"

Murdock shook his head negatively. He put his half-
empty glass on a window-sill. "You'd better tell me about
it."

The girl hesitated, looked away. "You mean, how
—why I came here the way I did?"

Murdock did not answer. His face was somber, but
there was a trace of a smile at the corners of his eyes as
he watched her, sized her up.

She was more attractive now than she had been up-stairs. Her tanned face was clean now, without make-up. The lips were just as red, but now they looked soft and moist; her teeth, surrounded by the darkness of her skin, were so white they glistened. Her hauteur, her coldness, had vanished. She was a little girl now, or maybe it was the green dressing-gown which swallowed her and made her seem so.

She was not a pretty, fluffy, pastel type; slim, tailored, rather. Young, fresh-looking now, vital, with a vitality that seemed to be smoldering and threatening to break its bonds. For all this, she was utterly feminine; the folds of his dressing-gown could not hide the curves of her body. It was caught tightly at the waist, he saw, and the long V of the neckline was deep. Shadows played there at the base, softened the rising arches of her firm breast, which, barely visible, curved off into the green flannel. He did not think she was aware that the V was so deep, because when he did not answer and she looked at him her pose remained natural, completely unaffected.

"I came back to the Redfield apartment for my bag," she said and her voice was low, pleasingly husky. "I suppose it was silly. It was terribly late, I know, but I thought someone would be up. I pressed the buzzer and tried the door. It was open and I stepped inside and—"

Murdock stood up, crossed to the telephone. As he lifted the instrument, the girl sat up in the chair, alarm flooding her face.

"What are you going to do?"

"Call the Lieutenant."

"No. You—"

"So far I've trusted you, haven't I?" Murdock asked flatly.

"Of course and—"

"But I can't take any more chances if you're going to lie about it. I've got to know where I stand."

The flush in the girl's face was evident in spite of the tan. "All right," she said weakly. "I thought—how did you know?"

Murdock put down the telephone and went back to his chair. He took another sip of his drink, stared out across the river before he spoke.

"You didn't have a bag when you came here. And the police didn't find anything like that lying around upstairs." He put down his glass, inhaled, and smoke came out with his words. "You went back and you saw Redfield and you got trapped up there. All right. Now I want to know why you came back."

"To see if Howard was there." This simply, a statement of fact.

"Howard Archer?" Murdock leaned forward, stared.

"Yes."

"Why?"

"Because"—the girl sighed and her resignation was evident—"because he's my brother. I'm Joyce."

"Oh." Murdock dragged out the word and leaned back. "I didn't know he had a sister."

Joyce Archer's shoulders lifted, dropped back. Her tone was slightly bitter. "You wouldn't, I suppose. I guess I've been pretty thoroughly forgotten." She smiled then, but there was a lack of humor in the effort. "I've been abroad for three years. Went to school there. It's a family complex. An uncle in England gave the idea to Mother. Howard was at Cambridge, you know. But I didn't mind being away, because I knew how little my friends got out of staying here and—"

She moved one hand on the chair arm, looked down at it. "But that's not important. I came back after Father and Mother were killed in the accident. Since then I haven't been in town at all, there was no reason for staying here. Most of my friends are married, and those who aren't"—she shrugged again—"bridge and cocktails and dances and a lot of talk about men and sex."

She was genuinely bitter now, her voice sullen, a bit contemptuous.

"And none of them doing anything about it. And the men just as bad—those that are left. But there was a girl in Hartford. We went to Bermuda, to Block Island, to Oyster Harbors, and had a good time doing nothing but swimming and riding and playing golf. Then a week ago I came back and found Howard running around with Rita Redfield. I know her." Joyce Archer leaned across the chair arm. She could not have put more emphatic disgust into her words if she had shaken her finger at Murdock. "She's shallow, she's mercenary, she's —a nymphomaniac."

"You're pretty positive about it," Murdock said sardonically. "I understood they were old friends. She never thought much of Redfield, anyway, did she?" He waited for an answer, but when none came, he added: "If you were so disgusted about it, why did you go to her party?"

"I wouldn't have," the girl flared, "if it wasn't for

Howard. I wouldn't think of going. It *was* disgusting. A celebration party for an ex-bootlegger that Mark Redfield had kept out of prison. And the people!"

"Yeh," Murdock said dryly. "A flashy criminal lawyer, an ex-bootlegger, a newspaper photographer—a button-pusher—"

"That isn't what I meant." The girl colored.

"Perhaps not, but—"

"You're different."

"How?"

"Well, you look like the sort of men I know; your clothes and—well, appearance. But you're not. You're different; maybe it's because you do things. You even talk—"

"Like a bum, you mean," Murdock said, grinning.

"No. I mean you talk to me one way, and you talked differently to that detective. And upstairs—"

"I'm versatile that way," Murdock said dryly. "To you, now, I talk in my own natural jargon. If you heard me when I'm out on a job you'd think my antecedents traced back to the slums. And there's another way—on my dignity—when I get out the tails and white tie. But it never gets me anywhere."

He broke off with a sardonic grunt, brought his thoughts back to Joyce Archer's story. "So you went to the party because he wanted you to."

"I went because he didn't want me to. We had a fight about Rita. I came to cramp his style if I could—anyway to see just how bad it was. Howard's a beast. It was sickening. Actually fighting over her."

"Fighting?" Murdock snapped the word, and his brows came up.

"Well—" The sharpness of his tone broke the girl's mood. She continued defensively: "Almost. Mark Redfield was drunk, you saw that much. But I didn't blame him. The way Howard was fawning over her. I don't know what he said, but I know the other men almost had to pull them apart. They practically threw us out." Her scorn was appalling. "And of course Howard got melodramatic about it. He said the thing wasn't finished— he'd settle it in private—that sort of talk."

"I see," Murdock said. And as his mind fought to reconstruct the facts he had learned from Bacon, he added dryly: "So you tagged along with your brother and brought your grudge and nursed it all the time you were there. You didn't want to miss anything; that's why you were alone by choice, huh?"

Joyce Archer colored, dropped her eyes. "You don't like me much, do you?"

Murdock did not answer. It is doubtful if he heard her, because he was struggling with the time element of the murder. Bacon would learn of this argument and threat easily enough. And with this knowledge he would have a motive sufficient to embroil Archer thoroughly.

Joyce Archer glanced up, saw that Murdock was looking out the windows. She took the opportunity, denied her before, to study him.

She wondered if she liked him because he was different. That she liked him she accepted without conscious thought, had accepted it from the moment he played his part in the shower. And this liking increased with association.

A newspaper photographer? He did not look it, at least not like her conception of a newspaper man, certainly like no reporters she had ever seen. Perhaps the first reason for this attraction was that he was clean, scrupulously so; she had noticed this upstairs. And there was a virile hardness about him that spoke of competence and honesty towards himself.

And his dress. The brown business suit, the polished oxfords, the knot in his tie and the way it nestled firmly against his collar, the fresh handkerchief in the breast pocket. The keynote of it all was a conservative, careless correctness with no trace of foppishness, without the stiff perfection of a magazine advertisement.

She had not been able to decide about the color of his eyes, but she liked them because they looked right at her when he spoke. And his peculiar little smile that crinkled the corners of those eyes and lifted two-thirds of his mouth and gave a glimpse of his teeth.

But perhaps it was not his appearance at all. Perhaps it was just that he seemed dependable, competent. And most of the men she knew did nothing well; they drank too much and talked too much about it and the women they made. . . .

"So you went out together? Then what?"

Joyce Archer's thoughts jerked back to reality. Not until then did she realize that she had been staring at him and that he had been watching her stare. She looked down at her hand on the chair arm and said:

"We came downstairs and started to get in the roadster.

"You weren't on the story," Murdock said. "Brady was upstairs with the rest of the gang when I came out in the hall. Nobody assigned you, did they?"

"Hell, no."

"And you're not on the lobster shift. How come you were prowling around at six o'clock?"

"I was late," Doane said, his round face cracking wide in an infectious grin.

"Late?"

"Yeah. I didn't get off till three and there was a poker game and—well, I was goin' home and I saw two police cars out front, so I—"

"So you horned in," Murdock grunted. "And you didn't get anything."

"It's that Keogh," mumbled Doane, suddenly grouchy. "Do I hate that guy! Just a thick-headed copper with an ingrown grudge. He wouldn't let me in." Doane's smile returned and his eyes got hopeful. "But you were there. Can't you give me—"

"No. Brady's got the story."

"Well—" Doane cocked one brow. "You can at least let me in here."

"No," said Murdock, but he was weakening; he always did before the youth's guileless assault.

"Can't you give me a drink?" pleaded Doane. "Hell, I been up all night and—"

"All right, all right," sighed Murdock, standing aside. "But one quick one and out you go. I got things to do."

He went out to the kitchenette, poured Scotch and soda, brought the drink to the living-room, and found Doane lying on the davenport, a picture of utter contentment, his knees in the air.

Murdock grabbed one shoulder, lifted the youth to a sitting position, handed him the drink.

Doane said: "Thanks," as he accepted the glass; then: "What, no ice?"

Murdock reached forward. "Gimme!"

"No!" Doane recoiled, panicky. "I was only foolin'."

Murdock grinned, but he stood there and made Doane pour down the drink, took the glass, and guided him forcibly but gently to the door. When he finally worked the youth into the hall in spite of the fervent protestations, Doane said:

"Now listen. If you run into anything—"

"Will you do me a favor?" Murdock asked wearily.

"Sure, Kent." Doane was quickly serious. "Anything you say."

"That's swell," Murdock said. "Then go 'way. Go any-where—as long as it's away from here."

"But—"

"You're wearing me down." Murdock put one lean hand on Doane's chest and shoved. The door slammed on Doane's wail.

Murdock shook his head for a moment and continued to grin at his thoughts. Then the grin faded. He shrugged, went over to the window and tasted the remainder of his drink. The soda was flat and he crossed to the daven-port, picked up Doane's empty glass, and took them both to the kitchenette, knocking at the bedroom door as he passed.

Opening the cupboard, he took out the Scotch-bottle, uncorked it. Then, glaring at it, he put the cork back in, replaced the bottle, and muttered a soft curse as he stared at the empty glasses.

He was in a jam and he knew it. She did not know about Howard. He did not want to tell her—yet. But she ought to go and tell her story to Bacon. He knew it, felt guilty with this knowledge. Never one to kid himself that he was able to do police and detective work on the side, Murdock had been content to help when he could and pay attention to his business—the taking of pictures.

One reason why he was successful at his job was that he enjoyed the confidence of the headquarters men and most of the precinct commanders he knew. He was holding out now, and he knew it. And let Bacon find out and— He cursed again and went into the bathroom.

Pink silk shorts and brassière were wadded on the bath-mat; the sodden mass of dress, jacket, and wrap lay in the center of the tub, the slippers on top of them, the stockings draped over the rounded sides. The sight brought an unconscious grin to his face and he stepped into the living-room, saw that Joyce Archer was again in the wing chair.

She said: "Who was that?"

"A friend of mine." Murdock hesitated. "We'd better get some breakfast up here."

"I'm not hungry." She looked at him over her shoulder.

"You will be before you get out."

Her lips went round, like her eyes. "You mean I'm to stay here until—"

"I mean you've got to stay here—today anyway." Murdock advanced, stood over her, his expression faintly amused. "You're not counting on wearing that outfit you splashed all over the bathroom, are you?"

She smiled at him. "I was too comfortable to pick up."

Murdock said: "I'll take them out when I go, get them dried and cleaned for you."

"How long will that take?"

"That's not the point. The police are looking for you. Fortunately they don't know you are here—yet. But they'll watch this building for a while and—"

"Couldn't I get out the back way?"

Murdock jammed his hands in his pockets and looked annoyed.

"You'll stay here and do as I say. I'm in this thing, and I want to help; but that isn't all of it. Ethically, I have no compunction about your being here. But if I didn't have a few friends on the police force I'd be looking for another job."

"You mean you're afraid—" Joyce Archer stopped uncertainly.

Murdock grunted impatiently, stepped to the straight-backed chair, and sat down. For a moment he studied the girl and then, hands still in pockets, he stretched out his legs and studied the polished wing-tips of his oxfords.

"Bacon and some of those fellows have got the idea that I'm a square shooter and on the level with them. Maybe they're funny that way, but I think they sort of like me. And this is the first time I've ever double-crossed them."

Joyce Archer said: "Oh."

Murdock stood up. "Yeh. So you either stay here and do as I say—until tonight—or you call headquarters and tell them your story. I'll try and pacify Bacon while I've still got a chance."

"I'll do it your way," Joyce Archer said and smiled at him. "But I'm not hungry."

Murdock grinned and moved over to a hall closet, got out a brown felt and a brown tweed topcoat. Tossing them on a chair-back, he went into the bathroom and a moment later Joyce heard him say:

"What do I do with 'em? Wring 'em out or what?"

She laughed and got out of the chair. The bathrobe nearly fell off, did slip from the shoulders. She snatched it back, tightened the belt, and went into the bathroom. Five minutes later Murdock had a newspaper-wrapped bundle under his arm.

"I was going to have breakfast with you," he said, stopping near the door and taking his little camera from the larger case. "But if you must be difficult about it—"

"I'd like it," Joyce Archer said quickly.

"It's too late," Murdock said. "My second thought is better. I'll get rid of this junk"—he tapped the bundle—"and get down to work." He turned the door-knob.

"I'll have some orange juice and toast and coffee sent up from the corner drug-store—and a sandwich for this noon. What do you like? Chicken? Ham and cheese?"

"With tomato."

"And I'll pay for it," Murdock added crisply, "so when the stuff comes you can tell the boy to leave it outside the door. Don't open up until he leaves."

8

DETECTIVE MAHADY WAS on duty in the lobby when Murdock stepped from the elevator. He nodded to the desk clerk, angled round a potted palm and a stone urn, stopped in front of the detective, a sour-looking man with an expression of acute displeasure.

"Bacon still up there?"

"No. Only I got to stay and watch for that dame."

"Nothing new?"

"How would I know?" muttered Mahady. "I'm just one of the boys."

Murdock said: "Tough," and slapped through the revolving door, turned left under the marquee, with a "Good morning" to the doorman.

The early autumn morning was fresh, crisp under a bright new sun that had thrown off daylight's muddy screen. Murdock breathed deeply without knowing it and lengthened his stride. He waved a hand at the traffic officer on the Avenue, continued on to Newbury Street, and turned into the drug-store. He ordered tomato juice and coffee, drank unhurriedly, then gave the order for Joyce Archer and paid for it.

The tailor-shop he sought was near by, a one-room, second-floor shop. Murdock climbed through a dusty-smelling half-light, his feet clicking sharply on the narrow wooden stairs, worn in smooth hollows by a generation or more of use.

The frosted glass panel of the door at the far end of

the drab hall said: "A. Abramson," and Murdock went into a square, high-ceilinged room that had a long rack, filled with neatly pressed suits; three benches, also filled with suits, but making, in the aggregate, an almost hopelessly snarled mass; a steam-table, and two spindly chairs.

A tall, gaunt man was at work at this pressing-table. He continued to work without looking up, and the escaping steam kept the room filled with its moist stale odor. Murdock walked over to the fat little Jew with the three days' growth of beard who sat cross-legged on a bench near the two windows.

"Listen, Abe"—Murdock tossed his bundle on the fellow's lap—"when can I get this back?"

"When do you want it?" parried Abe, attacking the wrapping. When he drew out the dress he said: "Oy," and squeezed it with both hands, like a sponge. "Soaked." He separated the rest of the garments, held up the brassière.

"So," he said finally, nodding his head up and down. "You're doing all right by yourself now-days."

Murdock grunted to repress a grin. "Never mind. I asked you when can I get them."

"Tomorrow."

"Today."

"Am I a miracle man? Feel. Silk. Soaked."

"Today," Murdock argued. "Or else."

"I can't guarantee it," Abe said, weakening.

"I'll be back at five—or six."

Murdock took the subway at Copley and ten minutes later swung into the photographic department on the third floor of the *Courier-Herald* building. Nodding a greeting to two other camera men who lounged in the anteroom, he took off his coat, hung it on an oak hatrack, and went down the darkened corridor to one of the cubby-hole-like dark-rooms.

He had developed his film and was putting it through the fixing bath when someone called down the hall: "Hey, Kent! Wyman wants to see you."

Murdock called the fellow into the dark-room, held the film up to the ruby light. "The five at the end," he said. "Finish 'em and blow 'em up to four or five if they'll stand it."

He went upstairs, through the city room, and into a corridor at the rear, stopping in front of a door which said: "T. A. Wyman." Knocking once, he went in.

The office was small, simply furnished with a brown rug, a massive, new-looking desk, a filing-cabinet, and three chairs, all made of metal which was supposed to imitate wood. Wyman glanced up from the desk as Murdock entered, took the cigar from his mouth, and said:

"Sit down, Kent."

Murdock took a chair at one end of the desk, settled into it, and crossed one leg over the other knee, waiting while Wyman gave his attention to some papers on the desk.

The *Courier-Herald* Publishing Company had morning, evening, and Sunday editions. Theoretically Wyman was managing editor of the *Morning Herald;* actually he was the *Courier-Herald* Publishing Company. He did not own much stock, his financial interest was comparatively small, but he ran things just the same.

He was a stocky man, partly bald, with a heavy face

lean face. He spoke in slow, almost absent tones. "It taught me to like nice clothes and how to drink; it taught me to appreciate good books and good pictures and—in short, it taught me to like most of the things money can buy. The hell of it is, I never was able to pick up any very good ideas of just how to go about getting this—"

"Have it your way." Wyman said shortly. "Where you going to get that future you want?"

"Newspaper work is a young man's game."

"It's anybody's game that can take it. I thought you could."

Murdock flushed, and Wyman continued:

"You wouldn't be satisfied if you couldn't take pictures."

"Probably not." Murdock flexed his crossed ankles. "But there are other fields besides newspapers. I thought I might go to New York and see if I couldn't get in with some advertising photographer—maybe even portrait stuff. Do some real camera work. There's money in it. I wouldn't be any Steichen or Nelson maybe, but I wouldn't need to be. Look at Bourke-White—a girl. Look at this guy Lohse—Remie Lohse. He's got an outfit like mine and look what he's done with it—*Vanity Fair* stuff.

"I've been interested in cameras ever since my father gave me a box outfit for my twelfth birthday. A hobby. It helped me through college—I had a pretty fair lay-out by that time, did a pretty good business with sports pictures. But I thought I wanted to be a newspaper man. Was I dumb?"

Murdock's smile was disparaging and he kept his eyes on his shoes.

This time Wyman remained silent. It was not entirely newspaper experience that put him at the top of the heap. He could never have climbed there if he had not been a keen judge of men. And his interest in Murdock was both personal and selfishly business. He knew he had not exaggerated when he said Murdock was the best camera in the city.

He was popular. He had a wide acquaintance in all levels of society, because he was the sort of fellow who could talk nearly everyone's language; he was equally proficient at balancing a cup of tea and a piece of cake on his knee and acting as if it belonged there, or busting his way through a crowd with a camera and plate-case. He was loyal, square, intelligent. He could fight. He took a black eye or a torn suit in his stride. He got pictures if anyone did, and a lot more that other photographers missed.

"So I tried it," Murdock went on, "for three years." He looked up and grinned. "I was a damn good leg man, too. But I couldn't write. So I came over on the picture side. I guess that's worse than the other. But I've done some nice work with a camera; I've got an idea I could cash in on it better if I—"

"Wait a minute," Wyman said. He looked at his cigar, turned it between thumb and forefinger, and stuck it in one corner of his mouth.

"I've been thinking about this for a long time. It's not original; plenty of papers are doing it. See how it sounds. We've got two papers—fourteen cameras; and it's about time we made a regular department; put a man in as the head of it and let him run the whole picture side instead of letting the editors give out assignments. Of course he'd have to work hand in hand with the news men, but there'd be more freedom, plenty of latitude to work with. What do you think? A photographer running the photo department. Don't that sound better than having a news man give all the orders?"

"Sure."

"Then take the job, try it out. If it works you can write your own ticket; I'll give you a contract."

"An inside job," Murdock muttered. "Take the blame for every camera and get no credit and not much chance to work on anything of my own."

"Ah—" Wyman clamped his heavy jaws on the cigar and pushed back in the chair. "You cry because you're afraid your legs'll give out, but when you can't get out and dig, you cry about that too. What you oughta do is go out and get drunk. Take a couple days off and—"

"It isn't that." Murdock pulled in his legs. "I've changed my mind about quitting anyway—since last night. I want a leave of absence—a couple of weeks."

"What for?"

"Well"—Murdock spread his hands—"you were partly right. I've had some wife trouble and I can buy her off. I understand the Bar Association is putting up a five-thousand reward on that killing last night. I was in at the start and I might get lucky. I'd like to—"

"How much of the five would you get even if you were lucky? You'd have to split with a half-dozen detectives and—"

"That's just part of it. The *Eagle* is offering five thousand for the exclusive story of the arrest and conviction of—"

"Oh," Wyman said. "You're that kind of a chiseler, huh?"

"That's the kind I'm going to be until I get a divorce," Murdock said flatly. "And I'm asking for the leave—"

"All right," snapped Wyman. He snatched the cigar from his mouth and threw it into a brass cuspidor. "I can think of some guys that would take salary checks from the business office and then, if they did get the story, sell out to the *Eagle* under an assumed name. You at least asked for the leave. So go get the story. You haven't got a prayer—not even you—but go get it. Get it and I'll match the *Eagle*. But this is just between you and me—and I've got to have pictures."

Murdock sighed in satisfaction and reached for the telephone. When he got the photo department, he said: "Bring those prints to Wyman's office, Eddy. Mac blew them up and they ought to be on the drying-rack."

Wyman's eyes snapped as Murdock hung up. "Got something?"

Murdock said: "Bacon gave me a break," and waited until a freckled, tow-headed office boy came in with five damp prints. Murdock glanced at them and passed them to Wyman.

The managing editor's eyes went wide and there was a sudden feverish cast to his face as he grabbed for the telephone. He kept pawing at the pictures with his free hand until he got his connection. Then he bawled:

"Stop the presses!"

Murdock jerked to his feet. "No!" he rapped, and clamped his palm over the mouthpiece.

Quick anger flooded Wyman's heavy face, flashed in his eyes. He fumed: "What the hell do you mean, no!" and tried to wrench the telephone free. "Why didn't you bring 'em up before?"

Eddy stood in the doorway, goggle-eyed.

Murdock said: "Wait! You're only running the bull-dog."

"What of it?" Wyman ceased struggling, as though he sensed that there was a real reason for Murdock's tardiness.

"Pictures in mail editions have been stolen before," Murdock said levelly. "They can't do much of a job with 'em, but it's been done. You won't lose any circulation in the country whether you run 'em or not. You'll pick up twenty-five thousand in city circulation if you have those shots exclusive."

Wyman banged down the receiver and glared at Eddy, who hastily withdrew. He took out a fresh cigar and stuck it in his mouth without biting the end.

"That's what burns me up about you," he growled finally. "You can think. You're not just a photographer, your a newspaper man. But there's no future, huh? Well, get the hell out of here, I got work to do."

Murdock smiled, and moved towards the door. "Okay. I just wanted to give you the first installment on this private assignment."

Wyman's brows came down. "Wait," he said skeptically. "How'd you get these? Have the outfit at home?"

Murdock shook his head. "My private rig. On the side.

For the glory of the good old *Courier-Herald* and—"

The shrill of the telephone interrupted him, and Wyman said: "For you."

Murdock leaned across the desk and accepted the instrument.

The voice at the other end was hoarse, jerky. "Murdock? This is Sam Cusick. Did you tip off the cops about seeing me last night?"

Murdock felt his pulse quicken, but he kept his voice level as he answered: "I might have mentioned it."

"Oh?" The word was a sneer. "You *might* have, huh? Well, get a load of this. You forget you saw me. You made a mistake, see?"

"I hear you, if that's what you mean," Murdock told him.

"You hear me, and you'll do what I say. I'm not gonna let 'em frame me for that job just because you saw me there. I got a way of keeping guys' mouths shut. And I'm gonna stay in the clear until I'm damn sure you can't do me any harm."

"What am I supposed to do?" growled Murdock, "Go down and—"

"Figure it out for yourself. You made a mistake."

The receiver clicked in Murdock's ear. He replaced the telephone and straightened up.

Wyman, watching him suspiciously, asked: "Who was that?"

"Just a pal of mine," Murdock said. A grim little smile pulled back his lips as he opened the door and stepped into the hall.

9

Tom Doane was loitering in the main corridor of police headquarters when Murdock arrived at three that afternoon. The young reporter grabbed Murdock's arm, started to accompany him to the elevators.

"What you down here on?"

"Bacon wants to see me," Murdock said.

"Hah!" Doane grinned, and stepped into the elevator, banging against the plate-case slung over Murdock's shoulder.

They rode to the fourth floor, turned right into the hall, and walked down to the far end where an open door led to a small anteroom. A uniformed officer at the desk nodded to Murdock, who crossed to the door in the right wall and knocked.

Keogh opened the door. Murdock stepped past him with Doane at his heels. The Sergeant scowled and grabbed the youth by the arm.

"Hey, you," he growled.

"I'm with him," protested Doane, reeling back through the doorway under Keogh's unrelenting propulsion.

"Not now you're not," Keogh said, and his broad face took on a satisfied grin.

"He's all right," Murdock said.

"He's a pest," Keogh said, and slammed the door.

The room was not an office, really; it was more like a conference room. The walls were bare; there was a long table of golden oak, scarred along the edges by official and unofficial heels. A half-dozen chairs were strung along both sides. Lieutenant Bacon, sitting at the far end of the table, was the only one in the room.

He said: "Sit down," and Murdock moved to a chair beside him. The photographer unbuttoned his coat, shrugged off the plate-case, and put the box-like camera on the table. Bacon asked: "You got anything new?"

"Not much," Murdock said. "Only Cusick made a friendly call."

"Cusick?" Bacon was all interest. Keogh circled the end of the table and sat down opposite Murdock. "When? What did he want?"

Murdock told of the telephone conversation, then lit a cigarette and pushed back his hat.

"We'll get him," Bacon said grimly.

"And I want to be there when we do," Keogh added. "He blackjacked a guy from Station 6 early this morning. That was before we knew about this other and the fellow met Cusick and started to question him about something else."

Keogh scowled, glanced out the window. "Somebody's gonna have a lot of fun when we get him."

Bacon hooked his thumbs in his lower vest pockets and studied Murdock a moment before he spoke.

"Archer and Redfield had a quarrel—a fight, last night."

"So—" Murdock said, and tried to look interested while Bacon gave familiar details.

"And we know who that dame is now," the Lieutenant finished. "Archer's sister. I can't hook her up—unless she helped somebody else."

Murdock asked: "Did you find the gun?"

Bacon nodded. "A twenty-five. It was in an overcoat, in that closet where we think the girl was hiding."

Murdock's brows lifted. "Prints?"

"Smudged."

The brows came down and Murdock, pulling thoughtfully on the cigarette, finally asked: "How about Spike Tripp?"

"We're letting him out on bail. We worked him over a bit, but it didn't add up to anything. That girl that was passed out was the one all right. Her story's the same as his: he was supposed to call for her. And anyway he's nothing but a cheap punk. He never was a killer and I can't find any motive. Right now we can't score any runs with him, and we can always pick him up if we want him."

Bacon rubbed the side of his nose with a bony index finger, pulled at a thick gold chain until a thick gold watch came into view. "We're waiting for Archer—and Girard. I said I'd give you a break. You can sit in."

The uniformed policeman on duty in the anteroom opened the door as though Bacon's speech was a prearranged signal. Nodding his head briefly, Bacon moved aside and Howard Archer stepped across the threshold, stopped there, and surveyed the room with cold blue eyes and a distasteful expression.

Murdock stood up, said: "Hello, Archer," and pushed his camera along to the other end of the table, picked up his plate-case, and moved it beside the chair which was farthest from Bacon.

Archer nodded and the Lieutenant said: "Sit down,

Mr. Archer—over here." He indicated the chair Murdock had left. Howard Archer strode forward. Keogh moved his chair so that he could lean back against the wall, and propped himself there, his feet dangling.

Archer sat down, frowned, and said: "Well," with a bored, patronizing inflection.

"You had a fight with Redfield last night," Bacon said.

"An argument," Archer corrected coldly.

"I heard different," Bacon said, "but let it pass. Anyway, you made a threat."

"That's right."

"And the fi—the argument was over Mrs. Redfield. It's true, isn't it, that you've been pretty friendly?"

"I've known her for years."

"But more so than ever lately, particularly while Redfield was busy with Girard's trial. Maybe more than friendly."

Archer's thin, tanned face flushed and his blue eyes were hostile and narrowed. "I resent that remark and I resent your attitude."

"That's too bad," said Bacon, unperturbed. "But maybe you've forgotten that this is a murder case we're talking about. I want information and I'm going to get it. We're not going to bulldoze you or high-pressure you." He waved his hand to indicate the room at large. "There's no stenographer. If you want to get your lawyer, that's all right with me. But if I were you, I'd take it easy and try and help us out. We're making no formal charge, and we're not going to arrest you—yet. We may have to if you hold us up."

Archer stroked his blond mustache and waited, his

eyes still hostile, disdainful.

Bacon went on in the same level tones. "In fact," he added, as though there had been no interruption, "I believe you considered the idea of running off with Mrs. Redfield."

Archer colored, snapped: "Have you talked with her?" Bacon nodded and Archer added: "Then why bother asking me about it? I've been friendly, yes. To be exact, I'm in love with her. She was practically forced into marrying Redfield, and she was sick of her bargain. Redfield was drunk last night, and he ended by making a scene. I left at about three o'clock."

"With your sister."

Archer hesitated uncertainly, then finally said: "Yes, with my sister."

"Where is she now?"

"I don't know."

"She go home with you?"

"Certainly." This sharply.

"Then," said Bacon wearily, "how come we find your car parked round the corner from Redfield's place at six-thirty this morning?"

"I left it there," Archer said, and Murdock, watching closely, thought that Archer lied very well and very promptly. He liked him for that, the first time he had ever liked anything about him at all.

"But you didn't drive it away."

"I forgot I left it there. I was thinking about other things."

"Then you came to the apartment house and went upstairs. What happened then?"

"I tried the door and it was locked, so—"

"So you sneaked out the back way," Bacon cut in dryly. "You must have or the operator would have seen you come out."

Archer took a deep breath, made an obvious effort to control his annoyance. "All right," he said. "You seem to know more than I thought."

"We have to," Bacon said.

"I came back," Archer lipped, "to see Ri—Mrs. Redfield, and to have it out with Mark then and there if necessary. I had been waiting for the chance to tell him how she and I felt about each other. We could have gone away together, but I preferred to tell him first. I was angry enough to want to do it last night and have it over.

"I came through the lobby and the operator looked as if he was asleep. I went upstairs and pressed the buzzer. When no one answered, I went in. I found Redfield dead in the library, found Rita in the bedroom. I couldn't rouse her. I didn't have any alternative; I had to get away.

"But I remembered the boy in the lobby. I thought if he was asleep I'd be a fool to take a chance of his waking when I went out. I knew if I was seen I'd be implicated. So I went downstairs and out the back way."

"What time did you come back?" Bacon asked.

"About four-fifteen, I think, but I'm not sure exactly."

Murdock had opened his plate-case and camera. As Archer answered, he screwed a flash-bulb into his synchronized flash-gun, adjusted the shutter and focus. When he put the camera to his shoulder and glanced through the metal frame of the finder, he saw Bacon's eyes shift to him. But for once Murdock was getting one-hundred-per-cent co-operation from the police. The Lieutenant gave no sign that he saw anything out of the ordinary and, glancing at Archer, said:

"All right. Thanks very much. You'd better plan to remain in town for a few days; we may need you again."

Archer smiled and stood up. As he turned, Murdock pressed the button, and the flash-bulb exploded light into the room. Archer's facial reaction was instantaneous. Anger flooded his cheeks, and he opened his mouth, closed it, finally spoke contemptuously.

"That's just about the sort of cheap trick I'd expect of you, Murdock."

Red spots jumped out on Murdock's cheek-bones. It was the one thing about the job he hated—having to take this sort of thing from fellows like Archer. He reversed his plate-holder to give himself something to do while he got control of his voice; then he said:

"Would you have given me the shot if I'd asked for it?"

"I should say not."

"That's what I thought." Murdock placed the camera on the table. "And it's my job to take pictures. So for fellows like you who have an exaggerated idea of the importance of their privacy, I get them the best way I can."

When Archer went out, Keogh spat out a curse and bounced the front legs of his chair down on the floor. "I hate guys like that. Smart. Throwin' that high-hat stuff around." He glared at Bacon. "You were too easy on him. A couple slaps in the mouth would soften him up a bit."

"Sure," Bacon said, sucking his lips. "And then I'd wake up out in the sticks and you'd be back in uniform. You can get rough sometimes; sometimes you can't—and you do too much thinking with your mouth. Damn it! I don't even dare hold him but—"

"He looks good to me," Keogh snorted, "next to Cusick. If I was going to make a choice between them I'd have to toss a coin. His story's screwy. Going out the back way. Hell! He was nuts about Redfield's wife and he came back looking for trouble."

Murdock's resentment still smoldered from Archer's attitude. But he thought of something in the man's favor and he spoke his mind.

"Don't forget about the telephone flash from Redfield's apartment at five after four. Archer didn't come in till fifteen after, the kid downstairs told you that."

"It can be figured," Bacon said, and scratched behind his ear. "If he went out the back way, he coulda come in that way before." He twisted in the chair, drummed the table-top with finger-tips. "It's his sister that's got me worried. A woman can pull a trigger and—"

"I doubt like hell," Murdock sniffed, "if she could bust Redfield's finger like that."

Bacon looked up quickly, caught Murdock's sardonic gaze. He took a deep breath, blew it out resignedly, seemed about to speak when a knock sounded on the door and Nate Girard came into the room followed by two well-dressed, somber-faced men. One was tall, slightly stooped; the other, thickset and swarthy. The eyes of both were the same: alert, hard, a bit cruel as they swiveled about the room.

Keogh said: "Well, well," sarcastically; "you got your cowboys back again, huh?"

"I'm going to keep them," Girard said, "until you fellows get on your jobs and round up Sam Cusick."

"Yeah?" Keogh said. "Well, leave 'em outside, you won't need 'em here."

"If that's a promise," Girard said easily, "okay." He turned to the two bodyguards and grinned. "You stay outside, boys; it seems the Sergeant objects to your company."

Nate Girard was an unusual figure, both in personality and in matter of record. It would have been difficult to convince the average man that during prohibition he was the most successful operator in the illicit liquor traffic in that part of the country. And this difficulty was not hard to understand. Girard had nothing in common with the run-of-the-mill bootlegger except the nature of his business.

Physically he was a handsome, striking figure, a man who dressed like a banker and whose conversation, manners, and general conduct—when necessary and advisable —were above reproach. In addition he was shrewd, intelligent, well-educated—probably the only college graduate in his line of business.

Even his police record was innocuous enough. Until the recent murder charge, resulting in his acquittal, he had just two counts against him, both technical liquor charges and both settled with fines. In the past ten years of his operations he had never been accused of murder or hijacking. Perhaps the strangest thing of all was that, among those who had business dealings with him, he had a reputation for honesty, a business word that was scrupulously kept.

During the recent trial reporters had scoured every available source to uncover facts about his personal life and habits. Always the sort of personality that makes news, he had received much publicity in the past, not all of it unfavorable. But his private life was cloudy, kept under cover. Just one new side of him came to light, unearthed by a sob sister on the *Courier*. As a human interest yarn, the story had everything: Girard the philanthropist.

And he had not been cheap or flashy about it either. He did not scatter nickels to poor children nor get his picture taken delivering Christmas baskets to the needy; but he had, for several years, kept a dozen families on his payroll, sending them a weekly check to pay for their food and shelter. There was no ulterior motive or obligation, no grandstanding about it; Girard did this for the satisfaction and enjoyment it gave him.

Murdock thought of all this as he studied the man and watched him move up alongside the table and sit down in the same chair Archer had used.

"Well"—Girard smiled at Murdock, glanced at Keogh, turned back to Bacon—"let's get on with the inquisition."

The Lieutenant leaned back, his gray eyes thoughtful. "Where were you last night between three-thirty and five? That's all the inquisition there is."

"Why?"

"Because I want to know. You've read the afternoon papers."

"In other words, you want to know if I have an alibi."

Girard rubbed his clipped mustache with his thumb. "Well, fortunately I've got one. Unfortunately I'm not at liberty to disclose it."

"There are ways of making you tell it," Bacon said sharply. Girard did not answer, and the Lieutenant went on: "Understand, I'm not saying you killed Redfield, but—"

"There's no reason why I should."

"There could have been."

"What is it?"

"You paid Redfield twenty-five thousand when he took the case; you gave him the other half yesterday. Luckily for you, we found that twenty-five in his apartment safe or there might have been a reason. But we don't pretend to know everything. You—anyone at that party might've had plenty of reason for putting him away. We suspect everybody. I want to know where you were after three-thirty. The man we sent to check on you found you at your place at six o'clock. Did anyone see you come in?"

"No."

"When did you get there?"

"I don't believe I want to tell that now, either," Girard said calmly. "Not until I find out whether I've got to tell the rest of the story. It involves a woman and—"

"Utsnay!" snapped Keogh irritably. "We've heard that one before. You got an alibi. Then spill it. We've made tougher guys than you talk."

Girard was unimpressed. "Maybe. But I don't have to tell you here, and you know it. If you want to make a pinch, I'll get hold of a lawyer and—"

"And you won't have Redfield to spring you, either."

"—and find out where we stand," Girard finished, ignoring Keogh's interruption. "I can tell if I have to, but if you make me and can't justify your arrest—"

"When did you hire those bodyguards?" Bacon said, giving Keogh an angry sidewise glance.

"This morning."

"Why?"

"I told you. Cusick and his brother tried to take me for twenty thousand and they got four years. Redfield and I put them away—Redfield because he was really working for me, although the D.A. prosecuted. I didn't kill Joe Cusick and—"

"You were acquitted anyway," Keogh leered.

Girard's profile was sharp against the light from the windows, and Murdock saw the jaw stick out, saw the neck redden and bulge with anger that could no longer be controlled. Girard stood up, walked to the door, opened it, and looked out. Closing it softly, he came back and stood spread-legged, looking down at Bacon. Finally he took out a cigar, bit it once or twice, and sat down.

"No dictograph hooked up here?"

Bacon shook his head, his thin face puzzled, wary.

Girard grabbed his chair, spun it about, and straddled it as he sat down, turning slightly so he could see all three men. He crossed his forearms on the chair-back, leaned on them.

"Here's something I never told anybody," he said and it was apparent that he was still angry. "I couldn't tell it until last year, and I've had no reason to make any confidences since. But you fellows are beginning to wear me down and"—he glanced at Bacon. "Oh, you're all right.

I know you've got a job to do, and you're a good copper in your way. If there were more like you it would be different. But this one"—he jerked a thumb at the scowling Keogh without looking at him—"is just a tough mug that with a little different break in environment or circumstances would've made a first-class thug. And—"

Keogh came to his feet with a bound. "Listen, you!" he grated.

Girard untangled his arms and stood up. "I'm listenin', smarty," he said, and he said it insultingly.

Keogh cursed and his quick temper got the best of him. He struck out with his left. Girard either moved with astonishing speed or he anticipated the blow. In any case he took it on hunched jaw, rolled with it and crossed his right, a clean hard smash that landed on Keogh's cheekbone.

Girard's punch had timing and power. Keogh bounced back against the wall and sat down. Sheer surprise kept him there a moment; then he was up, eager to continue.

Bacon yelled: "Lay off!" and jumping in front of the Sergeant, jammed him down on his chair.

Keogh started to struggle, stopped suddenly as he realized whom he was struggling with. Bacon sat down again and shook his head, his eyes exasperated as they met Murdock's interested gaze.

"Jesus!" he groaned, "do I get co-operation?" He eyed Keogh wrathfully. "Sometimes I wonder why I put up with you."

"He can't pull that stuff with me," Keogh growled.

Girard adjusted his cuffs, glanced at Murdock. "You were a witness if anybody wants to make anything of it."

"Take it easy," Bacon begged. "Who wants to make anything out of it?"

Girard, apparently unruffled now, folded his arms over the chair-back again. The cigar was crushed and broken now, but he did not seem to notice it; he chewed on it and began his story as though nothing had happened.

"I was brought up on a farm in a part of the country where newspapers are a luxury. We were poor—poor as hell. But I had the luck to have a mother who had ideas. She talked college to me from the time I was old enough to walk four miles to the country school. And she didn't know anything about college either. It was just an idea. She'd read something about it some place. She worked and slaved and saved her pennies and made me work out summers and bring every cent I made home to her. It got so I hated the idea of college, but her will was stronger than mine. Anyway, I went—to a cheap State affair. And I worked there, and she helped me. She couldn't come to see me graduate because she didn't have anything but house dresses. Maybe you can imagine how I felt when I got out. I was old enough then to realize, to appreciate, what she had done. And there was only one thing I wanted: to make some money and repay her. And what happened?"

Girard broke off with a little grunt, chewed on his cigar. No one spoke, and when he continued, his voice was absent, its keynote a grim bitterness that was unmistakable.

"I couldn't get a job, that's what happened." He hesitated again and looked out the windows, then went on as though reliving that part of his life.

"I was broke, and I couldn't let her know. I washed dishes, and kept furnaces and mowed lawns for my room. I waited on table and ran elevators and mopped out offices; finally I got a job as helper on a truck. For over two years I had just enough cash to keep going. And then I began to get scared. She had taken ten years off her life working for me. I could tell from her letters she was tired out. And I couldn't do anything about it. I was afraid I couldn't get that money in time."

Girard seemed to snap his reverie.

"That's why I was a bootlegger. It never bothered my conscience. I had a lot of public sentiment on my side because the public was a partner in the whole damn works. But even if they'd been against me, it would have made no difference. And I made money; and the more I made, the more I could grow.

"But I ran my business with brains instead of machine-guns, and you know it. I lost some money that way; I lost plenty of truckloads to hijackers. But I worked out a system whereby my own drivers didn't know where they were going half the time. Sealed-order stuff. It worked. And I found out there were some surprisingly honest men in the same business with me. I could have made more money with a gun; I made enough for me without it. None of my drivers ever carried a gun. When they were stuck up, they just got down off the seat and walked in. There was no shooting.

"And if I had it all to do over again, I'd follow the same groove. Because my mother had the things I wanted to give her before she died. My name is not Girard. As far as I know, she, or her few friends, never knew my business. My reputation was local, sectional anyway. My picture would never make the newspapers she finally had time to read. A sob story, huh?" Girard laughed, but there was no mirth in his tones.

"Don't get the idea I'm trying to justify my actions to you; in my own mind I don't need justification. But to tell you what I wanted, I had to tell it all. And here's the pay-off: For ten or twelve years I broke the law and was tangled up with killers and crooked cops and government men. The gun ruled, generally. Yet in all that time I never used one or put the finger on a man. Then I turn legitimate; I try to live a moral law-abiding life. And what does it get me? A lot of grief.

"I've got money; I've invested it as wisely as anyone can these days. I like a good time, but I mind my own business. And what's the result? Twice you've had me down here on gang killings. The Cusicks try to take me for twenty thousand and land in jail. One of them is killed and for that you did your damnedest to get me the chair. And now this Redfield thing."

Girard took out his cigar, looked at it, threw it on the floor, and stood up.

"Well, I'm fed up. Through. I'm sick of having you fellows push me around."

He hesitated, glanced challengingly about as though waiting for some answer. But no one said anything. There was nothing to say, because Girard was convincing; when he talked like that, you believed him. Bacon had not moved since Girard began; neither had the glowering Keogh. Murdock realized he was holding his breath and let it out softly.

Girard put on his coat, picked up his hat, and glanced around once more, then walked to the door.

"If the reason for this forensic display is cloudy, put it down to lack of practice. If it gives you the idea that I'm sick of the whole God-damned business, you've caught my meaning."

He put on his hat, his other hand on the door-knob.

"If you want me again, subpœna me and I'll come down with my lawyer. But if you're figuring on building me up for this Redfield job, you'd better work fast. Because I'm going down and see when I can get a good boat to Europe. I'm going to try the south of France for a while and see if they'll accept me at face value or try and pin the Stavisky job on me."

Girard opened the door. "I'll call you up, Bacon, and let you know what day I'm sailing."

The slam of the door broke the spell. Keogh stood up, went to the windows, and looked out. He cursed softly for a moment, then turned, said: "Damned if he didn't sound as if he meant it."

Murdock stirred in his chair, grinned at Bacon. "He kinda told you off, huh?"

"Yeah," Bacon sighed, "didn't he?" He stood up, continued dryly. "The hell of it is, I still can't think of any answers."

10

Kent Murdock stopped at the office on his way home, but there was no assignment for him and there was also no story to be passed along about the confidential questioning of the afternoon, so he continued on, stopping at Abe's for Joyce Archer's clothes and arriving at his apartment before six.

Joyce Archer was still curled up in the wing chair as he had left her. She put aside the book she had been reading as he entered, and when he moved closer he saw it was *Green Mansions*.

"Like it?" he asked.

"I don't know—I think I do. It's so different. But it's a beautiful thing, isn't it?"

Murdock said it was and took off his coat, laying it across the back of the davenport, placing his hat on top, the package of her clothes beside it. He thrust his hands in his trousers pockets, walked over to the windows and glanced out across the hammered steel surface of the river, frowned at it unconsciously as his doubt-filled mind picked out one thought and turned it over and over, reluctant to drop it.

"I like your place."

Murdock turned. The frown vanished, but the eyes remained troubled. "Why?"

"I don't know, unless—" She hesitated and he watched her glance slide about the room, touching the davenport with its coffee-table, the simple curtains, the heavy-looking secretary in the corner. She looked at each of the four prints—three etchings and a lithograph—in turn. He thought she liked them, particularly the Benson and one of Morgan Dennis's dogs.

"Well," she continued slowly, "the few bachelor places I've seen are either disorderly or too fastidiously neat."

"And what's this?"

"Why"—she smiled at him—"neat and disorderly."

He returned the smile now. "You've been snooping."

"I've been looking around."

He came towards her slowly, stopped in front of her. The dressing-gown had apparently settled to a fixed position with wearing. The V at the neck, curved and rounded by her breasts, was still in soft focus. Her face still looked fresh and alive and healthy.

A wad of waxed paper, the wrapping of the sandwich, lay on the reading-table. He saw that the generous bronze ash-tray was filled to overflowing with cigarette stubs. He gave her a sidewise glance, opened the jade cigarette-box. It still held a half-dozen cigarettes, but he was not satisfied and crossed to the red enamel box on the mantle. This one was empty; the one on the stand by the club chair, a carved rosewood affair, held but a single cigarette.

He grunted, said: "You smoke too much," and went over to the secretary, where he took a fresh carton from the top drawer. He tore off the wrapping, took out a half-dozen packs, and replaced the carton.

"I'll help you." Joyce Archer straightened her legs, and when she stood up, the robe fell away and there was a flash of bronzed thigh.

"You get dressed," Murdock said, and nodded towards the bundle on the davenport.

When Joyce Archer re-entered the room, she looked as he remembered her the night before; better, because there was no make-up to spoil the natural red of her lips, the freshness of her skin. And, he realized for the first time, she was tall for a girl; the shoes helped make her so, he thought.

He said: "That's better."

She grimaced and looked at her feet. "The shoes," she said, and he saw then that they had a stiff, cracked look about them.

He said: "I want to talk to you."

Her brows lifted, but when he did not add to the remark, she came forward, this time sitting on the davenport. Murdock dropped down on the opposite arm and she said:

"You act as if you were getting ready to scold me."

Murdock's grin came and went quickly. When the girl looked away, he studied the profile, admiring again the long clean line of her jaw. For a moment he thought about the girl herself. He liked her being here and could not explain the reason for it. She did not belong. She was, he told himself, too young and irresponsible and spoiled, yet—and he admitted it grudgingly—unspoiled in some ways that he liked. Genuine, that was it.

And she bothered him and—with no warning, his mind jumped off on a tangent, bringing with it a new bitterness that had lain dormant since last night. Hestor. Trouble settled over him. He cleared his throat and plunged ahead with the speech he had originally intended, his voice brusque, hard.

"I've been down to headquarters. They had your brother down there. He went back to Redfield's after he left you."

Joyce Archer's "Oh!" was a sucking sound. Murdock hurried on, telling what he knew in short, clipped sentences.

There was not much color in the girl's face when he finished. "Have they—" she managed to say—"is he arrested?"

Murdock shook his head. They don't dare—yet. But I wanted to tell you how it was. He's under suspicion—and you can't blame the police much for it. A murder case—particularly a case like this one—brings the public and the newspapers down on them with a hue and cry that they can't escape. They have to do the best they can."

Murdock shrugged and stood up. "He didn't involve you in any way, but they don't believe all of his story. I think you'd better go down to headquarters and talk with Bacon."

Joyce Archer's chin came up and there was something deep in her eyes that he could not fathom, something determined, like a little boy making up his mind to face a whipping.

"Do you think they will make me stay there—arrest me?"

"No."

"Then what good can it do?"

"No good probably," said Murdock sharply. "But they know who you are. They're going to keep on looking for you, and you'll worry your brother, and all the time you'll be taking the chance of having some tough cop picking you up and dragging you down."

"Of course," she said, standing.

Murdock nodded. "I'll go with you if you like."

"But you said if the police found out what you'd done, they wouldn't trust you any more."

"I can probably laugh it off," Murdock said shortly, "talk them out of it."

Joyce Archer shook her head. "There's no sense in that. I can go alone just as well. And I can tell them that I was able to sneak out the back way last night; I don't have to answer all of their questions."

"They'll trip you up," Murdock said. "You might as well tell the truth. You've got to explain the car you left round the corner and—"

Joyce Archer's hand went to her throat, and her mouth came open before she spoke. "I forgot."

"Your brother said he brought it. Those fellows down at headquarters are pretty good; it's their business to be. They'll make liars out of both of you."

"Then," her tone was stiff, annoyed, "I'll tell them I came in a taxi. You needn't worry."

"I don't," Murdock said.

"I appreciate what you've done." Her tone was accusing. "I've been a bother, haven't I?"

Murdock shrugged wearily and some of the harshness went out of his voice.

"Don't mind me," he said, "I'm just a photographer; a mug with a lot on his mind."

Joyce Archer stopped with her hand on the door-knob.

"Why are you a photographer?"

Murdock lifted one hand. "I like cameras and taking pictures—or maybe I'm just funny that way."

She opened the door, her voice again low. "Why don't you like me?"

"Maybe I do," Murdock told her, then added: "There's no detective downstairs now. You'd better go home and change those clothes before you talk to Bacon."

Murdock picked up the wadded sandwich wrapper, tossed it up, caught it, and then clenched it in his fist. He crossed over to the windows; he looked out for several minutes and saw nothing.

She bothered him.

From the time he had begun to earn his own living until he married Hestor, he had, in retrospective moods, thought about the girl he would some day marry. Always the girl had been like Joyce Archer. Lately his thoughts had focused upon being free; that and nothing more.

Within twenty-four hours it had become the all-important thing. Because if there ever was another girl, he did not want to wait, to make her suffer from past liaisons. Once free—

He was eight or ten years older than Joyce Archer. And his mode of living was not geared to hers. He had but few illusions left, and even those were beginning to fray around the edges. He was a newspaper photographer. He might go to New York anyway, try to find a different sort of opening. But even then there was nothing much he could offer a girl. Certainly not bridge and horses and houses in the country.

"Nuts," he muttered, and spun away from the window. Why in hell did he have to think about her anyway? What started it? Couldn't he meet a girl, have her in his rooms, without fighting to build dreams and knock them down all at the same time.

There had been other girls sitting in that wing chair. Not many, and not often, and not for long. But what of it? He didn't start worrying about them, did he? He didn't want them there all the time, did he? He reached for a cigarette, saw the tightly wadded sandwich paper in his fist, and threw it viciously towards the fireplace.

He lit the cigarette, inhaled once, and moved over to the chair. He sat there for a minute or so, immobile, one hand and forearm stretched on the curving arm of the chair. The cigarette ash lengthened and fell off, made a scattered heap on the dark rough fabric.

His eyes caught the ashes finally and he grunted, blew them off, and went over to his coat. Taking the folded copy of the *Courier* from a pocket, he came back to the chair and sat down. The late-edition head was smaller than the previous ones:

LAWYER SLAIN AFTER PARTY

He read the story, which jumped over to page three. It contained nothing new. There was a smaller one-column head adjoining the account.

GANGSTER SOUGHT IN
REDFIELD SLAYING

Sam Cusick, notorious South End gangster, listed in the District Attorney's office as Public Enemy number 14 and wanted by police for questioning in the Redfield murder, was still at large late this afternoon.

Through a statement offered by a man whose identity the police are unwilling to divulge, it had been definitely established that Cusick was at the scene of the crime in the early hours of the morning. Detective Fallon of Station 6, who recognized Cusick on the street before the killing was discovered, and attempted to question him . . .

Murdock snorted impatiently and threw the paper aside.

He stood up, crushed out his cigarette, and started towards the kitchenette. He was about half-way across the room when he heard the door open, and he turned quickly, then stiffened there as his muscles tensed.

A small, scrawny-looking man stood on the threshold, a heavy automatic in his hand. He had a thin sallow face with close-set eyes and a long, drooping nose that looked boneless. His blue coat was tight-fitting, his felt hat was the lightest of grays, and his gloves matched the hat. In the moment that he stood there motionless, the rat-like eyes flicked about the room, seemed to move in all directions at once. And they seemed satisfied with what they saw.

He spoke over his shoulder to the squat, bull-necked man who had pressed in behind him. "Looks like it's okay, Hymie," he grunted. He put the automatic in the coat pocket, where it pulled the cloth out of shape and made a threatening forward bulge. He came slowly forward as Hymie closed the door.

Murdock made his voice casual. "Hello, Cusick."

11

𝒫HIL DOANE PROWLED around police headquarters for some time after Keogh slammed the door in his face, but his prowling, from the standpoint of news values, was fruitless and he finally returned to the press-room on the first floor.

He watched the penny-ante game for a while and was tempted. He went into the washroom and counted his change. Twenty-eight cents. Might as well be broke as this way. Well, maybe not. He had to get some supper and there had been some trouble about credit at the Greasy Spoon.

He went back, sat down on a window-sill, and watched the play.

Larkin of the *Globe* picked at his nose, screwed his eyes on Mason of the *News*, who sat at his left, finally said: "I wonder has he got 'em."

Mason lifted the cigarette from the charred groove in the long table; he puffed once on it with a bored, uninterested lift of the brows. "For a nickel," he said airily, "you can find out."

"Somebody's got to keep him honest—"

Doane looked away, stared out on the parked cars in the walled courtyard with sultry eyes. Damn Keogh. Why the hell did he have to be on homicide? A guy as unreasonable and thick-headed as that ought to be out walking a beat.

Eight months Doane had been working for the *Herald*,

and he had made out fairly well until he had that trouble. He flattered Keogh, kidded him along, gave him cigarettes, bought him beers, finally got in his good graces. And then Keogh had given him a little break and let him in a cheap room in the South End where a girl had committed suicide—on the promise that Doane would see that he got some publicity.

And so he had written the story. It was a honey. Good for a column, anyway. He turned and spat on the floor. How the hell could he know Van Husan would queer everything?

"Very nice," the city editor had said when Doane put the neatly typed story on the desk. Van Husan had nodded his head without looking up, so that all Doane could see was the sandy hair and green eyeshade bobbing up and down. "Very nice. You've got some swell adjectives; the spelling is good. Real human interest, too. But"—Doane remembered how the voice cracked—"who the hell ever heard of this dame? Nobody living at that address is worth more than a paragraph, and I'm probably double-crossing the public at that!"

But you couldn't explain that to Keogh. His name wasn't in that paragraph and that was all that mattered. To hear him tell it, Doane had lain awake nights thinking about this way of playing him for a sucker.

He looked over Mason's shoulder. Why, the nut was holding a kicker to a pair of jacks and drawing two cards! Well, to hell with it; let him get burned. Doane stood up and went into the adjoining press-room, now deserted.

He took off his sweat-stained felt, tried to put a new crease in it, and found the task impossible. Searching the

pockets of his old herring-bone suit, he found a crumpled pack of cigarettes. There were three left and he
took the one that looked the loosest, straightened it out,
and lit it. He dropped into a chair, tilted it back, cocked
his heels on the table, and let his eyes wander.

There was a brown steel locker in the corner. He wondered what the hell it was for and quit wondering when
he realized he didn't give a damn. Murdock. Now, there
was a guy with something on the ball. The only thing to
do was to stick close to him. He was always running into
something, and this Redfield thing—why, he'd even been
on the party.

The conviction grew without much assistance. Murdock got peeved and grouchy and he bawled a guy out
sometimes; but he did not do it in a nasty way. And he'd
give you a break if you were around. It would be better
to stick with him, maybe even follow him around, than
go back to the office and have Van Husan stick him on
some Ladies' Debating Society meeting. One good story
was all he needed—just one good enough to make Van
Husan push up that green eyeshade. A story like that
would put him right.

The thought grew, and the more he considered it, the
more delightful it became. The prospect lulled his worries. He yawned and slipped farther down in the chair
and pulled the hat down over his eyes. Only he ought to
get more sleep nights. . . .

"Come on, snap out of it! Hey!"

Doane groaned, half fell out of the chair as he started
to rise. Finally stumbling erect, he blinked into the grinning face of Tyler, the *Courier's* regular police reporter.

Doane said: "What?" stupidly.

"You gotta cut out the snorin'," Tyler said, going back to the other room, "you're spoiling the game. We can't concentrate."

Doane looked out the window, and a sudden chill settled over him, brought with it the weakness of dismay. It was still light out, but it was getting darker; the gloom within the room was thick. Then the return of the thought which had put him to sleep jerked him to sudden action. He slid into the corridor and ran down its length, heels rapping on the tiled flooring, coat-tails flying. At the little information desk just inside the entrance, he flung to the uniformed policeman on duty:

"You see Kent Murdock? He come out yet?"

"Murdock?" The policeman scowled. "Sure. He left about fifteen-twenty minutes ago."

Doane groaned and his spirits collapsed. He went down the steps and out into the cool shadows of late afternoon, walked down to Boylston Street, and found a public telephone. He counted his change, finally dropped the nickel into the slot with the grudging, desperate manner of a man spending his last penny.

The *Courier-Herald* operator informed him Murdock had been there and left, and Doane set out in the direction of Murdock's apartment, a stocky figure tramping sightlessly down the street, his head down, oblivious of the bustle and rush of the home-going crowds.

He approached Embankment Arms from the opposite side of the street and stopped there on the curb to light a cigarette and reconsider. As he tossed aside the match, a taxi pulled up in front of the marquee, and the doorman opened the door.

Doane was half-way across the street before he recognized the smaller of the two men who started through the revolving doors. The effect of this recognition was instantaneous, breath-taking. He stopped motionless and rigid in the middle of the pavement, trying to conquer the panicky excitement which gripped him. Uncertainty held him there until the driver of a speeding taxi which ticked his coat-tails as it passed told him to get out of the street with concise and explicit profanity.

"Boy!" breathed Doane as he gained the safety of the curb, "Sam Cusick!"

Murdock remained motionless, a tight fixed smile on his lips, until Cusick gained the center of the room; then he moved forward.

Hymie continued to lean against the door, and Murdock gave him a quick, searching glance. The glance was sufficient to show the type. A squarish face given over almost entirely to jaw; a flattened nose, and ears that were bent; long arms and a practiced scowl, as though the fellow had learned the routine in the wrestling ring.

Cusick's lips twitched in what might have been his conception of a grin. "You see the papers?" Murdock did not answer, but he nodded his head. Cusick bent down and picked up the copy which had been cast aside. " 'It had been definitely established'," he leered, " 'that Cusick was at the scene of the crime in the early hours of the morning'."

He threw the paper from him. "Now," he said grimly, "I wonder how they found that out."

Murdock picked his coat and hat from the davenport.
Moving diagonally in front of Cusick and ignoring the
man, he opened the jade box, took out a cigarette. He
flung the coat on the chair arm, still clung to the hat.
The movement seemed to anger Cusick.

"I told you about that over the phone."

"I remember," Murdock said, and struck flame to a
match. He sat down on the chair arm on his coat before
he lit the cigarette; he inhaled and blew out the match
before he spoke. "But I'd already spilled the story and
you know it."

"You went down to headquarters this afternoon, and
you were there two hours. You didn't go there to take
pictures—not that long."

Murdock looked at the end of his cigarette, and his
face was somber. He could not kid himself about Cusick.
He might mean trouble and he might not. He would
eventually if the police did not pick him up.

He looked up at Cusick, spoke flatly. "Why don't you
get wise to yourself? You can't run around loose forever.
They'll pick you up, and the longer you wait, the
tougher it'll be for you."

"It'll be plenty tough anyway." Cusick shifted his
position, moving slightly away from the door. "I'm in
a spot and I know it. They're gonna try and hang this
thing on me. There are two guys who know where I was
last night. You're one of 'em. I'm gonna treat you both
alike. Know what I mean?"

"Not exactly," Murdock said.

"With your experience you ought to. Without you
two guys I'm clear. I can go down and take my licking

for putting the slug on that dick this morning, but that'll be all. So you're not gonna talk. If you ever—"

The knock on the door was startling, so loud it seemed to shake the room. An explosion of hushed silence followed. No one moved. It was as if in a second they had all been struck dumb and immobile. Then Cusick's gun came out. Hymie sprang away from the door; a gruff voice called:

"Open up in there!"

Cusick, now standing about six feet from Murdock, recoiled into a quick crouch and the forty-five automatic bulked enormous in his skinny hand as it swung to cover the photographer.

Murdock sensed the trend of the man's reaction. The eyes squinted, widened, and again seemed to look in all directions at once as the irises dilated into whites. Cusick may not have come to kill, but the impulse, like that of a trapped animal, was there now, unmistakably, and Murdock knew it.

He whipped out: "There's a back door."

Hymie started for the inner hall. Cusick set himself with a shuffling movement of his feet and lipped: "Why, you bastard!"

Murdock was too far away from the gun to hope to reach it. He did the only thing he could think of in that instant's respite. He snapped the hat with a quick flip of the wrist, sailed it into Cusick's face as the trigger finger tensed, then threw himself backwards into the chair.

He did not see the hat strike, but he did see Cusick's instinctive duck. The gun roared as he fell. He went clear over, struck the floor on the back of his neck, carrying the chair on top of him. He huddled there until he heard the pound of racing feet, the slam of the back door; then he pushed the chair aside, rolled to his knees, and stood up.

The knock came again, sharply. Murdock moved to the door. His face was pallid, glistening with sweat; the hand trembled on the knob. And then, curiously enough, he remembered. The door was not locked. Why the hell— He jerked it open.

Doane, white-faced and slack-jawed, stood in the hall. There was no one else, but Murdock had to step out and look down the corridor before he would believe it.

He went back into the room and straightened the chair without saying a word. By the time he finished, the tremble had gone from his hands. He took out his handkerchief and wiped the sweat from his forehead.

Doane looked just as scared as ever, and the sight of him relieved Murdock's tension, brought a grudging smile to his lips. He said: "How come?" thickly.

"I saw him come in," Doane said huskily, and color began to seep into his round, youthful face. "I came up the stairs and found he'd stopped the elevator at this floor. I knew I wouldn't have time to get the police and— well, hell, I had to do something."

"Yeh," Murdock admitted, "and you sure as hell put the pressure on me. But you had an idea and the guts to try it. You were in there swinging, and that counts for plenty." He went over and picked up his hat and coat. "Come on, I'll buy a dinner."

Doane's face cracked wide open in a grin. "With cocktails?"

"And a liqueur."

"Hah!" Doane cried. Then as his face sobered: "But—I mean, how about the story? Couldn't I make something out of it or—"

"Call Van Husan when we get out," Murdock said. "I don't think he can fire you for this sort of thing."

Kent Murdock was reading when Joyce Archer came into the apartment at ten o'clock. A slim blond vision in a suit of brown herring-bone tweed, she stopped just inside the door, her hand on the knob. Murdock put down the magazine and stood up before he noticed the small black overnight case in her other hand.

Surprise was in his lean face, and when the surprise subsided he became conscious of something else, a definite tingling of his skin and a certain warmth of body as though he were meeting an old friend. This feeling persisted until she drew closer and the light revealed her face more clearly.

It was not make-up this time; it was a genuine flush. The lips were pressed into a thin line, and the eyes were smoky, as though to give warning of smoldering, hidden fires.

She said, finally: "Can I stay here?" and her voice was jerky, low.

Murdock's warmth died away. His face got impassive and he said: "No," a bit sharply, because he meant it.

Joyce Archer paled and seemed to catch her breath, but her eyes met Murdock's defiantly; she took a new hold on the overnight case and started past him. He took her arm, reaching down with the other hand to grasp the bag. When she let go of it he drew her over to the davenport, eased her down on it.

"Tell me about it."

"There's nothing to tell. I'm sick of my way of living."

"Maybe you are, but you can't stay here and you know it. You're too young to be carrying around that kind of a reputation."

"Reputation?" The word flared out. "Who cares about it? It's mine, isn't it?"

Murdock moved to the mantelpiece, offered her the red-lacquered cigarette-box, held a light. The first inhale seemed to help her. Her words were less sharp. She had control now, but she went ahead with her idea.

"What's the matter with me? I'm as good-looking as the average; I'm supposed to have a reasonably good mind; I'm old enough to know what I want, and I've got nice legs."

"You've got a lot more than that, but there are some things you can't waste."

"You mean you don't like me well enough."

"I mean I'm married, for one thing, and—"

"Oh. Then I'm the one doing the compromising."

The tone was contemptuous now and Murdock, stung by it, flushed darkly. He tried to go on, to speak reasonably.

"You could at least be consistent. You're not coming here like a girl offering herself on the altar of love." The sarcasm crept in in spite of himself. "You came here with a grouch and you want me to—"

"I came here because I liked you and the decent way

you acted today. I thought I could get a little kindness and perhaps some understanding. I'm old enough to know what I'm doing, what I want."

"What did they do to you at headquarters?" he digressed.

"Nothing. They were courteous and—it's not that. I want a friend, that's all. It's been a long time since I've had one, and no one can ask me to believe the world is kind and good to everyone. I'm not equipped for an idealist."

Murdock said: "Suppose I make a drink. Maybe you can be honest with me then. But whether you can or not, you can't stay here this way."

He saw her color rise and he felt awkward before the hurt look in her eyes. He wanted to help, but he knew there was something behind the girl's outburst, something that had possessed her temporarily and destroyed reason. He wanted her to stay, hated himself for it so that he became more determined than ever to make her see things as they were.

He turned towards the kitchenette, but the knock came at the door before he had taken a step. Lifting the startled girl and her overnight case in one stooping movement, he swept her into the bedroom and closed the door.

The knock sounded again as he went back to the wing chair. He settled himself, called: "Come in."

Howard Archer came into the room like a whirlwind, slammed the door, and stopped so quickly his coat curled around his legs. Unmistakable anger suffused his thin face, and he gave Murdock no chance to speak.

"I suppose you know you're a dirty swine, Murdock," he lipped.

"Yeh?" Murdock returned easily. "Sit down and tell me about it."

Archer ignored the invitation. He strode forward, glancing suspiciously about the room as he moved, and finally stopped directly in front of the chair.

"Where's my sister?" he growled.

"Your sister?" It was the best Murdock could offer then, because he knew now why Joyce had come to him, why she had seemed so overwrought. An accepted sliver of bitterness followed on the heels of his disappointment. He had known she had not come on his account, but—

"Your innocence amazes me," leered Archer. "Well, I've come to get her."

"You're taking a lot for granted," Murdock said flatly, "and I'm not sure I like your tone."

Archer's eyes fastened on the doorway to the inner hall. They swung to Murdock, back to the hall. He started forward. Murdock came out of the chair and intercepted him before he reached the doorway. Stubbornness rose within him. He had argued to make the girl leave, now he was arguing with her brother to prevent his taking her.

He said: "Where did you get the idea you could break in this apartment and search it as you pleased?"

Archer's look was angry, contemptuous, so that his upper lip curled as he spoke.

"I know what happened last night and this morning. That wasn't enough, I suppose. You had to keep her here all day. And now, when we have a little quarrel, she runs to you like the spoiled kid she is, and you take her in."

Murdock kept silent with an effort. It was not his fight. He had to keep his head—accept this because Howard was her brother.

"Well," Archer went on, "that part doesn't surprise me. It's just the sort of thing you're looking for, isn't it? The sort of cheap rotten trick I could expect from a fellow with your background. A newspaper photographer."

The words were deliberately insulting and Murdock's face went gray and stiff.

"You're the kind," Archer flared, "that would take anything he could get and—"

The bedroom door opened violently. Joyce Archer's angry face appeared in the opening and her eyes were blazing.

"Howard, you're a beast! An obnoxious beast!"

The effect of this was to rob Archer of further speech. Murdock just turned and stared at the girl for a moment, then a slow grin tugged at his lips.

"I thought so," Archer finally muttered, pulling himself together. He stepped towards her, seized her wrist roughly. "Well, young lady, you're going home with me."

"I am not!" she tried to pull away.

"Are you out of your head?"

She set her lips.

"I ought to whale hell out of you. You can't do a thing like this and—"

"I can't? Why can't I? I'm of age. If you can chase around after Rita Redfield—and behind her husband's back—I can do the same thing. You wouldn't listen to me; why should I listen to you? Who do you think you are to—"

"That's different," fumed Archer.

"It's just that narrow, double-standard mind of yours." Joyce Archer freed her wrist. She drew back into the doorway. Archer grunted savagely and grabbed for her again. At the same moment Murdock bumped against him, throwing him off balance. Then the door slammed, the lock clicked sharply.

Archer turned on Murdock, started to speak, then grabbed the door-knob, jerked at it, pounding the panels with his fist. Joyce Archer's muffled voice came through the panels.

"Pound! Go ahead and pound! I'm here and I'm going to stay here until you get some of the sense you think I ought to have."

Archer began to curse softly and continued to tug at the door until Murdock grabbed him, spun him about. In the shadows of the hall the two men faced each other, Archer furious, breathing hard; Murdock calm, cold.

"I don't believe I like you, Archer," he said, and there was an enigmatic menace in the metallic ring of his words. "I don't think I ever liked you. And right now you're intruding. Your sister seems to have something of the same idea, so it goes for both of us."

"I—" sputtered Archer.

"Or if you want it in plain American," Murdock interrupted, "beat it!"

Archer met his gaze for a moment, finally turned

stiffly away and went into the lighted living-room. By the time he reached the door, his voice was once more bitter, disdainful.

"If you think you can get away with this, you're mistaken. I'll be back with the police. She'd better not be here when—"

"The police?" Murdock's brows lifted in mock surprise. "She's of age, isn't she?"

"But you're married and—"

"That's right." Murdock's seriousness was sheer mockery. "But under the circumstances—she came here of her own accord—the one thing I can think of is circumstantial evidence of what the papers call a statutory offense. Drag her through that sort of a mess if that's the sort of a heel you are."

Murdock stepped round Archer and opened the door. His face was flushed now, the skin at the cheek-bones white and taut.

"So far," he warned, "I'm the only one here who's kept his temper. Get out before I lose it."

He stood staring at the panels for some seconds after Archer had slammed out of the room, and his sigh was like a shrug as he turned and started slowly across the room. He went down the hall, knocking at the bedroom door and calling: "All right, he's gone," as he passed.

At the kitchenette cupboard he took out the Scotch-bottle and a glass. He poured a drink and took it neat in an absent sort of way, not bothering to replace the bottle. When he came back down the hall, the bedroom door was still closed and he knocked again. This time her voice called: "Come in."

Murdock hesitated wonderingly, then took the knob. It turned freely and the door opened. He took a step forward, stopped on the threshold as his nerves tightened and something whipped the blood through his veins with an accelerated speed and left his ears pounding.

Joyce Archer was in bed. She had pulled the covers up under her armpits so that there was exposed only the tanned shoulders, two thin straps of heavy-looking tea-rose silk. Her blond hair, fanned out on the pillow, framed a face that seemed unnaturally pale.

"You can't—" Murdock began.

"I can." This stubbornly.

He did not answer then. He looked away, saw the tweed suit draped on the chair-back, some silken things on top of it. He took out a cigarette, but he did not light it. After a while he stepped to the bed, sat down on the near side, away from her.

"So that was the reason," he said and made his voice casually humorous. "Spite."

"It's nauseating," she answered quickly. "The way he's been chasing her. Oh, I suppose it's not his fault entirely. I know her. But even now, after what happened last night— You'd think this was the one thing they had been waiting for."

"You're not very complimentary," Murdock mused. "He wouldn't listen to you, and you had a fight, and you got a mad on and came rushing over here with your dramatics."

"I hate you!" Joyce Archer flushed and flipped over in bed, her head turned away from him.

"And," Murdock went on, unperturbed, "I almost thought you came here because you wanted to. Suppose I had believed you? Suppose your brother had not come to explain for you?"

She turned back. "Well?"

"Oh!" Murdock smiled a little then. "So you were willing to go that far to spite him."

"I'm going to stay right here," she said obstinately.

"All right." Murdock stood up. "You're going to stay right here until you bring him to his senses. That it?" When she did not answer he went on slowly as though to accent his words: "Well, if that's the way it is—"

He came round the foot of the bed to the closet door, opened it. He took off his coat and waistcoat, hung them on a clothes-hanger. He pulled out the knot of his tie, took it off, and began to unbutton his shirt. Then he reached into the closet and brought out a pair of tan pyjamas and the green dressing-gown.

In all this time he had not looked at her. Then he turned suddenly, in time to catch her expression before it changed. The blue eyes were very round. The bedside lamp made non-existent hollows with the shadows of her cheek-bones; the red, full mouth was slightly open. When it closed under his glance the effect of her face was an unnatural tenseness and he grinned, genuinely then, and sat down on the bed.

"You're scared, aren't you?"

"W-well," she stuttered defensively, "wh-who wouldn't be?"

"I'm glad you are." The corners of Murdock's eyes wrinkled in a grin that was unusual for him—it seemed a bit wistful. "And you're a good egg, and I hope I'm not that much of a mug. The odds have got to be more even."

There may have been a trace of disappointment along with the relieved surprise in Joyce Archer's glance. Murdock could not be sure. He stood up, reached into the closet again, and hauled out a blanket. At the door he stopped.

"The davenport is long enough. I measured it before I bought it."

He opened the door. "You know, I think I'm beginning to like you."

12

WHEN KENT MURDOCK reached the office the next morning, Phil Doane waylaid him and tagged along to the photographic department.

"Got anything new?" he asked.

"On what?"

"Why, the Redfield thing."

"No," Murdock said, "and I'm not expecting anything." He stretched out in the chair. That davenport wasn't as good as he thought. His neck was stiff. Joyce had been fast asleep when he left—and the door was unlocked. He had peeked in at her, then tiptoed in for another suit, but she had not wakened. He realized Doane was talking and the interruption on his more pleasurable thoughts irked him. "You're getting to be a pest."

"Aw, now—" Doane pleaded. "I just want to play along. You're one of those guys that's always stumbling onto hot pictures—and there's always gotta be a story, ain't there? If I—"

"All right, all right," Murdock cut in impatiently, but not unkindly. "If I get anything, I'll let you know. And if you've really got enough drive to help out, go find Spike Tripp for me. I want to talk to him."

"He's as good as found," Doane said.

This statement was a gross exaggeration. For the next two days developments in the Redfield murder were of no importance. Newspapers were filled with stories headed with variations of: CUSICK STILL AT LARGE and ARREST EXPECTED IN REDFIELD CASE. Murdock's assignments were routine: a fire, the results of automobile accidents, the arrival of an Italian cruiser.

Then on the third morning Doane had barged into the office, his face flushed and eager. "I found Tripp," he gasped.

Murdock snapped aside his newspaper. "Where?"

"Down at Teddy's place."

Murdock stood up, grabbed for his hat and coat. Undecided upon taking his regular camera and bulky plate-case, he compromised by taking his small camera, which was still in his desk.

Doane said: "Can I go?"

"I suppose so," Murdock answered, but paid little attention to him. They went out to the corridor, started down towards the elevators side by side. An office boy rushed out just as they were getting into the car.

"Hey!" He grabbed Doane. "Van Husan's looking for you."

The young reporter went all to pieces. He sputtered, looked pleadingly at Murdock, who had entered the car.

The office boy said: "He's waiting."

The elevator boy said: "Make up your mind."

Doane turned away, a forlorn figure, his rubicund face melancholy, dejected. "Don't forget, now," he begged, "if you run into anything."

Teddy's place, just off Stuart Street, between Broadway and Eliott, is a long, narrow, gloomy room opening on an alley. The bar is old, heavy-looking; the floor is a linoleum imitation of tile, and the half-dozen tables at the rear are of the kitchen variety with no covering. The brightness of daylight was in Murdock's eyes when he entered the place, and at first the only thing he was conscious of was the smell of stale tobacco smoke and beer.

When the eyes adjusted themselves, he saw that aside from a solitary beer-drinker who was scowling into his glass at the bar, the only other customer was a man at the rearmost table next to the door. That man was Spike Tripp, and he looked suspiciously at Murdock, seemed uncertain about his next move.

Murdock's attitude was confidence itself. He said: "Hello, Spike," cordially and pulled out a chair. "What're you drinking?"

The invitation helped. Spike thawed out a bit, grunted a greeting, adding: "The same—rye."

Murdock called the order, taking a beer himself. He said: "Where you been hiding?" as he sat down.

"Me? I've been around. Why?"

Murdock reached for a cigarette. He was not ready to say why until Tripp's suspicions were allayed. The main reason, he admitted to himself, was little more than a hunch. Just something that Cusick had said that night when Doane had scared him off: "There are two guys who know where I was last night." If Spike Tripp was one of them—

A waiter with a dirty white apron and long pointed mustaches brought the drinks, and Murdock paid him. He gestured a silent toast to Tripp, tasted the beer, and studied the fellow over the top of his glass.

Born Tsiknas, Spike Tripp had been a fair welter-weight until the grind of training became too much of an ordeal. Then, because work was anathema to him, he had drifted about, trying whatever easy-money chance presented itself. His activities in past years had been many and varied, all of them questionable. It is doubtful if any one person knew the extent of his endeavors, but his police record—a not particularly vicious one as police records go—gave some indication of his natural talents.

He had been a bootlegger of the split-case variety. He had been a collector for a nigger pool impresario; he had served an apprenticeship with slot machines until two rival factions went to war with guns. Spike did not like the heat. He got out. More recently he had been a race-track tout and his current venture was on his own: running a tipster sheet on the Rockingham meeting.

The police and the underworld have a word for the type: *punk*. Ordinarily good-natured, reasonably harm-less, he was a slow-witted, thickset fellow in his middle thirties, broad-jawed, with no bridge to his nose, and the leathery skin of his face decorated at one cheek-bone with a strip of adhesive tape.

"Why?" Murdock repeated the word as he put down his glass. "Because I didn't get a chance to talk to you that night at Redfield's place. I heard you were out on bail and—"

"Sure. They got nothing on me. I told 'em that. But those guys ain't happy unless they're workin' over some poor mug like me that ain't got any influence. Take a gander at this"—he pointed to the strip of tape on his cheek-bone—"always the smarties, markin' a guy up."

"It was a raw deal," Murdock said, making his voice sympathetic. "But, at that, it must've looked fishy, your hiding up in that hall closet."

"You've got to hide from guys like Keogh. How the hell did I know somebody had bumped Redfield off? Would I been hangin' around there waitin' to get picked up if I'd known it? What do they use for brains down there at headquarters, anyway?"

Murdock took another sip of beer.

"Did you try to run out on them?"

"Well—" Spike shrugged. "I see all these dicks swarmin' over the place—"

"From that closet you could see Redfield's door okay, huh?"

"Sure. I could see the door and the elevator and the back stairs, and when I lamp the coppers, I lay low till things quiet down. As soon as the hall is empty, I take a sneak for the back stairs. Only I'm one of those guys that never gets a break. Keogh sticks his pan into the hall just as I pass Redfield's door, and there I am."

"They'd probably got you anyway," Murdock said.
"They would have searched the halls and closets." He
hesitated, continued casually: "But from where you were,
you could see everybody that went in and out of the party,
huh?"

"Sure, I—" Spike broke off as though he had chewed
off the next word. He picked up his whisky glass, tossed
down the drink, and reached for the chaser of water.
When he looked up again, his little eyes were shifty,
wary. His voice was suddenly suspicious.

"You're tryin' to prove something, huh? What?"

Murdock sought another answer, picked up an idea
out of thin air, and went ahead with it, his voice confidential.

"Listen. Don't get me wrong. I'm not a cop. And right
now I'm not even a photographer. But I've had some
trouble with my wife. I was at that party for a while.
Girard was there with her. I thought maybe you saw them
come out."

Tripp seemed to relax, and his voice sounded relieved.

"Oh, I get it. Well—" He hesitated, fiddled with his
glass, and seemed undecided. When he went on, however,
there was no trace of uncertainty in his manner. "I didn't
see 'em. It's like I told the cops. I didn't come in till
quarter of five and I—"

The suddenness with which Tripp stopped the sentence jerked Murdock's eyes from the table. The man's
gaze was riveted on some distant object over his shoulder;
his feet shifted and both hands were on the table edge,
white-knuckled, tense. He sucked in his breath and

pushed up before Murdock could turn around, pushed up and spun away from the table into the adjoining doorway with a feline quickness that was born of his ring training.

The doorway was empty when Murdock said: "Hey!" He grunted disgustedly and turned around. A tall and rather thin silhouette was moving through the street entrance. Murdock recognized the outlines after a moment and went to meet the man who was moving slowly towards him.

He said: "He saw you coming."

"Tripp?" Lieutenant Bacon stopped dead still, fairly shouted the word. Then, cursing under his breath, he ran down the length of the room and out the back door.

Murdock was waiting at the bar when Bacon returned two or three minutes later, and the Lieutenant took him by the arm. "Why didn't you stop him?" he charged. "Damn it all! What the hell good are you if you can't—"

"Wait a minute," Murdock said flatly, and pulled his arm free. "He was facing the door; I wasn't. He saw you first and he was out before I knew what it was all about. If I can help, okay. But I'm a photographer, not a cop."

Bacon spun about without a word, glared at the bartender, and started for the door. Murdock followed him out, and when Bacon got in the rear seat of the police phaeton, Murdock crowded in behind him without waiting for an invitation.

Bacon did not seem to object, did not seem conscious that Murdock was beside him until after he had given the uniformed chauffeur an address on Hemenway Street.

The car pulled out from the curb sharply, rolled down

the one-way street and round the block to Stuart Street.
Neither man spoke until they crossed the railroad bridge
and angled into Huntington Avenue. Then Bacon, whose
annoyance had subsided somewhat, leaving his lean face
impassive, turned and spoke suspiciously.

"What were you talking to him for?"

"I had a hunch," Murdock said evenly, "a hunch that
maybe he saw more than he told you about. I wanted to
see if I could get him to admit he was in that upstairs hall
at any time before a quarter of five."

"How long you had the hunch?" pressed Bacon
sharply.

"A couple days. But I couldn't locate him and—"

"You held out." Bacon's tone was irritated, accusing.

"Held out?" exploded Murdock. "Don't be silly. It
was just a half-baked idea. If I ran to you with every one
I got, I'd run myself ragged; you too."

"Maybe," Bacon said morosely, "only this time you
were right."

"Oh." Murdock's brows knotted at the bridge of his
nose.

"Yeah." Bacon leaned back on the seat, hesitated as
they turned right on Massachusetts Avenue. "If I could
do all the checking myself I could get some place, maybe.
But no, I let some fat-head do routine stuff and where
does it get me? In jams."

Bacon did not elaborate, and seconds later the driver
slanted in towards the curb, stopped in front of a gray
brick apartment house of four stories, one of a long row
that, no longer trying to be smart, now seemed content

to rest upon its uncertain age and a reputation of reasonable respectability.

The girl who opened the door of Apartment 3-B was the entertainer whom Murdock had last seen lying on the bed in the blue room of Redfield's apartment. She was small, trim-figured, and young-looking. Her black hair was cut short so that it lay upon her round head like enamel. The face, pinched slightly, powdered a bit too heavily, was pretty in a common sort of way.

She said: "What do you want?" and her dark eyes were wary.

"We want to come in a minute," Bacon said. He said it so casually that the girl did not realize that he was putting his words into action until he had eased her aside and was half-way through the door.

The girl's eyes glazed angrily then and she tried to resist, but fell back under the steady pressure of Bacon's shoulder on the panel.

"You can't bust in here," she raged. "I've got friends and—"

Bacon said: "Hello, Spike," and then Murdock caught a glimpse of the fellow over Bacon's shoulder.

The girl quieted down immediately. Murdock shut the door and she followed Bacon, who moved over to the plush-covered, hot-looking sofa and sat down on one arm at the opposite end from Spike Tripp.

Murdock glanced around a small, over-furnished living-room that tried hard to be smart and failed miserably. He circled around by the windows at the right side,

dropped down in an imitation Windsor chair in front
of a cheaply veneered Governor Winthrop desk. The girl
remained standing, but the rise and fall of her solid-
looking bosom was rapid, spasmodic.

Tripp shook his head wearily. "Christ! You guys are
worse'n the itch!"

Bacon said: "What did you run out on me for down
at Teddy's?"

"Run out?" Tripp's brows lifted and made an expression of surprise. "It wasn't that. Only I had a date with
Marie"—he glanced at the girl and grinned—"and I
thought you might start askin' me a lot of questions, and
then I'd be late, and Marie always makes trouble when
I'm late."

Bacon's face got red. He looked at Murdock and shook
his head.

Tripp continued innocently: "What was it you wanted,
Lieutenant?"

Bacon said: "Let's take a ride."

"Ride?" Tripp forgot his act. "What for?" he growled.
"I'm out on bail, ain't I? You can't—"

"Who says so?" Bacon rapped. "That night operator
at Redfield's place said you came in at four-forty-five and
we let it go at that. The guy I had checkin' the building
muffed one—as usual. I only just found out today that
they've got a night maid on duty there. She saw you go
up the fire stairs at three-fifteen that mornin'. She was in
the fifth-floor hall and she saw you go round the corner
and start up. And then I found that my friend the operator remembered he had to go to the can at just about
that time. He was off the desk for about five minutes. We

were concentrating too much on the time after three-thirty to follow through. What were you walkin' up for?"

"Because I didn't know how the sixth floor was laid out. For all I knew, the elevator might've gone right to Redfield's entrance. I just thought I ought to get off at the fifth and walk up; then I'd be sure not to get thrown out."

"That's all right." Bacon nodded in satisfaction. "I just wanted to know if you were there."

"But I went right out again," Tripp protested. "When I heard the music, I knew the party wasn't gonna wind up right away and so I went out and came back at a quarter of five."

"So you say," Bacon grunted. "But if you did you went out the back way. And that's one I called right. Remember? I said you came back for an alibi."

"I didn't," Tripp argued, "I came back in to get Marie."

Bacon stood up. "Maybe I can make you remember better down at my place. I got a room that was built for guys like you. And I'll tell you what really happened; let's see if I can guess right twice. You hung around up on the sixth floor until some time after the party broke up—waiting for her"—he nodded towards the girl, whose face had gone white. "And while you were there you stuck in that closet and saw what you could see. Because you're that kind of a guy. We've had a tip before that you made a few dollars in blackmail. And parties like that might mean business, huh? And you stayed right there. And I want to know who came back after that party broke up—and what time and all about it."

Tripp's little eyes shifted from Bacon, sought the girl.
As they fastened upon her he shook his head. It was just
a slight, almost imperceptible movement, yet it was
enough for one with her schooling.

She was standing less than two feet from the Lieutenant, and he was not looking at her. So when she jabbed
out with both arms stiff and all her weight behind them,
he slid off the end of the davenport and fell over towards
the middle of it with his face on the cushions.

Murdock was on his feet in an instant, but the flash of
Tripp's arm as he sprang from the davenport was even
quicker. The small automatic appeared from nowhere
and swung to cover him. Tripp backed into the inner
doorway just as Bacon recovered and regained his feet.

Bacon cursed, snapped: "Put it down before you get
in trouble!" He took a step forward.

"Lay off!" rasped Tripp. "You're not gonna take me
down and beat the pants off me. Not till I get a chance
to—"

"Put it down!" Bacon's voice was sharp with the ring
of authority. If he felt any uncertainty, he did not show
it. He did not reach for his own gun; he just moved
slowly forward, his manner assured, confident.

Tripp stopped in the doorway. His face went gray and
his gun arm stiffened; the knuckles of his hand got white.
Murdock held his breath, was the first to notice the blur
of motion behind Bacon. In those four or five seconds no
one had paid any attention to Marie, and for the second
time she did her part.

She cursed shrilly and threw herself upon Bacon's
back, her arms around his neck, her hands clenched under

his chin. Bacon spun angrily, whirling the girl's feet high off the floor. Tripp disappeared through the doorway. From somewhere beyond, a door slammed as Murdock leaped forward and Bacon threw the girl roughly to the davenport.

Murdock and Bacon reached the locked door together. Bacon hammered at it, and Marie was upon him again, pulling at his arm.

"Break it!" she shrilled. "Break it, you lousy police bastard, and I'll have you—"

Bacon jerked away from the door, bumping into the girl and knocking her to the floor. He continued down the short hall to the kitchen, with Murdock right behind him. There was a single window here and Bacon threw it up, leaned out. Murdock squeezed into the frame beside him.

There was a fire-escape touching the adjoining window of the locked room. Murdock saw that this window was open. Then, looking down, he saw Tripp just disappearing round the corner of the building into the alley.

Bacon pulled his head in and closed the window. He looked at Murdock, groaned from deep down in his long body. "That was a damn fool thing to do. We'll pick him up, all right. But now we'll have to get real rough with him."

Marie was lighting a cigarette in the living-room when they went back. Her face was still flushed, her eyes hard, gloating. Bacon picked up his hat and she said: "If you want to make anything of it—"

Bacon said: "So far you've done all right." He stepped towards her, his wrist cocking. "But how would you like a slap in the mouth for yourself?"

Marie completely forgot her bravado. She squealed and threw up a protecting hand as she cringed. Bacon grunted and strode to the door. "Come on," he said to Murdock. "There's a way of handling tarts like her too. But what's the use? I shoulda got tough before."

13

STOPPING IN AT his apartment as he did at three o'clock that afternoon was something that Murdock would have been hard pressed to explain to an outsider. On his way back to the office with some unimportant pictures of an Industrial Exhibit he passed within two blocks of his apartment. And just about that time he decided he was thirsty.

For the first time in three days there was no one to greet him as he opened the door. Ever since the night Howard had come to take his sister home, the argument between Murdock and the girl had continued. But each time she won out, at least to the extent of staying on.

She was, he realized, as stubborn about this one thing as he was. It had become a complex. She would stay, she ruled, until Howard had the decency to drop his affair with Rita Redfield. It was no longer a question open to reason. Howard Archer's actions could be justified or not, but Joyce had determined her own course and she hewed to the line. So far it had done no good. Howard Archer had not come back.

Murdock placed the camera and plate-case on the floor just inside the door, tossed his hat into the wing chair, and lit a cigarette. He was, he realized, no longer thirsty. He sat down, crossed his legs. The past three days had been much the same as before. He worked; he did not know how she spent her time. It was the evenings that made the difference. They had dinner together each night. After that they came home and read—except the time when they went to the movies and stopped for a few dances at the Copley.

There was no longer any uncertainty about the ending of the evening. Each time she was the first to uncurl from her spot on the davenport and go into the bedroom. And, after the first night, she brought out a sheet and a blanket and a pillow and made a bed for him. Nothing was said, directly or by inference, about that first night.

"I hope she took her bag with her," Murdock said, and straightened his legs. "I'm about due for a good night's sleep."

He stood up and went out to the kitchen, resisting the almost overpowering impulse to look in the bedroom. He'd done his part, hadn't he? He had given in to her all along the line, treated her decently, considerately. He knew she liked him for this acceptance, this manner of treatment. But the thing couldn't go on indefinitely. She was old enough to know that.

He spent a long time with the drink, dumping the ice cubes, rinsing three of them, pouring the Scotch, and squirting in the foaming soda from the siphon. It was a relief, all right, to be alone and feel he could do as he pleased, forget everything else. Newspaper work and liv-

ing alone were making him crusty, set in his ways. He had
to watch his language when she was around or he'd be
talking like a photographer.

Tasting the drink, he went into the living-room. It
seemed empty. He'd been there too long, that was it.
His odd, virulent mood sought an outlet in criticism and
he glanced around, an expression of distaste on his wide
mouth. Nearly two years now. Since Hestor. One thing:
nothing of her influence remained. She had taken most
of their things with her. The few she had left he had
gradually replaced. But he needed a change. Rents were
a lot cheaper now. He could do better with a quieter
place, or one higher up. Get a bigger place for the same
money.

He drank some more of his drink, paced the floor with
the glass in his hand, finally stopped at the davenport and
stared morosely at the print of Cameron's Whitby Bridge
which hung above it. A newspaper photographer, huh?
A button-pusher. Even some high-hat reporters disdained
the craft. The college training. What good was it? Taught
him how to be dissatisfied, taught him to like good
clothes, to appreciate good books and pictures; taught
him very little about how to get these things.

He turned abruptly. What the hell made him so rest-
less? Then the answer which had repeatedly pounded
against his consciousness broke through and he grunted
softly, his lips dipping at the corners.

"Watch yourself, fella!" he said under his breath.

The object of this cautionary soliloquy burst into the
room and startled him as he finished. She had on a dark,
tight-fitting dress, a mannish polo coat, a trim dark brown

hat. Her face was quite pale; her eyes were bright, glaring.

Murdock started to grin. "Hello."

Joyce Archer began to peel off her gloves. She put them together and slapped them against her palm and turned on him. She seemed to have trouble speaking. In that moment Murdock had a hard time remaining where he was. To try to live up to his resolve, he raised his glass, finished his drink, and made his voice casual.

"I was on my way to the office and decided I was thirsty."

If Joyce Archer heard him she gave no sign. "They're running away." The words were throaty, sharp.

"Who?" asked Murdock although he knew what she meant.

"Howard—Rita."

She came to him, held out her wrists. Red finger-marks stood out across them above the tan of her skin. She jerked her hands back, spun about, and started to pace the floor.

"He had to drag me out before I'd go. He's beastly, insane. He doesn't know what he's doing. I went home and saw his trunk packed, two of his bags gone. I found them upstairs. And Mark Redfield buried yesterday."

Trouble settled over Murdock. He sat down on the davenport, put his empty glass at his feet, his forearms on his knees so that the wrists were limp, dangling the hands between his knees.

"I told him what I thought. I can't understand him. It isn't only Rita. He's been this way ever since he came back from England. He's got just enough money tied up from father's estate to have the good time he wants. He's mad. And she—"

The girl broke off, stopped pacing to face Murdock.

"It's her fault too. I told her so. And if Howard had kept his hands off me I—" She checked herself. "You've got to stop them."

Murdock looked at her without raising his head, and in looking his brows furrowed, giving him a hard, quizzical expression. "He ought to know better. He's a witness, a material witness. If he runs out, the police will drag him back. Let him go."

"I can't. Not that way. And have him hunted as if he were a criminal? He knows nothing of the murder."

"He hasn't convinced Bacon of that yet."

"But you don't think—" Her mouth went slack.

"It makes damn little difference what I think. If you want to stop him"—Murdock stood up, his face somber and a roughness in his voice—"call police headquarters."

She gasped at that and he crossed to the telephone. "No!" she said, frightened now. "Please."

Murdock did not pick up the instrument. He stood there waiting.

"Listen, Kent." Joyce Archer came to him and took both of his arms above the elbows. "Do this for me, will you? He's running away. You can stop him. But I can't call the police. If they see that he's going, it will make it all the harder; it will make him look guilty. You see that?"

Murdock just nodded, watched her humidly. Traces of resentment appeared among his thoughts. He felt jealous of Archer and his hold on the girl; and then he felt ashamed of his jealousy. She spoke first.

"It's not just this. I never had many friends. Travel. Packed off to school, and kept in school—abroad most of the time. To get me off my parents' hands. But Howard was close to me. There's seven years' difference in our ages, and that matters a lot to a girl growing up. And he was sweet to me. He'd come to Paris on his vacations. He made me feel as though I was his girl. He had lots of others, yes, but he had a little time for me too. I think he knew I was lonely. And now he's changed and I've changed and I know he's beastly and acted like a cad to you, and yet, next to you, he's the only one. Maybe if I could make him see this other thing through he'd have time to—" Her voice choked slightly as it trailed off.

Murdock's palms were damp and he rubbed them against the outside of his coat pockets. There was an unnatural thickness in his throat, a lumpy something that made it hard to swallow. A faint perfume rose from her hair, bothered him. He pulled gently from her grasp, stepped over to the wing chair, and picked up his hat.

She followed him. "You'll try?"

"Yes," Murdock said, and because he felt a certain helplessness before the unashamed display of her emotions, because he could not cope with the genuine reaction set up within him, his voice was unnecessarily gruff.

"But even if you have the right to meddle with his life, with two lives, this way; even if you have—and you haven't—I think you are overconfident about my powers of persuasion. Why should I succeed with him when he failed with you the other night?"

Her eyes, fixed upon his as he began to speak, were

trusting; and then, when he finished, he read the hurt in their depths. He forgot about everything else. His arms went around her waist. They were standing close together and he drew her tight against him with a quick rough embrace. Her back arched and as he kissed her, the lips were stiff for a fraction of a second; then they were alive and hot and her arms were around his neck, straining so that the hardness of her muscles surprised him and he felt a twinge of pain in the cords of his neck.

He dropped his hands, pushed her away, and caught his breath. His face was hot. He stooped, snatched up the camera and plate-case. He had to look at her as he opened the door. Her eyes held him. They were bright and shiny, just a little frightened from reaction. Or it may have been something else; he could not be sure.

The maid who opened the door, a small, sandy-haired girl with a generous waist and plump arms, said: "Mrs. Redfield is not in."

Murdock slipped through the doorway in front of her, put the camera and plate-case on the foyer floor. "I'll go in and wait."

The maid closed the door hurriedly and then had to run to intercept him. "But—but she's not—she won't be—"

"I know," Murdock said, reaching for the door-knob; "I'll wait."

His confidence shattered the maid's resistance. He opened the door and stepped into the huge living-room beyond. Rita Redfield and Howard Archer were at the opposite side. His arm was about her waist, her hand on his arm, and, facing the terrace windows, they turned their heads and looked at Murdock over their shoulders.

Archer dropped his arm. Murdock kept coming across the room. There was a silver tray on a small table, a tall cocktail-shaker, two glasses. Beside the grand piano four compact, light-weight traveling-cases stood in a row.

Archer stopped stiffly in front of Murdock, blocking his path. The thin, tanned face was angry, the pale-blue eyes hard, like steel disks. "Sorry," he said curtly. "We were just going out."

"Yes," Murdock said. "Your sister told me."

"She sent you up to—"

"She thought I might be able to persuade you to postpone the trip until this—this murder case is cleared up a bit."

"Sweet of her," Archer said irritably. "But in the light of what happened the other night—"

"I understand she had a reason for that too."

Archer turned. "Ready, Rita?"

Rita Redfield came towards him, stopped to one side and slightly behind Archer. Murdock's eyes moved to her; it was difficult to look elsewhere. Her beauty, in spite of its showiness, the vital fullness of the figure beneath the severe line of her oxford-gray two-piece suit, was commanding. Her dark eyes, full on Murdock now, were expressionless—or so they seemed. The expression came from the droop of the painted mouth, the lifted arch of her brows over the upward-slanting eyes. Here was a woman. Murdock was at once aware of her allure, could understand better now than before just why Archer had planned to go with her. In some ways, and he had time in

his study of her to think of this, he did not blame the
fellow. One thing: they had much in common. They
might get along.

"And waiting," Rita Redfield answered without taking her eyes from Murdock. "I'll have Williams take the
bags down."

"Never mind," Archer said. "I'll take them myself."
He turned, juggled them up so he had one under each
arm, one in each hand. Murdock moved back to the door,
stood in front of it. Archer had to put down the bags
again. His voice snapped dangerously.

"You're being damned obnoxious and—"

Murdock said: "Wait just a minute. Let's leave out all
personalities. Let's see if there is any logic in this business." He looked at the woman. "Your husband was
buried yesterday, and, passing over any moral question,
are your affairs in shape to run out so soon? How long do
you plan to stay?"

"Indefinitely," Archer snapped.

"There is very little to be cleared up," Rita Redfield
said, and there seemed to be something of amusement
in her gaze, as though, somehow, she enjoyed this set-to
between the two men. "And fortunately I insisted upon
a trust fund when I married him."

The complete assurance of the woman's manner ruf-
fled Murdock and he went on stubbornly:

"It's not so simple with you, Archer. If it's of any
interest to you, I've been pretty close to the police on this
thing. They're not at all satisfied with your story. I know
this. Run out on them like this—even if you get away with
it—and they'll bring you back."

Archer's chin came out. "Get out of the way!"

"Understand," Murdock went on grimly, "it's nothing to me personally. I don't like you and I never did. But Joyce asked me—"

"It's Joyce now, is it?" Archer leered. "Well, get this, Murdock: You practically threw me out of your place the other night. There was nothing I could do. If she wants to give herself to a fellow of your class, a newspaper photographer—"

"Watch your words!"

"—I suppose it's her affair. But for you to presume that you can come up here and—" Archer broke off as his rage got the better of him. "Get out of the way!"

Murdock's lips pulled back in a weird little smile. Then Archer hit him, a quick straight punch full on the mouth.

The blow was not hard, but coming as it did, with Murdock off balance and unable to get set, it staggered him. He took a backward step. Blood came out on his lips, and his face darkened. His reaction was instinctive and he caught himself in time to stop his counter-punch. He dropped his hand.

Archer's face was white, his lips set. He was afraid of what he had done or what he thought might happen. It was in his eyes; he was afraid. As though he realized there was more to follow, he moved back a step and whipped a small automatic from the pocket of his raglan topcoat.

"Get out of that doorway or I'll shoot!" he said huskily.

"They'd bring you back for that, too," Murdock said, trying to keep a check on his temper and natural anger.

"I wouldn't have to kill you. A bullet or two in the leg—"

"They'd bring you back."

"They'll probably try and bring me back anyway."

Murdock held Archer's furious gaze a moment, then shrugged and stepped aside. "You're not scaring anyone," he said as he took a handkerchief from his breast pocket and wiped his bleeding lips, "waving that gun. But if you should be fool enough to shoot, it would be difficult all the way around, particularly for Joyce."

Archer turned to Rita.

"Can you carry one of the bags?" She picked up one and he managed the other three since they were neither heavy nor bulky. He still clung to the gun. "Don't try to follow us. You stay here until—"

"You might have some justification for shooting here," Murdock said disdainfully, "since I rather broke in on you. But outside, Archer, I'll do as I please." He waited until the two of them left the room; then he followed. At the outer door he picked up his camera, slung the plate-case over his shoulder.

All three waited for the elevator. Murdock cocked one eyebrow at Rita Redfield, smiled. "I hope the rest of your trip is less melodramatic."

She returned his smile with a certain hauteur, more than a little amusement. Murdock glanced at the still glowering Archer, who was looking somewhat ridiculous and beginning to sense it. "You're going to look funny barging through the lobby with that thing in your hand," he said dryly. "Suppose it went off?"

14

*K*ENT MURDOCK OPENED his camera as he followed Archer and Rita Redfield through the downstairs lobby. As he stepped under the marquee, he saw that there was a taxi at the curb, but no other in the block. While the doorman pitched baggage into the front seat, Murdock adjusted his shutter, focused the camera, and threw it up to his shoulder.

He called: "Archer!"

Rita Redfield had one foot on the running board, one foot on the floor of the tonneau. Archer was right behind her, his right hand on the door-handle. Both turned at the call, and in that instant Murdock pressed the shutter-release. Rita Redfield disappeared in the cab; Archer's mouth worked silently and his blond mustache twitched like a thing alive. Then the mouth clamped shut. He flung himself into the cab and slammed the door.

The little smile on Murdock's lips and in the depths of his dark eyes was static. He reversed his plate-holder and again put the camera to his shoulder as the cab slanted into the middle of the street. His next picture caught the back end of the car—and Rita Redfield's face pressed against the rear window.

Murdock had to walk to Commonwealth Avenue before he caught a taxi. He said *"Courier-Herald,"* and flopped back on the seat. The smile disappeared. The reason was not that he had failed with Howard Archer. He felt sure, when he had promised Joyce, that there was small chance of success. He had done the best he could under the circumstances, but the only sure way to stop Archer was to call Bacon—to have called him before he left his apartment.

It was this thought that erased his smile and filmed his eyes with trouble. For the first time he was not playing ball with the police. And Bacon— Damn it! He justified his actions, tried to justify them, with the thought that this case was different. In the first place, he was out to collect something in the way of a reward, at least a part payment to Hestor—if he was lucky. In the second place, there was Joyce.

He had crossed Bacon by hiding her at his apartment. True, it had not mattered in the end. And he was crossing Bacon again. With this sort of information about a stranger, Murdock would surely have tipped off the police. *And Archer could have killed Mark Redfield.* He grunted savagely and stared morosely out through the cab window at the traffic jam on Tremont and Boylston.

"For a guy who's supposed to be on the level," he grunted in his throat, "you're turning into a lousy, double-crossing heel."

By the time he had reached the office, Murdock had made his decision. He could check up himself and see just what Archer was going to do; and he could go part way with Bacon, do a little something to salve his conscience. He called headquarters as soon as he reached his desk.

"Anything new?"

"Naw," Bacon grunted.

"Pick up Tripp?"

"Didn't I say there was nothing new?" Bacon was almost petulant.

"Then get a load of this and don't say I'm holding out on you. Archer skipped out this afternoon—with Rita Redfield."

Murdock waited until Bacon's explosion subsided.

"I can't tell you," he said in answer to the Lieutenant's demand for more information. "All I know is that they pulled out of the Embankment Arms about ten minutes ago with four bags. Maybe they're going to hide out; maybe they're leaving town."

"But what—"

"How do I know?" Murdock cut him off before he could state the question. "Do I have to do all the leg work for the police department? Check it—and quit crabbin'!"

He hung up on Bacon's "Thanks." Staring at the mouthpiece, he said: "That's the best I can do."

Wixon, another camera man, who had his feet cocked on a desk across the room and was reading the sports page, said: "What?"

Murdock said: "I was thinking out loud."

"It's possible then, huh?" Wixon asked, grinning.

Murdock opened his plate-case and took out his exposed plates of Archer, of the Industrial Exhibit. He went down the narrow corridor connecting a row of adjoining dark-rooms. He turned into the black cubicle at the end and set to work. All of the pictures were good, and when he had made the prints, he took them into the photo-engraving room and dried them over a flame. The assignment pictures he sent upstairs; the two of Archer and the taxi he studied a moment, then put in a call for the Green and White Taxi Company.

It was dark when Murdock located the driver of Archer's taxi in a stand at the corner of Boylston and Providence Streets. The driver, a beetle-browed husky with a fog-horn voice, was suspicious, surly, when Murdock started to question him.

"Sure," he blustered, "sure I had a fare from the Embankment Arms. What about it?"

Murdock described Archer and Rita Redfield.

"Suppose it was them?"

"I want to know where you took them," Murdock rapped, irritated by the man's manner.

"All right," scoffed the driver, "you want to know. So what? You're no copper."

"Listen," Murdock said, "you're not smart—just dumb. And it bores me to hear you talk. But I want some information. I work for the *Courier-Herald*. I'm willing to give you a fin, but if you're not interested I'll go to headquarters and you'll tell them for nothing. So make up your mind."

"That's different," the driver said. "Hell, why'n't you say you was a newspaper guy." He eyed the bill in Murdock's hand. "They went over to the airport."

Murdock climbed into the cab. "Let's go."

When the driver skidded the wheels to a stop on the cinder bed of the airport, Murdock went into the administration building, showed his press card, said: "You keep the names of passengers, don't you?"

The clerk said they did, that the last plane had left

an hour ago. Murdock asked for the passenger list, found only one woman in the group. He asked the clerk what she looked like.

"Middle-aged," he said. "Sort of fat and wore glasses."

Murdock lit a cigarette, frowned thoughtfully. "Who rents planes around here? I mean for fairly long trips? The people I'm looking for hired one around four-thirty or so and—"

"Sure," the clerk said, brightening. "I remember. A Tri-State outfit job. They're down in that second hangar, that blue one. I don't know if there's anyone there, but—"

Murdock went out before the clerk finished. An east wind whipping in from the ocean tucked his coat-tails between his legs and he had to buck it all the way to the blue hangar, which, in the shadows of the floodlight on the peak of the roof, looked all black.

There was no one there except a mechanic, but he gave freely the information Murdock sought.

"Yeah. Shorty Regan took off with 'em in a three-place Eagle. He was supposed to take 'em to Newark. Funny, too. If they'd waited a half-hour they coulda got the transport. I had a hunch maybe they were honeymooners or something."

Murdock passed the man a dollar bill and snapped up the collar of his coat. "Not a bad hunch either."

Phil Doane slid off of Murdock's desk in the photographic department anteroom, his round, good-natured face eager, flushed with excitement.

"Hey, you know what?"

"Yeah. What?"

"Archer skipped out—with the Redfield dame."

"Yeah?" Murdock looked surprised. "How did you tumble?"

"I was lookin' for you at the Embankment Arms— Where the hell you been?" Doane did not expect an answer. "And Bacon and Keogh and a couple others swarmed into the place. For once I was right there when it happened and Bacon gave me a break. Told me to get a coupla pics from the morgue and run them too. And Van Husan," Doane continued elatedly, "was tickled silly."

"Did he say so?" Murdock asked dryly.

"Well, no," Doane said, sobering a little. "He said: 'It's about time.' But all he did to the yarn was put a 'ead on it and make a couple minor changes."

"That's swell," Murdock said. "You're safe for another week. Now beat it, will you? I got things to do."

Doane did not protest. He started out whistling, stopped at the door. "But don't forget—on this other thing. You're gonna let me in on it if—"

"Go 'way!" Murdock said, but the way he said it amounted to yes, and Doane knew this and went out, picking up the whistle contentedly.

Murdock took off his coat and hat, hung both on the yellow-oak hat-rack. He sat down at his desk, slouched there for some minutes, staring at the practically nude figure of a dancer that someone had cut out of an old *Police Gazette* and pasted on the wall. His eyes followed the generous lines of the figure automatically, but he was not aware of what he saw, of anything but his thoughts.

He stood up and began to walk around in circles, his head down, hands jammed in his coat pockets so that the fabric was tight across the buttocks. He stopped the circular pacing abruptly after a minute or so, went to his desk, and swept up the telephone, his lean face dark, his eyes intense, fixed straight ahead.

When he got his connection he said: "Fenner? Murdock." A pause. "Yeah, and I've got another job for you."

Another pause.

"No, this isn't about her. This is easy. But listen, Jack, this is confidential as hell. It's got to be that way. Between you and me."

Another pause.

"Sure, I know, but this is important enough to me to make sure you got it straight. Here it is. An Eagle plane from Tri-State Airways took off from the airport about four-thirty this afternoon. A private job, see? The pilot was a lad named Shorty Regan and he was hired to go to Newark. I want you to find out if he did go there. Get him when he gets back—I don't know when it'll be—and find out where he went."

Another pause.

"That's all. I told you it was easy. Call me when you find out."

15

A THOUSAND LITTLE THINGS, all of them converging on Joyce Archer, flashed through Kent Murdock's brain as he crossed the lobby of the Embankment Arms and stepped into the elevator. He would have to tell her about her brother and how he had failed. But he could do that, and she would understand he had done his best for her. He would also have to tell her exactly what the situation was, tell her how much he had told the police and why; tell her about Fenner and the plane.

Maybe she would think he had double-crossed her. He hoped not, but in any case he would have to risk it. She deserved the truth and he could give her that much.

This was decided when he stepped from the elevator. But the other— It all came back to him so that he practically relived the moment. The scent from her hair was in his throat. He could feel the warmth, the sweetness of her lips, that hard young pressure of her arms at his neck. And the thought tormented him. That first night, when he had found her in his bed. The subsequent nights. On the surface, casual, with a friendly intimacy and understanding; below the surface, a strained, unnatural surging and quickening of the pulse that was almost constantly accelerated until it had become a torrent of desire, ungovernable without the strictest concentration.

And if the thing had happened before, if he had not resisted until the impulse broke through his restraint that afternoon . . .

He stopped in front of his door and took out his keys. He unsnapped the button of the pigskin case, thrust forward the door-key, then stopped it an inch from the keyhole. He stood there rigidly a moment until he realized his breath was short, that he was sweating from the pressure of his coat and his thoughts.

Turning suddenly with an almost savage movement, he jammed the keys into his pocket, glanced around. The corridor was quiet, deserted. He knelt quickly, lowered his head until he could see the crack between the bottom of the door and the sill. The yellow sliver of light from the room told him what he wanted to know.

He stood up and walked quickly back to the waiting elevator. His pace was jerky, stiff-kneed; his lean face was twisted somehow from the tightly pressed lips so that it looked worn and haggard, with a tautness that was reflected in eyes that did not seem quite well.

There was a drug-store two blocks away. Murdock turned in there and walked back to the telephone booth at the far end of the soda counter. Lifting the receiver, he waited until the operator answered, realized finally that he did not know his own number. The interval while he hung up and looked through the directory served to snap his tension. When Joyce Archer's voice finally came over the wire he had control of himself, and his voice was normal—or just a shade brusque.

He said: "I drew a blank."

"You what?"

Murdock laughed shortly. "That was the button-pusher talking. What I mean is, I failed you with Howard."

"Oh." The voice was dull.

"It was a case of a brawl or nothing. I couldn't quite see it that way. They were at the point where a little thing like reason is inconsequential. I'm beginning to think I know how it is."

"How what is?"

"I had to tell the police," Murdock said, ignoring the question.

"But you couldn't do that. You—" The voice was frightened and trailed off miserably.

"I couldn't hold out on Bacon entirely. Try to understand that. But I did not tell all I knew. They would have found out anyway. They were bound to check on him. All I did was to tell them a little ahead of time."

"Yes," the voice said listlessly, "I see."

"There's something else," Murdock went on doggedly. "I got a picture of them, the cab they used. I traced it to the airport. They hired a plane to take them to Newark. I'm having a friend hunt up the pilot when he returns and find out for sure where they went."

"You didn't tell—"

"That's just for our own information."

There was a pause then and Murdock pushed back his hat and reached for a handkerchief. The stuffiness of the booth was oppressive; the air was getting hot and sticky.

"That's why I didn't call sooner," he added.

"I thought a lot about it while you were gone. I was worried when I didn't hear from you. But I'm not surprised really. Disappointed. But it was too much to expect. I guess I set the example."

"They may hit it off together if—" He did not add: "the police don't find them."

"Where are you now?"

"Downtown."

"Are we going to eat together?" The voice brightened slightly, as though shrugging off its disappointment.

'Not tonight. I've got work to do," lied Murdock.

"Oh. Well—when will you be out?"

"When you go."

"When I—"

"He's gone now."

There was no answer.

"That's what you came for, wasn't it?" Murdock pressed stubbornly. A new bitterness crept into his voice. "You wanted to make him see reason; sauce for the goose, inverted. And we've both botched the thing some way. I mean, you can go home now. You did all you could do."

There was no answer to this either.

"You can't use that as an excuse any longer," Murdock blurted.

"I didn't think I needed an excuse." Joyce Archer's voice was stiff now, cold. "What I told you was a long time ago—it seems a long time. I thought things were changed. But it was a mistake, then, this afternoon."

"It was a mistake with things as they are with me." Murdock wiped his face, crumpled the handkerchief in his fist.

"Then why don't you come here and tell me so to my face?"

"Because I'm scared."

"Of me?"

"Yes. Of me, too. Of both of us."

"Need you be?" The voice was relieved now, low, vibrant.

"You know. I'm old enough to know when to be scared. I'm just a mug, a newspaper man. I've had most of my illusions knocked out of me. But I'm not that much of a mug—or if I am, not with your kind of a girl."

"Then you still have an illusion or two left."

"I know what it is to do a thing impulsively and re-gret it."

"It wouldn't be impulsive now, would it?"

"You'd better go home."

"I won't."

"Go home and stay there and think it over and then—"

"It wouldn't make any difference unless—"

"Unless what?"

"It wouldn't make any difference."

Murdock wiped the handkerchief across his face again.

"If you stay there," he said sharply, "you'll stay there for good. And here's something else. You've been there three nights. I've tried to be polite and considerate and decent because you're young and temporarily dissatisfied, and disgusted with your brother and life in general. You'll react to all this emotional drive some time and see things as they are. Then you'll hate me and yourself and—"

"I hate myself now, most of the time."

Murdock cursed softly in his exasperation. "Anyway, I think I'm going to New York."

"Why?"

"I'm fed up with my job."

"I thought you liked newspaper work."

"Maybe I do, but I can't know how well until I get away from it. I want to try some advertising work, some portrait stuff, and see—"

"Well, why not? Couldn't I go?"

"No."

A woman's purring voice broke in. "Deposit another five cents, puleeze."

"Wait a minute," growled Murdock and he fished for the handful of coins in his pocket. He had one five-cent piece left, jammed it into the proper slot, and the gong-like bell rang in his ear. "Hello."

"Thank you."

"Hello."

"Why can't I go?"

Murdock felt momentary relief at the sound of the familiar voice again; then his face grew taut and his eyes were miserable in the shadows.

"Because I won't take you. I'm married and until—"

"I know that." This impatiently. "You're not seducing me. I'll be glad to get away from here, to be with some-one, even if only for a short while, who will try to understand and maybe be a little kind."

"I won't take you."

"I don't blame you for not respecting me. But do you hate me as well?"

"Hate you?" exploded Murdock.

"Then why—"

"All right." Murdock felt the pounding of the blood at his eardrums, the hot stifling pressure of the little booth. His mouth, his throat, seemed dry and parched. He went on in a quick, almost savage voice:

"If you want to know, I love you. I don't know what else could make me this way. You're what I want, what I've always wanted. I like the way you talk; I like your mind and your spirit and the nerve that made you run away and break into my room. I like the way you feel about your brother and your naturalness and frankness and the lines of your body and the way you walk across a room. I like— Damn it! I like it all. But I don't want a sample. I want it for good. If you want to wait, maybe I can work the thing out. I've got to work it out. But—"

"It took you a long time to say so." Joyce Archer's voice was alive and throaty, joyful.

"If that's what you wanted, you've got it," Murdock snapped.

"I thought I was right. It's so much nicer to be sure. Because I'm that way. And that's why I said things had changed and why I don't want any excuse any more. If we are honest with ourselves, we don't have to wait. It's silly."

"Not to me. Because I've sat there in my place three nights and thought about you and fought with myself, knowing that whether you liked me or not you were a good enough sport to keep your part of the bargain. You came to spite your brother and you would have carried on rather than back out. I've gone this far. I'm going to wait until we can start out right. It's worth it. We can see each other, all right, and go places and do things, but—"

"How long will it take to get your divorce?"

Murdock groaned. "Hestor knows how to spite, too." With the weight of his confession off his mind, with the knowledge that Joyce had accepted it and felt as he did, his tone was lighter. Some of the stiffness went out of his lips and he forgot about the sweat on his face and forehead. "I'm beginning to think it's a woman's complex."

"You mean she won't give you one? On any grounds?"

"No," Murdock said flatly. "Not till she's ready. I can

buy her off; that's the only way."

"How much?"

"Ten thousand."

Joyce Archer's laugh, distorted by the instrument, shrilled in his ear and he flared: "What's funny?"

"Nothing. I'm not rich enough to scare you off, but I've a little. Enough to—"

"Oh, no," Murdock cut in. "It's my mess. I've got to clean it up."

"But I'm in it now."

"Yes, but at best I'll probably be a lousy guy to have around the house. I balled things up once before. Maybe I've learned something. But at best I'm no bargain—even without cost. You're entitled to something better—to the best break I can give you."

"But what does it matter if—"

"No!" warned Murdock. "A bought husband, huh?"

"Don't be a grouch!"

The silky-voiced operator broke in upon him again. "Your time is up. Deposit five cents, puleeze."

Dismay settled over Murdock. There was no other nickel in his pocket. He said: "Wait!" Then, fairly shouting: "You go on home because—"

He heard Joyce's laugh again, heard: "I suppose I'll have—" and then the line went dead.

16

*H*ESTOR MURDOCK LAY in the perfumed depths of her bath and parboiled herself blissfully. Her legs were stretched out. She had a rubber-covered and luxuriantly soft pillow behind her head so that she could lean comfortably against the slightly sloping head of the tub. Her arms lay idly along the sides and the steaming water, a pinkish color now, came to her armpits; her back was slightly arched, bringing her breasts close to the surface so that the occasional movement of her body set up miniature ripples which threatened to bare them at any moment.

This, the first five minutes, was always the best. She did not want to stir herself. The warmth, the lift of the water, gave her an ethereal sense of floating, of hanging suspended, naked, motionless, in hot, lush space. But it did not last. It was never until she felt chilled that she realized the water had cooled. Then it was too late to recapture the ecstatic mood; too late to do anything but hurry out of the tub and take a brisk rub-down and tell herself she would not make the same mistake next time.

But there was time enough tonight; the water had nearly scalded her. And Girard would not call until ten o'clock. He had wanted to pick her up at the studio. But to get the most enjoyment out of these hours with him, she had to start off right.

The broadcasts always left her nerves ragged and high-strung. It was not like the stage. Nothing to judge how she was going over except by the dead-pan audience beyond the glass panels. Trained seals. Polite. Clapping when it was expected of them. Filing in and out like a jury. It was time, she told herself, she got used to this. A year and a half she had been broadcasting. Not an important program, but the hundred and fifty a week was three times what she had made in the chorus. It was that time-clock efficiency with which everything was conducted that keyed her up like this.

A hot bath, though, a cocktail, and a change of clothes —these made a difference. She stirred in the tub, and the pillow slipped down her back into the water. She picked it out and tossed it on the floor, sat up, and reached for the lavender-colored soap.

When she had finished she called: "Anna," and a moment later a stout Negress with a good-natured face and gold ear-rings in pierced ears came into the room. She had a towel over her arm, which she unfolded and held up in front of her. The towel was so long she had to peer over the top to see that her position was correct to receive her mistress. When Hestor stepped from the tub, she turned her back and Anna wrapped the towel about her and let go of it.

The orchid bath-mat was as thick as a rug. Hestor seemed to flatten her feet on it. When she had the towel adjusted to suit her, she turned around.

"Did you bring the shaker in?"

"Yes, m'm." Anna bobbed her head up and down.

"Then lay out my black velvet."

Anna's head bobbed again. "Anything else, m'm?"

"That's all." Hestor started to dry herself, and Anna moved to the door. "Oh, Anna, and leave the door unlocked."

Anna went out. She was a good investment. Lucky to get one as good for part-time work. She had no need of a full-time girl. She was never up until noon, was she? And she never needed Anna after nine o'clock or so at night. Of course, it *would* be nice to have a full-time maid; she'd have one some day.

Hestor dropped the towel at her feet, slipped into feathered mules and picked up the blue crêpe negligee on the white chair. As she started to go out, she caught her reflection in the full-length mirror and stopped in front of it. Facing herself this way, she studied her image for a few seconds, then replaced the negligee and presented her left side to the glass.

She cocked her head with the chin up and surveyed herself from the corner of her eye. Not bad at all. In fact— Her hands moved up to her breasts, moved under them to support them. They were still firm, the skin smooth and rounded. And they did not need support. Her hands came away. Thank goodness, she had not yet lost her figure.

She was thirty. If she watched herself, took a little exercise, and ate sensibly she would be just as good at forty. But why not? Her figure had never been anything but a source of pleasure. It had never troubled her; she had never had to baby herself. Her hands moved to her stomach. Rounded, yes. But she was not the flapper type. Slender enough, but not depending upon a dress to proclaim her sex.

She smiled, turned away, and picked up the negligee. She did not put it on; she carried it into the bedroom and tossed it upon the ivory four-poster. Opening a round, flowered box of powder, she reached for the puff. The handle was eighteen inches long, gently curving; the puff itself was about the size of half a cantaloupe.

What, she wondered as a cloud of powder settled about her, would be the upshot of Girard's attention. He was a bachelor; there might be a possibility of marriage. But if not, if the affair was of any duration, he would probably make some sort of settlement. She had heard he was generous. And certainly there was money enough. Besides, he was a gentleman. An ex-bootlegger, but a gentleman. Until she had met him, six months before, that line of business had designated a type. Girard was different— well educated, polished. She liked the way he talked, the way he wore his clothes, the way he ordered dinner. And there was a deference, an almost inborn deference, in his manner towards her.

She smiled at herself and put down the powder-puff. The black velvet lay on the bed. It would be a job getting into it, but it was worth the effort and, once on, its sleek tightness made a girdle unnecessary, and the effect was— she had seen men look at her in night clubs—well, adequate, certainly. She contemplated the dress a moment, then stepped over to the bedside table and picked up the cocktail-shaker, a severe cylinder of chromium and black enamel. She shook it five or six times, poured dark red liquid into the single silver cocktail cup. Manhattans were her favorite. She liked the sweetness of the Italian vermouth, the jolt of the rye whisky. But she had to be careful. They were heavy. At least to her. Two, not more than three, or she felt sleepy and thick-headed.

She drank the first cocktail quickly, poured the second and carried it to her dressing-table, sat down on the cushioned bench. Her make-up did not take long, because she was an expert, her training and experience dating to pre-burlesque days. Fortunately her eyelashes were good—long and with a natural sharp upward curve; mascara was unnecessary. Stroking them with a tiny brush for a few seconds, she surveyed her handiwork with satisfaction, touched the stopper of the perfume-bottle under each ear, then finished the second cocktail.

She sat down on the bed, picked up the sheer silk stockings, her thoughts reverting to Girard. Then, as she crossed her legs, the sound of the door-buzzer broke her reverie. She stood up, slipped a foot into the mule which had fallen to the floor.

He was early; too early.

She caught up the negligee, shrugged into it, and tied the sash tightly about her waist as she moved into the living-room. Then, instead of going to the door as she had intended, she turned and went back to the inner hall, turned again, and called: "Come."

The smile died on her lips as the door swung inward. Kent Murdock stepped through the opening, stopped there with one hand on the knob, the other removing his brown felt. Irritation and resentment flared up in Hestor's face. The lips dipped at the corners, and her shoulders sagged slightly. For a second or two they stood there staring at each other; then Murdock closed the door and Hestor started towards him.

"I'm going out," she said flatly.

"All right," Murdock said, just as flatly. "I won't stay long."

Hestor stopped in the center of the room, seemed about to speak. Instead she shrugged, took a cigarette from a plain silver box, and spun flame from a lighter. She forgot about holding the negligee. It gaped open at the throat and friction loosed the sash slightly. Murdock sat down on a chair arm, let both hands and the hat hang loosely between spread knees. Hestor turned and threw herself down on a chaise-longue with a striped silk damask covering.

"You can stay five minutes," she said, "but it won't take me that long to say no."

Murdock's thin smile was mirthless. "Who is it, Nate Girard?"

Hestor did not answer immediately; she simply watched Murdock through the spiraling smoke from the cigarette and did a lot of thinking in a very short time.

Suppose she gave him his divorce. She would have to give him one eventually; she would want one herself. And if she was not careful— She knew him well enough to realize that, comparatively easy to get along with up to a certain point, Murdock was not the sort to take too much from anyone without fighting back.

So far she had been careful, and lucky, in that Murdock apparently did not care what she did. Men, the companionship of men, were as necessary to her life as food. Yet until Girard there had been none sufficiently important or attractive to warrant even a semi-permanent liaison. During the time Girard's trial was in progress Andrew

Sprague had seemed attractive to her, but now that Girard was out again—

She said: "I'm going out with him tonight, if that's what you mean."

Murdock nodded, turned the hat between his hands. "Why don't you do something about it? It might cramp your style some time, being tied up to me."

"I like it that way now." Hestor felt her irritation mount. "What's your trouble, the Archer girl?"

Murdock's eyes narrowed slightly. He hesitated. To tell the truth would only serve to rekindle Hestor's already smoldering spite; to deny— His chin came up; he spoke sullenly.

"Yes."

Hestor smiled with taunting sweetness. "Really?" Her voice thinned out. "Well, what can you do about it?"

Murdock watched her and she met his gaze defiantly. Let him wait, then. She was in no hurry. She liked to see him squirm. Damn him, anyway! There was something about him, even now, that attracted her. Perhaps it was his similarity to Girard—or perhaps Girard's similarity to Kent furnished the spark for this new affair. They had much in common. Something vital and clean; a hardness, but an innate fairness; intelligence and educated minds that she did not entirely understand, but which she knew enough to respect. And she had come a long way herself. These last two years had made a difference. With her present knowledge, with the right sort of handling, she could have held Murdock—at least longer.

But it was just as well. If he was still attractive to her, so was Girard. And Girard had money. He was older; he would probably demand but little and she could find other outlets, given money and leisure, for any surplus of desire. Her experience with Murdock would help her with Girard. She would know how to handle him now. She'd know when to hold back. And—she revived the thought with sudden bitterness—she could never bring Murdock back, even if she wanted him.

What did he expect in marriage, anyway? Look what she had given him. And he had spurned it; that was it, spurned her. Well, let him wait. Let him see how it felt. What if she really tricked him into marrying her? Hadn't she done her best to fulfill her obligations? She brought him youth and a beautiful body, an intensity of feeling that he could not get from one woman in a hundred. And it had not been enough—or, paradoxically, it had been too much. She had tried too hard. She could not tune him to her pitch. The thought of the quick cooling of his ardor—what little he had—infuriated her and—

Let him wait. Awhile longer anyway. She was in no hurry with Girard—and besides, she did not know whether she could get him or not. If she kept her hold, Murdock might get that ten thousand, or part of it. It was worth the effort, because if he did get nasty, she could always—

"I can think of two things," Murdock said grimly, cutting in on her thoughts.

"What two?"

"I can run out on you. I've been thinking of it anyway. I don't have to stay here, and without your weekly tax you wouldn't be so keen on holding me."

"Oh," Hestor said, and her lip curled. "And how about

your girl friend? She'd run away with you, I suppose. And will she be surprised when she finds out what she's run off with? When you let her down like you did me."

"She's different from you, Hestor," Murdock said, and his voice was thready. "I think she has a slightly different sense of values. The criterion would not be the same."

"Is that so?" Hestor flashed, and twisted on the chaise-longue so that the robe slipped from the legs stretched straight out and crossed at the ankles. "Well, you won't run out. You've got too good a job right here. You couldn't pick up another like it, and you know it. If you want your freedom, get the ten thousand. The girl ought to be worth that much. Just because you got me for nothing—"

"I've paid plenty."

Murdock stood up, walked stiffly around the room, came back to the foot of the chaise-longue. He stopped there, spread-legged, hands on hips, fanning out the tails of his topcoat.

"But there's another way," he said finally. "So far you've been lucky. When we separated I made up my mind to let you live your own life, do as you pleased. You have. I've never checked up on you. Frankly, I haven't been interested. But I am now." His face was dark, determined; the lips were stiff. "I think if I cramp your style from now on you may change your mind."

"You? Cramp my style? How?"

"I'll have you watched. And I'll be big-hearted about it and tell you in advance. You'll stop chasing or get caught. Either way is all right with me. Because I know you, and you can't stop. And with the odds the same for both of us, I can stand it better than you can."

Hestor's face flushed with sudden anger. Her lips drew back against her teeth and she seemed about to speak. It was with an apparent effort that she controlled the impulse. She tossed her hips petulantly and one side of the robe trailed off on the floor. Thigh, hip, one firm breast were suddenly bare. She made no move to retrieve the wrap. She just stared at Murdock.

Murdock's eyes flicked to the nude side of her body and he jerked them up to her face. It was he who colored. Hestor lay there watching him, her pose natural, indolent, her gaze mocking.

She said: "You can't bluff me."

"I don't have to bluff." Murdock held her eyes. "In fact"—he let his hands slip from his hips and tapped his hat against one leg—"I've already started."

Hestor sat up, yanking the negligee about her shoulders with an automatic and unconscious movement.

"You lie!" Her eyes were glaring slits.

"No," Murdock said levelly. "I've had an idea all along about you. I may have been wrong before, but I've got proof this time."

"Of what?" she challenged.

"You went to Redfield's party with Girard. You left at three-thirty and I had you followed."

"You dirty—" Hestor reverted to type, but Murdock hurried on before she could finish.

"I told you, earlier that same night, to watch yourself."

Hestor glowered at him, crushed out the cigarette stub in an amber ash-tray, then gathered the negligee about her, completely covering her body. One eyebrow lifted as she studied him. When she spoke, her voice was like a sneer.

"All right. What about it?"

"Just this. You came here, and Girard came in with you. He was still here at five-thirty."

To Murdock's surprise, Hestor made no immediate answer. For several seconds she merely stared at him. Then, slowly, her eyes widened slightly and there was a curious, enigmatic expression in their depths. The trace of a weird little smile tugged at her sullen mouth.

"You can't prove it."

"I think I can."

"Suppose I said he wasn't here. My word is as good as yours or any private detective's. You couldn't get a divorce on that bit of evidence."

"Maybe not. I could try—but I don't know that I shall. Maybe I'll just let it ride as the first step." Murdock watched her closely, aware of her peculiar, wary reaction, but unable quite to diagnose the mood. He buttoned his coat. "But a couple more of those little incidents might make the difference; I might be able to do some good."

Hestor Murdock spoke as he reached the door. "I'm going out with him tonight. Call up your detective and see what he can do for you."

Murdock opened the door and turned to face her, his hand on the knob. She was smiling at him, smiling with a taunting and superior twist of her mouth. And yet that enigmatic expression remained, as though her brain was puzzling over something that had so far escaped diagnosis. He thought she was going to speak, but when she

continued to smile silently, he put on his hat and went
out.

17

THE BUXOM *Police Gazette* nude on the anteroom wall
made a focal point for Murdock's gaze as he slouched
down in his desk chair. His study of the figure was unconscious, troubled, and if he was aware of the picture at
all, it was because of an automatic association set up by
his brain between this photographic reproduction and
Hestor.

His new attempt to persuade her to give him a divorce
had failed utterly. And she had accepted his announcement of Fenner's finding with an equanimity that surprised him. Perhaps she was becoming more expert at
disguising her feelings. In any case he had, however,
planted the seed of doubt. He was sure of that much,
and he wondered if he might have shaken her confidence
so that, if he could raise part of the ten thousand, say
half of it, she would be willing to compromise in her
demand.

His mind hung suspended on this thought until, after
a while, he laughed aloud, a short brittle explosion that
held no mirth.

He was right back where he started from. Solve the
Redfield murder and he could collect. Not ten thousand, but perhaps half of it. The Bar Association offer
was just one of those things that sound good, but are sel-

dom realized. For the arrest and conviction. That, with luck, would mean an indefinite wait; any money would undoubtedly be split several ways. Wyman's offer was different. Here he could collect, but—the contingency was the same: Solve the case.

Murdock stirred in the chair and lit a cigarette. The smile became fixed on his lips. "Fat chance," he said half-aloud. Exclusive stories of this nature were much like action pictures. It was generally some amateur who collected. Stories resulting in arrests came from insiders, or neighbors, or friends of the criminal who double-crossed him. Any pictures of violence, bank robbery, accidents, generally came from some fellow with a box camera who was taking a picture of the building across the street when it happened.

Actually to go out with the express purpose of finding Redfield's killer, to get the story and pictures, seemed ridiculous. Yet what else had he left? If he failed, and he probably would, he would at least have the knowledge that he had tried. And he didn't get pictures sitting around the office wishing for them. The point was that for the past two or three days he had thought about the case, but not constructively. He had an idea or two; but these ideas were hazy, general, with more hope than reason behind them. But now he was sure about Joyce, and Hestor remained adamant and . . .

The combination of thoughts spurred Murdock's brain to a receptive clearness. He sat up, puffed smoke clouds around his head and began to review each single incident of the case, until the germ of an idea crept into his brain, began to blossom. By the time he crushed out his cigarette he thought he had a starting-point.

Any general investigation, any attempt to solve each angle of the case, would be fruitless, silly. Contrary to newspaper stories and fiction, the police department of any large city is an efficient organization. It has the man-power, the equipment, the specialists, the right channels of information, the authority to go out and do things.

Murdock lacked all of these. What he did extract from the mass of facts and incidents that unwound in his brain was one feature that, so far as he knew, the police either had ignored or, more probably, had passed up temporarily in favor of more important clues.

Concentrating on this point, he began to see the importance of an answer. The more he thought, the more interested he became. Then, finally convinced of the importance of this potential clue, he struck a snag in visualizing some method to run it down. Single-handed, it would take him weeks. . . .

The answer—surprisingly simple when it arrived in completed form—came a half-hour later. The means lay within the organization of the *Courier-Herald*.

Murdock's dark eyes were bright when he finally stood up. The smile which still etched itself on his lips began to narrow the corners of his eyes. Determination had kept pace with his prodding thoughts; his interest was keen and made hopeful by imagination.

Opening a desk drawer, he pulled out the picture of Archer, taken at headquarters on the afternoon of the questioning. It had not been used, but he was glad, now, that he had it. He slipped it into his pocket, went up-

stairs to the morgue and library adjoining the front corner of the city room, which was now blazing with light,
reverberating with the sharp, persistent clatter of a half-
dozen typewriters.

With the help of Jerry, the librarian, a stoop-
shouldered veteran, Murdock collected a picture of
Nate Girard, one of Sam Cusick, another of Spike Tripp.
He went back down to his department and out into the
photo-engraving room. Squinting his way past the blue-
white brightness of the high-watt bulbs, he found the
foreman.

"Ben." Murdock drew the foreman over to a table at
the side of the room and placed the four photographs in
a row. "Make me a plate of these."

The foreman, a thick-chested husky in overalls and a
blue shirt, pulled at a heavy red nose and scowled. "It
ain't gonna look good. They're all different focus."

"Who cares?" grunted Murdock.

"What do you want 'em for?"

"For my own use. I want one plate—say four inches
high and let the width come. They don't have to be
jammed right together, just so they're reproduced on
one sheet."

"If you say so," Ben said, shrugging and picking up
the prints.

"Thanks, Ben." Murdock slapped the foreman's
shoulder. "And when you get it done, get about six or
eight good proofs and leave them on my desk—with the
plate."

The mezzanine floor was deserted, gloomily lighted

by a single bulb in the hall ceiling. At the far end of the corridor a yellow rectangle of light slashed across the opposite wall from the frosted glass pane of a private office. Murdock entered here without knocking.

The office was small and bare, boasting one desk, two chairs, a filing-cabinet, and a large map of the city which hung on one wall. Lolling far back in a spring chair, his heels cocked on the desk, was a short, plump man with black hair and eyes, and jowls made blue by a heavy beard. His coat was off, and his sleeves were rolled up; the unlighted stump of a cigar was wedged in one corner of his mouth, and his discolored felt hat was pushed forward so that it did not seem possible that he could read the newspaper he held spread out before him. He did not look around until Murdock said:

"Hello, Mac."

MacShane, city circulator of the *Morning Herald*, glanced over his shoulder, and his black eyes slid up and down Murdock's figure with a sort of surprised indifference before he spoke.

"My gawd!" He brought the paper together. "How the hell did you find your way down here?"

"I heard," Murdock said, grinning, "I heard there was a circulation department some place in the building. I wanted to be sure. Carson around?"

MacShane swung his feet down from the desk, swiveled around in the chair. "No. He's got sense. He goes home when he's through."

"Well," Murdock said, "you'll do."

"I was afraid of it. I'll bet it's trouble."

Murdock shook his head and sat down on the other

chair at the end of the desk. "I want a little help."

"It's the same thing," MacShane groaned. "The only time you guys on the news end know we're alive down here is when you need help—or when you got a complaint that some friend of your Aunt Emma's didn't get his paper."

Murdock said: "Nuts," and then his eyes fell upon the map on the wall. He stood up, crossed to it. Locating his own apartment house, he put his finger on it and, taking out a pencil, made four dots. One of these was in the Hill section, one was in Brookline, one was near Westland Avenue, and the fourth was off Arlington, near Columbus.

He beckoned MacShane with a nod of his head. "Come here."

MacShane stood up wearily and scowled. "I don't like the looks of this."

Murdock said: "How many district men you got?"

"Eighteen on carriers, six news-stand men, four—"

"Never mind." Murdock grunted good-naturedly. "I didn't ask the right question. Take a look." He pointed to the apartment location, indicated the four dots. "How many men have you got in that territory?"

"All of it?" MacShane asked. "Four."

"Hah!" Murdock breathed. "It hadn't ought to be too hard."

"I'll bet it's plenty tough," MacShane said. He came back to the desk. "And I don't like the way you say it."

"Listen, Mac." Murdock leaned across the desk, and the grin evaporated. "Can you get these four fellows down here tonight?"

"I doubt it," MacShane grumbled. "What the hell do you think we do, work all the time? What do you want?"

"I want to check on the telephone pay-stations in that territory."

MacShane threw up his hands. "There are thousands of 'em! Christ! You must be nuts!"

"Wait," Murdock snapped, and the crispness of his voice held MacShane. "It's not as bad as you think. All I want is the places that are open at four o'clock in the morning. Your circulation birds know a city upside down and backwards. Those district men ought to know every brick in the pavement."

"They do," MacShane flung out, "but what—"

"I'll bet there aren't more than fifty places in that whole district that stay open all night. A few drug-stores, a few lunch-rooms, and—"

"Hotels," MacShane rapped.

"Yeah." Murdock's tone was momentarily discouraged. "Well, they're probably out. If he went in a hotel—"

"Who?" lipped MacShane, clamping thick jaws on the cigar so that the muscles rippled below his cheek-bones. "What the hell is this?"

Murdock explained tersely. "I'll give you pictures of four men. You get these district men here and I'll have copies for each of them. What they've got to do is find the all-night places, find the fellow on duty, and show him the pictures. I want to know if any of the four made a pay-station call at four-thirty in the morning. If one of them did, the guy ought to remember it, because he couldn't be so damn busy at that hour. It won't be so hard. I tell you there won't be fifty places open and—"

"It's hard, even the way you tell it," MacShane muttered. "Suppose my boys locate all these places, that don't mean the guy on duty is gonna remember—"

"I know that," snapped Murdock. "I'll need some luck. But it's the only way I can think of. It's a chance and—"

"What night?"

"Last Friday."

"So—" MacShane's eyes narrowed. "Who are the four guys?"

"Cusick, Girard, Tripp, and Archer."

"Redfield?"

Murdock nodded.

"These dots are where they live?"

Murdock nodded again.

"Why just pay-stations?"

"I don't think a man would take a chance on his own phone. It might be checked."

"What're you tryin' to prove? I ain't had time to read much about it."

"Then what difference does it make?" Murdock asked. "It's got to be confidential anyway. I want you to talk to those four district men separately. If they don't recognize the pictures, so much the better. I'm working alone on this. It's just a hunch. You can give me a break, Mac. How about it?"

MacShane rubbed one blue jowl and scowled down at the desk; but even with the scowl the eyes were alert, interested. He was a circulation man, MacShane. As such he was accustomed to handling, and on time, the most perishable product in the world: a big city newspaper, which, with five editions, is conceived, born, and forgotten in a few hours.

Time was the all-important element. The answer to the problem, an organization so highly geared that there was no waste motion. When the editor and his reporters and camera men put the paper to bed and went home—or wherever it was they went when they called it a day—MacShane and his crew went to work. It was dirty, strenuous, nerve-racking, thankless work. But to a circulation man, it was his job. District men, carriers, street hustlers, truck-drivers, these were MacShane's tools; and he knew how to use them. The process made a pessimist out of him, but it did not decrease his effectiveness.

"Well"—he looked up at Murdock and grinned so that the dead cigar butt angled up sharply—"maybe we can do it."

Murdock exhaled noisily; his lean face broadened with his grin. "Atta boy."

"Don't get all hot about it," MacShane cautioned glumly. "It don't mean you'll get what you want."

"If you can't do it," Murdock said, standing up, "it can't be done. I'll put a case of liquor in the hat. You can split it with the boys, or I'll pay their taxi—"

"I heard you the first time." MacShane turned in his chair, leaned back, a quick grin fading. "But here's something. If it's a story you're after, and you get it, damn you if you don't make it break right for me. Don't forget, I work for the *Herald*. Next to that I guess the *Courier's* all right. But I don't want none of these other rags stealin' our stuff—"

"Give me what I want and I'll break it right."

MacShane grunted and reached for the telephone. "Bring in your pictures. I don't know if I can get these guys tonight, but I'll have something by tomorrow afternoon—probably a blank."

Murdock saw the first police car when he swung out of the taxi. It was near the mouth of an alley. As he shouldered his plate-case and started into the sidewalk shadows he saw that a second car had been driven into the alley proper so that its headlights splashed a weird yellow glow down the length of the walled canyon.

The policeman beside this second car stopped Murdock, who said: "Bacon sent for me. What's up?"

The policeman grunted, leaned close. "Oh, hello, Murdock. He sent for you, huh?" He hesitated uncertainly. "Then how come you don't know what's up?"

"Bacon's funny that way. He said: 'Never mind why, get the hell down here.' "

The policeman turned and called to Bacon. The answer came back profanely and the policeman said: "Yeah, I guess you're right."

Murdock squeezed between the car and the rear wall, stepped into the light-rays. A little knot of men were grouped about some object at the far end of the alley and over to one side. By the time he was half-way to the group, Murdock saw that this object was a man. Instinct, the urgency of Bacon's telephone conversation, which he received just after he had sent MacShane the halftone proofs Ben had made for him, told him the man was dead. But he did not know who the victim was until he pushed in between Bacon and Sergeant Keogh.

Spike Tripp lay on his back, his arms outstretched, his eyes open and staring. The examiner was still making a cursory inspection of the body, and the vest had been unbuttoned, disclosing a reddish blotch that extended clear across one side of the chest. This red-stained part of the shirt was stiff; the limbs, the set of the body, made an impression of complete rigidity that was unnatural, grotesque.

Bacon turned, glared at Murdock, spoke angrily. "A smart trick, huh?" he growled. "Run out on us yesterday and this is what it got him." He began to curse, stepped back from the body, and tugged savagely at the brim of his hat.

Murdock let the plate-case slide from his shoulder. He watched the examiner for a moment; then he, too, looked away. For some moments the thoughts which surged in a vortexing jumble through his brain made him forget his surroundings. Bacon had been right—he himself had been right. Tripp had been upstairs in the hall outside Redfield's apartment for a longer period than he had admitted. And apparently he had seen someone come back after the party had broken up. He had seen Archer and probably Joyce. Who else?

Sam Cusick's words came back to him on a rush of memory: "There are two guys who know where I was last night." Murdock exhaled through loose lips, thought: "I guess there's only one who knows now."

He glanced about. Night hung pitch-black over the alley. The windows facing it and extending up the side of the four-story loft building opposite caught this blackness, exaggerating and reflecting it. Surrounded by a neighborhood that was sordid and decadent, this man-made crevasse was abandoned. Dust, refuse, old papers, staves and hoops from a shattered barrel, littered the ancient cobblestone floor. And along this floor there swept a breeze which stirred the papers, giving them life, and spread a chill at Murdock's ankles which seemed to mount until it infused his thoughts.

Bacon turned back to him. "One slug, right in the ticker. He was in the doorway here." He turned and waved an arm at the shadows beyond the body. Murdock had not noticed it before, but he saw now that there was a doorway set deep in the wall of the building. The door was closed.

The examiner stood up and spoke irritably. "I can't do much more here. I'll have to get him where I can work on him. But he's been dead quite a while, probably around noon."

"It wasn't tough enough before," Keogh growled irrelevantly. "He has to go get himself knocked off and make it tougher." He began to swear.

Murdock, speaking to Bacon, asked:

"Just found him, huh?"

"Some kid found him. The killer tucked him in the doorway out of sight."

Murdock opened his plate-case and took out a tripod.

Bacon said: "I'm gettin' sick of this. I'm chiseling on the other button-pushers to give you a break, and what do I get out of it? Hell, get lucky or something!"

Murdock said: "It looks as if you'd have to find Cusick."

"It's his kind of a job," Bacon said. "And if we get some decent idea of when he was killed—"

"Decent?" exploded the examiner, who was just starting to leave. "What do you want, a miracle? You let him lay around for twelve hours and then expect me to work out the time of death by a mathematical formula."

Bacon held himself in check until the doctor left; then he snarled: "Noon, huh? And Archer skipped out at four-thirty."

"I told you he looked good to me," Keogh said.

"He looks good to me now," Bacon said sharply. "We found out he hired a plane at the airport. And when I get him back here—and I will—I got an idea I'm going to persuade him to tell us where he was at noon today."

Murdock did not say anything; he just busied himself with his camera and flash-bulbs and felt more worried about Tripp's death than he cared to admit. Maybe Joyce could give Howard Archer an alibi. But it would take something more than lack of an alibi to get convictions and he knew it. And here he was kidding himself that he could solve the Redfield case.

Murdock called MacShane when he got back to the office, told him about Tripp, and said that he had some pictures as first payment on the job MacShane was doing.

He reached his apartment a half-hour later. The door was locked, and when he stepped into the darkened room and snapped on the light, he was aware of just one thing: the chilled, complete emptiness of the place.

18

CHE POLICE DRAGNET was out. When Murdock arrived at headquarters the next morning at Bacon's request, there were already fifteen or twenty thugs and hoodlums of varied experience and reputation in the hold-over. All leaves and vacations were suspended; every plain-clothesman in the city was out on the street checking, or trying to check, Tripp's movements and looking for Sam Cusick.

The Commissioner of Public Safety had a long telephone conversation with the Mayor. His Honor had added his sentiments to those received, and passed them along to the District Attorney and the Police Commissioner. The main hall of headquarters buzzed with activity—the hum of voices, the rap of feet on the bare stone floors. Plain-clothesmen hurried in and out of the main entrance, rode the elevators, and occasionally brought in a suspicious character. The Bureau of Records clerks were pawing through fingerprint cards; the photographers and fingerprint men were still combing the alley for a worth-while clue.

The upshot of the whole thing, Murdock learned when he entered Bacon's office, was nothing. There were two newspapers on his desk. The *News* said: TRIPP MURDERED IN ALLEY. The *Herald* had one of Murdock's pictures on the front page, and a more conservative head reading: REDFIELD WITNESS SLAIN.

Bacon chewed on a cigar and nursed a grouch. Keogh sat disconsolately in one corner. Quinn, from the District Attorney's office, glanced at Murdock as he entered, and then took up his former position and stared gloomily out the window.

Murdock said: "Well, I guess there isn't anything new, huh?" He dropped his plate-case beside the door-frame, put the camera on an old sectional bookcase, his hat on top of the camera.

"Nothing new?" snapped Bacon. "No, damn it! But to read these lousy rags you'd think somebody'd murdered the Governor. What's the matter with me, anyway?"

Murdock waited.

"I give you a break and then your paper starts to yell for my job, for all of our jobs."

"The *Herald*?" Murdock snapped, frowning. "We didn't—"

"Well," growled Bacon, "the *News* and the *Globe* are the worst. Crucify us, huh?" He broke off, took out his cigar, glared at it, and slammed it into the battered cuspidor with a curse. The gesture made an essential outlet for his feelings and he continued more evenly: "The Super was just in and he kinda laid it on to me. From now on newspaper guys are out till we know where we stand."

Bacon hesitated and Quinn turned to look at him. Murdock took his hat down, put it on. He appreciated Bacon's position. In fact, he felt a certain sense of guilt that bothered him.

He'd gone along on his own hook and given Bacon or the police no help at all. True, what he had held back had no apparent importance. The Tripp thing yesterday morning had only been a hunch. Certainly he had not hindered the case, and he had not yet heard from Mac-Shane. He continued stubbornly:

"You got Cusick yet?"

"No, damn it!"

"Where was Girard?"

Bacon took a deep breath and looked at Quinn. "Girard," he said regretfully, "is in the clear. We couldn't figure him for the Redfield job anyway, and now we know he didn't do it."

"How?" pressed Murdock, stifling his interest.

"The examiner's turned in his report," Bacon said sourly. "He says Tripp was shot once in the heart with a forty-five slug. He was shot some time around yesterday noon—and before two o'clock, and—"

"A couple hours after he ran out on us," Murdock broke in.

"—neither Girard nor those two hoods he hired could've done it," Bacon continued, ignoring the interruption. "All three of them had lunch with McGurk and his secretary."

Murdock nodded and arched his brows. "The Representative?"

"Yeah. They had lunch early, so they could go to a double-header out at Braves Field. They ate at eleven-thirty and were out at the field at twelve-forty-five."

"Then," Murdock said, "that leaves Cusick."

"And Archer," rapped Keogh.

"Hell," pressed Murdock, "haven't you turned up anything that—"

"No," groaned Bacon. Then, forgetting in his despair that he was to give no further information, he added: "Nothing but this." He opened a desk drawer, took out a roll of bills, and tossed them on the desk.

Murdock stepped forward, straightened out the once folded sheaf of greenbacks. Bacon said: "Twelve hundred and forty bucks," but Murdock paid no attention to him, his interest held by the fact that of the total amount the greater part was in crisp new bills—fifties.

He picked up the money, counted it. The new bills amounted to one thousand dollars and he saw that the numbers ran consecutively. The rest of the amount was in old fifties and twenties.

"Figure it for me," he said dryly.

"What's there to figure?" Bacon grunted. "Tripp always had money. It coulda been his or—"

"Or," cut in Quinn, stepping away from the window, "he blackmailed somebody for that thousand—he's done it before. Somebody paid him so they could get a chance to turn around and knock him off."

Murdock stared at the new fifties for some seconds, finally stepped back and lit a cigarette.

"If he blackmailed somebody on the Redfield job, why wouldn't this guy take back the thousand after he'd killed him?"

"It can be figured," Bacon said. "Look." He sat up and put a fresh cigar in his mouth without biting off the end. "Tripp was in that upstairs hall all the time that party was going on. He hung around after it broke up, waiting for that dame of his. And he saw something. When we let him go he probably starts promoting the shakedown. Maybe that's one reason why he ran out on us yesterday; must've already made the date to collect. This guy—Cusick or Archer—says he'll pay. Why? To make Tripp think it's okay and get him out where he can crack down on him." Bacon spread his hands, and the cigar swiveled with his grimace of disgust. "Tripp falls for it and gets one in the vest."

"That doesn't explain why the money was left," Murdock said.

"What of it? Maybe the gun was scared off after he shot him; maybe he didn't dare wait around searching the body. Maybe he'd rather lose the thousand than take a chance; and maybe he left it on purpose just to try and ball us up." Bacon bit the end from the cigar, struck a match, and puffed a smoke-screen about his scowling face.

"Well, to hell with that part. I don't care a damn about that thousand. It don't mean anything. Tripp was blackmailing the guy that killed him. That's all we know. That's all we need to know. Cusick—Archer. Gimme those two and you can worry about the money."

"I doubt like hell," Murdock said sardonically, "if you could get a conviction if you had the two of them right here now—unless one of them had the murder gun."

"Yeah?" leered Quinn. "Well, ten'll get you twenty we convict. We've got a few things, but we can't connect 'em up right till we get a chance to work over Cusick —or this lad Archer. It makes a difference when we've got a fellow here. There's ways of persuading him, and once he starts to talk, things tie in fast."

"You could be right," Murdock said, pulling his camera from the bookcase and moving to the door. "Tried to check up on that money—those new fifties?"

"Starting from scratch," Bacon said, "it'll be hard. The bills are too small for banks to keep a record of who they gave 'em to—and they might've been drawn out for weeks. To hell with the money." He broke off suddenly as though just remembering his former instructions.

"G'wan," he grated sharply, but not unkindly. "Get out! Didn't I say no more inside dope? Show something and we'll play ball with you; otherwise you and all the rest of you calamity howlers are out."

Phil Doane, patrolling the main-floor corridors, spotted Murdock as he stepped from the elevator. "Boy!" he cheered. "How you take 'em!"

"What?" said Murdock absently, still trying to put together the information he had received in Bacon's office.

"You did it again," Doane wheezed. "Those pictures of Tripp. And I just missed you last night." He sighed and went on disgustedly: "Know where I was? At the Somersett getting some red-hot crap from the Independent Women's Community League; one of Van Husan's bright ideas."

Doane cursed, and followed Murdock out to the street. "You'd just left when I got back. Nobody knew where you'd gone. Why didn't you—"

"Bacon called me," Murdock said, hailing a taxi. "He wouldn't tell me what it was over the phone. I didn't know what it was all about till I got there."

Murdock got in the taxi, and Doane crowded in behind him. Murdock gave the driver his instructions and turned to the youth at his side. "Where the hell you going?"

"With you. I ain't supposed to be down here anyway."

"You'd better stick to Van Husan," Murdock told him good-naturedly, "or he'll tie the can to you."

"If I don't turn in something big pretty soon," Doane moaned, "I won't have any more job than a rabbit anyway."

Murdock got rid of the youth at the office. After discarding his photographic paraphernalia he went directly to the library and called Jerry.

He was a man grabbing at straws now. The police activities rested upon the capture of Cusick and Archer. There was nothing Murdock could do about that end. All that remained was to follow his lead with MacShane —if he had any luck in finding the information he wanted. And he was not content to sit around and do nothing while he waited. He had to keep busy. Anything to keep his mind occupied.

The only thing he could think of was to review the murder of Joe Cusick, Sam's brother, and the Girard trial. At the time, he had not been particularly interested, had not followed the case as closely as he might have done. But there might be something, some bit of information that would furnish a lead or—

Jerry shuffled into view round the corner of a bookcase, stopped in front of Murdock, and pulled steel-rimmed spectacles down from his forehead.

"Can you get me all the dope on the Girard trial?" Murdock asked.

Jerry nodded. "Don't know why not."

"And I want it all, Jerry, from the time the two Cusicks tried to give Girard the shakedown."

As Jerry turned away, the telephone rang. The call was for Murdock.

"I got the dope on that plane Archer hired," Jack Fenner said.

"I thought you'd died," Murdock said.

"Yeah? Well the lead wasn't so very exclusive. The police turned it up. They had a guy over here waiting for the pilot. He stayed overnight in Washington."

"Where'd he go?"

"Washington, you cluck!"

"Didn't know what happened to Archer?"

"Nope. Paid him off and took a cab."

"Okay, Jack." Murdock grinned at the telephone. "Send me a bill—and don't forget the cut rate."

Murdock pressed the receiver arm, held it a moment without hanging up. When the operator answered he gave the number of Archer's house in Brookline, asked to speak to Joyce. She was in and her voice did things to him, made him forget, for a moment or two, his worries.

"How did it seem," she asked, "to have your apartment back?"

"Empty," Murdock said. "I didn't like it. You spoiled it for me."

"That's encouraging."

"Why don't you be nice and say you missed being there?"

"I don't want to pamper you."

"All right." Murdock hesitated and his voice got casual. "I found out something about your brother. They went to Washington."

"Oh," the voice was dull. "Have the police—"

"They don't know any more than I do." He hesitated again, deciding against telling her about Tripp. She might read about it in the paper, but—

He asked: "When did you see him yesterday? What time did he come home and pack? Is there any servant there who can tell you where he was in the morning?"

She said: "I'll see," and left the telephone. When she came back a minute or so later, she added: "He went out about ten; he came back about a quarter after one and started to pack furiously. Why? Is there—"

"I was just wondering," Murdock said, and trouble clogged his brain.

He talked awhile longer, changing the subject immediately, and hung up. Again he got the office operator and asked for MacShane.

"Got anything?" he asked.

"Not yet," MacShane said. "Two of 'em have come back. Didn't find anything. And say, shouldn't we cross Tripp's picture off that gallery?"

"Leave it. He could have called," Murdock said flatly. "We got to make sure. Ring me up when those other two men come in. I'll be up here in the library until I hear from you."

Jerry came back with a half-dozen large envelopes in his hands. Murdock moved over to an oak table, pulled out a chair, and sat down. He began his work systematically by emptying all the envelopes and sorting out his material in chronological order. When he had finished his preparations he began to read, starting back four years previous when the Cusick brothers tried their extortion scheme on Girard.

By noon he had read little more than a quarter of the story. He rang for Jerry and asked him when he ate. Jerry said any time. Murdock got an office boy and sent him out for sandwiches and beer and pie.

Murdock liked Jerry. An old-time newspaper man who had become stuck on the copy desk, he had retired only to become irked with the sudden idleness. A job had been found for him in the library and, according to Jerry, he intended to keep within smelling-distance of printer's ink, within sight of the city room, until he dropped.

They talked as they ate, sitting there on the library's worn leather divan, and then, shortly after one, Murdock resumed his study of the clippings. He made notes as he read, jotting down the salient features of the story. Always one sentence kept cropping up in his mind, a sentence that, even when he finished the last clipping, shortly after six o'clock, was still unanswered:

"Acting on an anonymous tip, Captain Keller, Sergeant Anthony, and Detectives Reed and Crosetti of police headquarters found Girard alone in his apartment. . . ."

Murdock repacked the envelopes and stood up. He stretched, put both hands in the small of his back, arched it, and yawned. He said: "Acting on an anonymous tip," softly, and his lean face got somber, his eyes brooding and thoughtful. Then, driven by the impulse of inspiration, he went out into the city room and walked over to a desk near the windows.

A small man with a black mustache and prematurely gray hair looked up from his typewriter, surveyed Murdock with tired brown eyes, and said: "Hy, Kent."

Murdock answered: "Hello, Naylor." He slid one thigh over a corner of the desk. "You busy?"

"Not too busy. What's on your mind?"

"You're the one who followed through on Joe Cusick and the Girard trial, huh?"

"One of the ones," Naylor grunted.

"Come in the library for about five minutes."

Naylor looked puzzled, but he stood up and followed Murdock across the room and through the swinging wooden gate. Murdock offered a cigarette and Naylor accepted as he sat down on the divan. When they both had lights, Murdock said:

"I've been reading up on that job until I'm bleary-eyed. Listen while I unload, and check me if I'm wrong. I want to be sure I got the story right."

Naylor leaned back, smiling wryly. "Shoot."

"Four years ago the Cusicks tried to take Girard for twenty thousand dollars, and the plan backfired. Girard saw the thing through. Redfield refused to take their case and they went up. The night after they were released from prison, Joe Cusick was found dead in an automobile three blocks from Girard's apartment, shot once through the head. A roundsman found him at eleven o'clock, and about the same time he was calling in, headquarters got a tip. They beat it right down to

Girard's place, found him alone in the apartment, and searched the place. They found just two things."

Murdock hesitated, turned on the divan to face Naylor. "They found a gun with Cusick's fingerprints on it, and they found what looked like bloodstains on the rug." He glanced down at the slip of paper containing his notes and read what had been a headline: *"Blood Clue in Cusick Slaying."*

"On the strength of this they took him down, questioned him while they built up a case, booked him. A specialist testified that the spots on the rug were human blood, but at the trial the defense experts offered a rebuttal to show that this blood could not be definitely proved to be Cusick's. They found out that Cusick's fingerprints were on the gun picked up in Girard's place, but the hitch was that *this gun had not been fired—it was a different caliber from the slug found in Cusick's head.*

"The D. A. built up a good case, but it was circumstantial. Cusick had been seen in front of Girard's apartment, and the D. A.'s case was that Cusick came back to give Girard another shakedown, that Girard shot him and then lugged the body down the back way, put it in a car, and drove three blocks, to where the cop found it."

Naylor puffed on his cigarette and said nothing. Murdock frowned at his slip of paper, read: *"Absence of Clues Aids Defense."*

"Redfield's defense," he continued, "was merely a complete denial. No one had seen Girard on the street, but he admitted being out shortly before the stated time of Cusick's death. His story was that someone must have tried to frame him and had planted the gun in his apartment while he was out—but had made a mistake and left the wrong gun—and then had tipped off the police to come and search his place. He denied all knowledge of the crime and made no attempt to explain the blood-stains on the rug."

Murdock put the paper in his pocket. "Is that the story?"

"Just about," Naylor said, dropping his cigarette on the floor and stepping on it. "It was just one of those things where there was a reasonable doubt and Redfield was the sort of bird to make the most of it. At that, he had a hell of a job. Those bloodstains worried the jury, even though they could not be used as conclusive evidence."

Murdock said: "What's your own opinion?"

"Me?" Naylor stood up. "Hell! He was plenty guilty! Cusick tried to put the finger on him, and Girard beat him to it."

Murdock pushed his lower lip out to overlap the upper and got to his feet. Naylor started to leave the room, and Murdock watched him thoughtfully until he reached the door; then he called:

"Hey!"

Naylor turned.

"How about that tip?"

"That's one thing that worked both ways," Naylor said. "If it wasn't for that, the police wouldn't have got to Girard—not so soon anyway. And yet it helped his story. Because if somebody else had knocked off Cusick, it would be natural to plant a gun and tip the police to Girard."

"That's not what I meant," Murdock said. "What I mean is, have they ever found out where the tip came from?"

Naylor shook his head.

"It just came through to the telegraph bureau—" Murdock began.

"The guy asked for Captain Keller, told him that Girard had killed Joe Cusick, and hung up."

Murdock remained motionless, watching the door for some minutes after Naylor left. In his résumé of the story there had crept into his mind a half-developed idea which intrigued him. It was, he told himself, fantastic, far-fetched. Nothing in what he knew or had read gave him any reason to believe in this idea, yet it remained a possibility—a possibility that could never be definitely proved. Grunting softly, he turned, grasped the telephone from the table, and asked for police headquarters. While he waited for his connection a wry grin pulled at the corners of his mouth.

"Keller?" he asked a moment later. "This is Kent Murdock up at the *Courier-Herald*. I got a question I want to ask."

A gruff voice said: "Hello, Murdock. I don't know about the answer, but you can ask."

"You got the tip-off on Girard the night you searched his apartment?"

"Yeah."

"But you don't know where it came from?"

"No."

"Do you remember just what the fellow said to you."

There was a slight pause and then Keller seemed to

clear his throat. "He said: 'Nate Girard just knocked off Joe Cusick. If you get down to his place quick enough you might catch him before he can cover up.' "

Murdock's tight little grin etched itself deeper. There was a certain resigned bitterness in his expression, in the depths of his dark eyes. He said: "Thanks, a million," slowly, pulled down the receiver arm with a finger, and held it for several seconds without hanging up. Finally a recurring thought stirred him to action and he sighed audibly, moved the receiver arm up and down, asked for MacShane.

"You got anything yet?" he demanded.

"Yeah," MacShane said, and his voice was sharp with interest.

"Well, why the hell—" Murdock began.

"He just came in."

"I'll bet he's been in for hours and you forgot—"

"Nuts!" yelled MacShane. "I tell you he just finished telling me and—wait a minute"—he broke off—"he says how about the case of whisky?"

"He'll get it," Murdock rapped and knew now, with a quick tightening of his nerve ends, that MacShane had produced. "Who's the guy?"

"Nate Girard!"

Murdock's lips pulled back in a seemingly self-satisfied smile.

"You're sure?" he charged, his voice sharp, metallic.

"Sure I'm sure. It's one of those side-arm, all-night restaurants. On Charles." He gave the address. "The counterman says he remembers. What the hell do you want, a—"

"Okay, okay," Murdock cut in eagerly. "Thanks—"

"Thanks, hell!" rapped MacShane. "You gonna make anything out of it? Is there gonna be a story that we can peddle a few sheets on?"

Murdock spoke impatiently. "I don't know. I doubt it like hell. Just one of my screwy ideas that probably won't work out. But keep it under your hat and I'll have a crack at it."

"Don't forget to make it break right," MacShane warned.

"If it breaks"—Murdock glanced at his strap-watch, saw that it was nearly seven-thirty—"if it breaks at all, I oughta have something by nine or ten. How does that—"

"Made to order," MacShane cheered. "Now show something or I'll cross you off my list."

19

KENT MURDOCK ATE a hurried dinner at Durgin Park's and reviewed incessantly the information he had digested during the day. From the beginning he had had no set ideas about the murder of Mark Redfield. In the first place, he had never aspired to police work. Not one to nourish the idea that he could compete with the detective bureau, he was interested, ordinarily, in just one thing: taking pictures. His close contact with the police in the past had paid dividends; by playing ball with them he was able to get better pictures; often they were exclusive shots which were denied the run-of-the-mill camera man.

The chance which brought him the sight of Sam Cusick in the second-floor hall on the night of Redfield's murder had enmeshed him in the killing. But even so, he would never have suffered from any delusions of solving the case except for Joyce Archer—and Hestor.

There was the real reason: Hestor. The dramatic meeting with Joyce had introduced him to the case and heightened his interest in no ordinary way; through her he was interested in her brother. But his work would have finished with Archer's flight had it not been for Hestor. He would probably make a fool of himself trying to follow up fragmentary evidence that, no matter how he considered it, seemed too inadequate to be brought into court—even if he were right.

But by the time Murdock paid his bill and pushed out on Hayward Place, his mind was made up. If he was right, he could—although it was a will-o'-the-wisp conception—see two chances to win. Either would do, but he had to have one.

He went back to the office, got his camera and platecase. For once he was not particularly concerned about pictures, but the habit was strong; there was always a possibility he might get something exclusive enough to earn Wyman's bonus. He was not at all prepared for Phil Doane's interruption of his thoughts as he stepped into the third-floor hall.

He asked: "What the hell do you want?" irritably.

"Where you going?" Doane asked, unperturbed.

"Home."

"Then what you got the box for?" Doane cracked eagerly.

"Listen!" Murdock snapped, and his eyes were as hard as his voice. "I said I was going home."

"All right, you're going home," Doane said and the eagerness left his tone. "But," he continued stubbornly, "you're not gonna stay. You've got something."

"How do you know?"

"I can tell by the look on your pan."

Murdock battled irritation and uncertainty, started down the hall for the elevators. Doane, tagging behind, took the somber-faced photographer by the arm as they reached the little foyer.

"Aw, listen, Kent," he pleaded. "You said you'd give me a break. Van Husan's on the war-path. Hell, there's got to be a story if there's pictures, ain't there? I won't cramp your style, honest. Just let me—"

"I'm not going out on any tip," Murdock snorted. "I've just got a little hunch—"

"Your hunches are okay with me," Doane added.

"—and even if I'm right, there might not be a story. This is personal, see? And I may get in a jam."

"I like jams," Doane insisted. "I ain't been in one in a long time."

"All right, quit arguin'!" Murdock blew out his breath, looked annoyed until his sense of humor filtered into the situation. He shook his head sadly and felt the grin wrinkle his face. He could not help it; Doane was that kind. You cursed him, resisted the impulse to commit mayhem only with the greatest of inward struggles—and yet you liked him.

"Will you do what I say?"

"Sure," Doane blurted eagerly, his eyes brightening.

"And just what I say?"

Doane bobbed his head up and down, grinning broadly.

"Okay, then," Murdock said. He slipped the strap of the plate-case from his shoulder, held it out to Doane. "Then lug this and see how you like it. And if we don't get to first base—and we got two strikes on us now—don't crab."

When the taxi stopped in front of the Embankment Arms, Murdock told the driver to wait. As Doane started to push over on the seat, he added: "That goes for you too. Stay here till I come out."

Leaving his camera and plate-case in the cab, Murdock crossed the sidewalk, called a greeting to the doorman, and swung through revolving doors which had been pushed back. The softly lighted lobby was quiet, its only occupant, besides the clerk, a stout, middle-aged man in a dinner coat, wearing glasses on a black silk ribbon and pacing back and forth in front of the desk.

The clerk, a sleek, white-faced young man, motioned to Murdock and he detoured past the desk without breaking his stride. The clerk held out some letters. Murdock took them and continued on to the elevators without looking at them. When he let himself into his apartment he snapped on the lights and went over to the secretary; he opened a drawer and took out the leather case which contained his candid camera and its accessories.

With no great hope for any pictures, he had been in the business long enough to go out on any job prepared. And sometimes the miniature camera with its expensive and beautifully made lenses got pictures where his newspaper camera failed. The camera was already loaded with a supersensitive speed film, and he substituted a 1.5 lense for the 3.5 wide angle which had been attached. This done, he snapped shut the camera's individual case and slipped it in his topcoat pocket.

A glance at his strap-watch told him it was eight-forty. He crossed to the wing chair, sat down on the arm, and pushed the brown felt back from his forehead, revealing skin deeply corrugated in a scowl. He sat there staring at the print by Benson for some minutes; the scowl remained constant. Finally he lit a cigarette, said: "You're probably nuts," softly, and went into the kitchen.

Here he poured a drink and chased it down with water from the faucet. As though unable to make up his mind, he held the bottle up, saw that it was nearly empty; then he replaced the bottle with a quick noisy movement, spun about, and strode down the hall into the bedroom. Snapping on the light, he circled round the foot of the bed to the maple stand, opened its lone drawer, and took out a thirty-eight automatic.

He switched off the light again, inspected the gun as he moved slowly across the living-room. The clip was full, but there was no shell in the chamber. He pulled back the slide to throw one into position, snapped up the safety. He was balancing the weapon in his hand, staring at it with thoughtful eyes, when he heard a knock on the door.

There was just one knock; then someone tried the knob. Murdock had no time to pocket the gun, but he was able to swing his hand behind him when the door swung inward and Joyce Archer stepped into the room.

In spite of his surprise at seeing her, in spite of the doubt, the uncertainty, that had filled his brain, he recognized once more the odd, unaccountable energy and excitement she brought with her into a room. Her personality banished emptiness with warmth and fullness, and he stood watching her while she came to him and lifted her lips as naturally as though it were a practiced gesture.

He kissed her and felt again the tingle of his skin, the welcome sweetness of her mouth, the faint scent of her hair. His arms came out to encircle her waist before he remembered the gun. He dropped them awkwardly, got the right hand behind him as he lifted his head.

She glanced at him curiously then, her smoky blue eyes unusually clear; soft but penetrating. Under this scrutiny he flushed and did not know why. She smiled and he smiled back at her.

She asked, simply: "Do you still feel the same as you did last night?"

"If you mean do I love you," Murdock said, "I do."

"That's what I meant."

She looked at him a moment longer. This time there was respect and admiration and love in her glance, but these were deep down and Murdock had no time to speculate about it. He was at once aware of something else: the suddenness with which she had entered.

"What is it?" he said. She hesitated and he guessed:

"Have you heard something about—"

"Yes." She put a gloved hand in the pocket of the camel's-hair coat and took out a yellow folded sheet, passing it to him.

The color identified the telegram and he shook out the folds.

MARRIED HERE YESTERDAY STOP WILL
CABLE LATER LOVE   HOWARD.

He looked at the top line to find out where the message had been dispatched. "Miami," he said slowly, not looking at the girl. "And 'cable you'. He's going down to Trinidad or South America."

He looked up. She returned his look without speaking. He passed back the message and smiled. "Well, it could be worse. They must believe in each other to get married."

"Yes, but—" She hesitated, her eyes anxious. "I read about that man who was murdered in the alley, that Tripp. It says the police want Howard for questioning."

"Routine," Murdock assured her.

"But you called me and asked me to find out where Howard was yesterday noon. Does that mean you—"

"It doesn't mean a thing. I just thought—"

"You don't think he killed him?"

"No. I think Sam Cusick killed Tripp. I've got a hunch the police think so too." Murdock grunted softly. "Will you stop worrying about it?" He smiled, put out a hand to take her arm; too late he realized he had put out the wrong hand.

Joyce Archer saw the gun immediately; her glance

seemed to freeze on its shining blue surface. She looked up.

"What's that for?" Twice her eyes darted to the gun and she jerked them back. "Why do you need it?"

"Well—" Murdock glanced down at the gun, shoved it into his coat pocket with an awkward gesture. His tone was sheepish. "Sometimes I carry it."

"Why do you have it now?"

"I'm going out," Murdock said. "I'm on my way to a job, and I stopped here to get my other camera. I just happened to think of the gun and—well, it's sort of a tough job."

"It's dangerous or you wouldn't even think of it."

"Now wait," Murdock said, again reaching for her arm. "It's not dangerous, but there might be trouble. And trouble's part of my job. I'm used to it. Sometimes I need a little persuader and—"

She moved out of his reach and began to pace the floor. He watched her, realizing he liked to see her walk for the pleasure it gave him, she was so well put together. His smile was tolerant, amused.

He said: "Really, I've got to run."

Joyce Archer opened the comfortable-looking camel's-hair polo coat, pulled it together absently, and held to the lapels. Then she stopped and faced him.

"Is it this Tripp thing?"

Murdock nodded.

"Are you going with the police?"

"No," he said flatly and his smile faded.

"Why?"

"Because my idea is so wild they'd probably laugh me out of headquarters."

"Then why do you bother?"

"Because it is the only chance I've got." He took a breath and his facial muscles seemed to tense under the skin. "I talked with Hestor last night. She wasn't encouraging. But I've got a chance to work the thing out by myself. Even if it was a good idea, I wouldn't dare go to Bacon until I found out for sure just what the set-up was." He grunted bitterly. "So you see the sort of double-crossing heel I can be when it comes to the show down. I've got to try it—alone. I can't explain it, but if I win I think I can be free of Hestor. It's worth it, isn't it?"

She did not answer and he forced a short laugh, concentrated in the levity in his tone. "I've got to keep you respectable, haven't I?"

That did it. Joyce Archer shrugged and a faint smile played at the corner of her eyes, although there was anxiety in her voice. "When will you know?"

"In another hour or two. You go home and I'll call you—"

"I'll wait here," Joyce Archer said, and shrugged out of her coat.

"Well—"

"They've put a man to watch the house. I loathe the feeling it gives me." She stepped over to the davenport, tossed her coat on the back, took off her tight-fitting hat, and dropped it beside the coat. She put both hands to the side of her head in a supporting movement which fluffed out the ash-blond hair; then she came over to

Murdock, stopped in front of him, a lithe, firmly rounded figure in a snug-fitting red dress.

She said: "I'm sorry."

"About what?" Murdock's grin was puzzled.

"For butting in—about your job." She came close. "Whatever it is, I know you can do it."

She lifted her arms, clung to him a moment, and stepped back smiling. She spoke again as Murdock opened the door. "Only let me know as soon as you can."

20

PHIL DOANE BLEW out a sigh of relief. "Jeeze, I thought you'd gone dumb on me or something."

Murdock sank down on the seat beside him. "You're not supposed to think. And don't start counting on any story, either."

"Anyway," Doane said, "I get a ride out of it."

Murdock gave the driver an address on Mt. Vernon Street and fell silent. Doane sat erect on his side of the seat and the intermittent flashes of street lights filtering through the cab windows picked out a round boyish face that was eager, expectant.

Charles Street forms one boundary of Beacon Hill. A main thoroughfare in the daytime and an outlet for much commercial traffic, it was, at this hour, strangely quiet; a gently curving street walled in with ancient two- and three-storied structures that seemed drab and decadent in spite of an occasional shop or drug-store which spilled light on the sidewalks. The upper stories, offices, and lofts were dark; traffic was moving with the detached remoteness of a suburb.

The taxi-driver swung right into Mt. Vernon Street and shifted into second for the climb. The hill was dark, steep, deserted except for one or two vague-figured pedestrians coming down a half-block away. The houses here, narrow, outmoded structures remodeled into more modern apartments, made a staggered silhouette against the sky so that they seemed to climb the hill in huge, blackened steps.

The whining protest of the car's gears stopped abruptly as the driver angled in to the curb, stopped, then cramped his wheels to snub them into the curbing and take the strain off his brakes. Murdock got out in front of a thin four-story building with a severe brick façade built flush with the sidewalk. When he began to haul out his camera and plate-case Doane said:

"How about me?"

"Stay in the cab." Murdock glanced up and down the still deserted street, finally spoke to the driver. "Pull up a ways, clear of this entrance, and wait for me."

Doane said: "Who lives here?"

"Nate Girard."

Doane whistled. "You mean—"

"I don't mean a damn thing," rapped Murdock irritably. "I told you this was personal. I'm going in and talk to him—if he's there."

"What're you lugging the box for?"

"How would you like to go back to the office?"

"I didn't say a word," Doane added hastily.

"I'm taking it," Murdock said, somewhat mollified, "because only a sap leaves his camera around for guys like you to play with. I may be out in five minutes, I may be there for a half-hour. So stick around and if there's no story—and there won't be—you can have another ride."

"Don't forget," Doane said. "If anything should happen."

The taxi bucked up the hill. Murdock shouldered his plate-case and stepped to a doorway which was merely a hole in the wall and made an inclined, tunneled entrance to an all-wood door at the top of the steps. There was a row of mail-boxes on the right wall, but Murdock did not refer to them, continuing to the door, which was unlocked.

There was no foyer, no waste space. A hall stretched straight ahead of the door and disappeared in a semi-darkness beyond; adjoining this was a narrow staircase; the single bulb at the landing above apparently only served to make the interior more obscure. Murdock wrinkled his nose at stale, dusty-smelling air and started up on uneven steps that creaked protestingly under their carpeted covering.

At the third-floor landing Murdock turned right. There were only two apartments to a floor and he knocked at the door on his left. It opened almost immediately, swung back to a ten-inch crack, making a vertical frame for a thick swart face. Deep-set eyes that looked black in the shadows peered through the opening, which remained fixed.

Murdock said: "Girard in?"

"What do you want him for?"

"Is he in?"

"Who wants to know?"

"The name," Murdock said irritably, "is Murdock— M-u-r—"

A well-modulated baritone called: "Come on in, Murdock."

The thick face moved back and the door opened slowly, as though resenting the intrusion. Murdock stepped inside. The thick face became part of an equally thick body that would not have been out of place in a wrestling ring. Then Murdock saw Nate Girard in the cushion-back chair under a parchment-shaded floor lamp; and across the room, his hand in his coat pocket, a tall, stooped man who was well dressed, but whose hard thin face did not seem to belong to the clothes.

The door closed behind him, and Murdock glanced about. The room was large, high-ceilinged, and, in comparison with the building, singularly well furnished. The thick oriental rug was enormous; the furniture was heavy-looking, with coverings that appeared expensive. The half-dozen prints were good and there was a well-filled bookcase between the two windows. If the effect as a whole gave a slight impression of overcrowding, it did not disguise the good taste which had accumulated the furnishings.

Nate Girard watched Murdock push magazines to one end of a rectangular mahogany table and put his plate-case and camera on the cleared space; then he put aside the book he had been reading, a weighty-looking volume, and took a cigar from a silver humidor.

He said: "Sit down. What'll you have to drink?"

Murdock unstrapped his plate-case, opened the lid. He turned, saw the hard, suspicious eyes of the thickset man upon him. "I thought I might get a picture of you," he said easily, "at home. And I want to talk to you."

He stepped away from the table, surveyed the thickset man, then the tall one, with a sardonic, faintly amused smile. "Can you get rid of the gorillas, or—"

"Who's a gorilla?" The thickset man took a step forward, his face out-thrust and mostly jaw.

Murdock's brows lifted. "What do you call yourselves nowadays, synthetic gentlemen?"

The thickset man was instantly mollified; it seemed he understood the word *gentlemen*. He said: "That's better."

Girard watched the byplay with amusement. He said: "I was about to let them go for the day anyway." He nodded towards the door. "Run along."

"You sure?" the tall man began suspiciously.

"I know Murdock, if that's what you mean."

The two men took coats and hats from the steam radiator behind the door. The tall one said: "Tomorrow morning?"

"About ten," Girard replied.

Murdock moved over to the reading-stand beside Girard as the door closed. Picking up the volume which had been placed, cover up and opened, upon the stand, he said:

"*Ulysses*, huh?" He cocked one brow, and the little smile narrowed his eyes and lifted two-thirds of his mouth. "Because you like it or—"

"I started it," Girard said, "out of curiosity. I keep going because I like to see how many pages there are between the parts I understand." He bit off the end of his cigar with firm white teeth, rolled it between his lips before he lighted it. Still holding the burning match, he surveyed the lighted end, seemed satisfied, and blew out the match. He looked up at Murdock.

"Sit down." He indicated an arm-chair opposite. "You didn't come here to take pictures. What's on your mind?"

Murdock took the proffered chair, placed his hat on the floor beside him.

Girard said: "There's some cigarettes in that box." He nodded towards the hammered bronze affair on the top of a magazine-rack next to Murdock's chair.

Murdock took a cigarette, lit it, sucked on it thoughtfully for a moment, and watched Girard. The handsome face was friendly, but the dark-eyed gaze was steady, scrutinizing.

For a fleeting instant Murdock remembered that, as a man, he liked Girard. He had never been bothered by his past. Their acquaintanceship had been on the best of terms, founded on a mutual respect for personality. Then the instant was over and he concentrated on the idea which had brought him here.

He said: "I want to talk about Hestor."

Girard's eyes reflected a sudden inner reaction which it was impossible to diagnose. For a second or two his lean face was impassive; then he smiled and the clipped mustache moved laterally on his lip.

"It's not exactly a surprise, although—" He broke off, took the cigar from his mouth, and studied it. "I didn't think you were interested; I didn't think you gave a damn one way or the other."

He looked up, but Murdock did not answer. Girard put the cigar in his mouth and eased farther down in the chair, folding his hands across his waistcoat and crossing one leg.

"I like a good time," he said finally. "I went without that sort of thing for a hell of a long while. Even when I was bootlegging, I stuck pretty close to business. It's not until the past two or three years that I've stepped out. I'm making up for lost time. I've got enough money, so that it's not hard to get about what I want. And I can get it without stepping on anybody's toes, because there's no lack of material. I've never married, for obvious reasons. The sort of girl I wanted couldn't care for a bootlegger, wouldn't take the chance. I'm beginning to live some of that down and"—his voice took on an undercurrent of bitterness—"if I can steer clear of any more murder charges, I might get really respectable in a few years. Of course, I'm not getting any younger."

Girard took out his cigar, studied the inch of gray ash on the end, and gently tipped it off into an ash-tray.

"And meanwhile it's like I said. I'm going to enjoy life. I can do it without breaking up homes." His eyes swept back to Murdock, narrowed slightly. "Don't get me wrong. I'm not Sunday-school about it. If I was in love with a woman I'd go after her whether she was married or not. And if she felt the same way about me and I could get her, I'd take her."

His manner relaxed and again the mustache moved with his grin. "But I'm not that way about Hestor. She's all right. She's good company, she's good-looking, and she can dance. For a good time I like her. But even if I was crazy about her, I didn't think you'd be interested. I thought you two had called it off, had agreed to—"

"We have," Murdock said, sitting up and grinding out his cigarette.

"Then what's the kick?" Girard asked crisply. His tone got sardonic. "You don't want her and you don't want anybody else to have her. That it?"

Murdock shook his head. He straightened out in the chair, crossed his ankles, stared at them with sultry eyes. "We're through, definitely."

"But you don't want her running around?"

"For a while I didn't care. Right now, the more she runs around, the better I like it."

Girard scowled. "I don't get it. You say you're not interested and yet—"

"I didn't say I wasn't interested."

Girard flipped his hands up, let them flop back to his waistcoat. His voice was annoyed. "All right. You're interested. Cut out the fencing. In what?"

"In a divorce."

"Oh—" Girard's eyes widened.

"She won't give me one," Murdock said grimly. "I was a big disappointment to her. We agreed to separate and I'm paying her. I don't mind that. But I want a divorce—I'm going to get one."

"I see." Girard's shoulder moved in a shrug. "But why pick on me?"

"For one thing," Murdock said slowly, "I wasn't sure just how you rated her. I wanted to find out if you had any idea at all of marrying—"

"None," Girard said shortly. "None."

"And for another thing," Murdock went on as though he had not heard, "you've been attentive. I know there have been others, but at the time I wasn't interested enough to check up. I am now. And I'm tired of getting the short end of the stick."

Girard flushed, seemed about to speak. Murdock jerked up in his chair and continued in sharp, aggressive sentences. "You played around with her before the trial. You were out with her last night. You took her home the night of your party and—"

"You don't expect to make a divorce action out of that, do you?" Girard snapped.

"I've got a chance." Murdock lowered his tone, tried to speak reasonably. "There's nothing personal in it, Girard. I've got nothing against you. But I'm going to get a divorce; if you've played around and get hooked for—"

Girard's laugh was mirthless, sharp. "Talk sense."

"I am," Murdock flared. "And you're not quite as clear as you thought. I had you followed the night of your party. You took Hestor home, and you went in with her. You were still in there at five-thirty in the morning. Does that make sense?"

Girard came erect in his chair with a slow, studied movement. For some moments he did not speak, and the two men stared at each other silently, immobile. Girard moved first—his hands. When he spoke, his voice was casual—deliberately so.

"You can't win a case on that evidence."

"I can try," Murdock charged.

"You'd have to prove I was actually in her rooms all of that time." His voice was deprecating. "All you know is that I went in the building with her."

"That's right," Murdock said flatly. "But it just happened to come at the right time."

"How do you figure it?" Girard asked suspiciously.

"Like this." Murdock leaned forward and took special pains with his words. "If you weren't with Hestor all that time, you might have been out. And if you were out, say by the back door, you might—I say might—have been in Redfield's apartment at four o'clock."

Girard's eyes were like black metal disks, and his face seemed to stiffen. Otherwise his expression did not change. For a half-minute he sat there silently; then he took a breath and said: "I see what you mean, but—"

He never finished the sentence. The next word died in his throat because in the same instant the door swung open, slammed back against the wall. A squat, bull-necked fellow with a flat nose and a squarish face stood in the opening, a heavy revolver in his hand.

Murdock did not look at Girard. He just stared slack-jawed at the gun, at the man; and the color oozed from his face with recognition. Hymie. Cusick's playmate!

Hymie stepped into the room, said: "Just take it easy!" as he closed the door.

21

*G*ET UP!"

Hymie moved to the center of the room, waved his gun. Murdock stood up; Girard stood up. Hymie circled round behind Murdock and stepped to the doorway leading to the other rooms. Groping along the wall until he found a light-switch, he snapped it on; then he stood aside, said:

"Come on! Grab air and come on down here in front of me!"

Girard's face was stiff, his eyes smoldering. He raised his hands slightly, glanced over at Murdock, then back at Hymie, who said, "Maybe you think I'm foolin'," irritably.

Girard shrugged and a forced smile pulled at his mustache. He started for the doorway; Murdock followed him.

"Keep those hands up where I can see 'em," Hymie said. "Just behave. You're goin' down that hall and unlock the back door."

Murdock kept his hands shoulder-high, realizing bitterly that if he were first, there might be a chance to get his own automatic from the topcoat pocket. But with Hymie's gun in his back—

Girard stepped into a linoleum-floored kitchen and stopped in front of the door. Reflected light from the hall was sufficient to make visible the distinguishing features of the room. Hymie moved sideways, like a crab, keeping his gun in front of him, covering Murdock and Girard. He reached for the key in the door; he turned it without looking at it, stepped aside.

Instantly the knob turned. The door swung slowly, and Sam Cusick sidled through the opening. Murdock watched the forty-five automatic in his hand until Cusick's sharp, thin voice said: "All right, let's go back in the other room."

They moved out of the kitchen in single file. Girard, then Cusick, then Murdock with Hymie's gun in his back. In the living-room Girard started to sit down. Cusick said: "Wait a minute," and slapped his hands over Girard's pockets. He turned towards Murdock, motioning Hymie to watch Girard. He repeated his search until he found the gun in the topcoat pocket.

He took it out, tossed it up, and caught it deftly. He slipped it in a side pocket and grinned. "You won't need it now," he grunted.

Girard sat down in the cushion-back chair. Murdock lowered his hands and turned about so that his hips leaned against the rectangular table holding his camera and plate-case. Hymie moved over by the door and Cusick stood near the center of the room where he could watch both men.

Cusick said: "Hymie's been watching the place. I couldn't. They've made me hole up, the bastards! But it don't matter. Hymie saw the two cowboys come out." He glanced at the squat man. "You didn't tell me about Murdock. You're slippin'."

"He musta been in that taxi," Hymie growled. "I couldn't get a good look at him. Anyway, how did I know he was comin' up here?"

"That's why I sent you up the front way," Cusick said. "To make sure."

Murdock slid his hands along the edge of the table until his arms appeared to prop him up. He glanced at Girard, who was watching Cusick with an expressionless face and eyes that were fathomless.

And Cusick—Murdock studied the man. He still wore the same tight-fitting blue coat and gray gloves. He was so thin and small he looked harmless except for the heavy automatic and the gloating, pitiless look in the close-set eyes which kept guard over that long, boneless nose.

Murdock said: "Well, what's the idea?"

He made his voice level, a bit disdainful. And he was afraid he knew the answer to the question. If Girard thought enough about Cusick to hire bodyguards, and if Cusick thought enough about Girard to put Hymie watching the house, the answer was fairly obvious. But he wanted to talk, to get Cusick's mind on other things. He wanted to stall. It was apparently the only chance. Doane was outside and unless he should— He cursed himself for browbeating the fellow. Doane would probably stay right there in the taxi as he was told. But if he should take a chance— The front door was still unlocked and—

"Nate knows," Cusick broke in, "don't you, Nate?"

Girard did not answer. Cusick's voice got thin, stringy with emotion. "You put the slug on Joe. I'm gonna pay off!"

"You're wrong," Girard said finally. "I didn't kill your brother."

"That's what you say," Cusick sneered. "And you even got a jury to believe you. Well, if the law can't make you pay, I can."

"You're awfully damn sure about it," Murdock said.

"You're damn right I'm sure."

"How?"

"I'll tell you," Cusick lipped. "When Joe and me got out of the clink we were gonna even up with both Nate and Redfield. Maybe not knock 'em off, but make 'em pay for the jolt we got. But it was gonna be one or the other. And we flipped a coin. Joe drew Girard. And I know, see?" Cusick's chin—what there was of it—came out. "I know Joe came here that night to put the pressure on."

"Why didn't you testify for the State, then?" Murdock cut in. "It would have made a better case and—"

"Yeah?" Cusick sneered. "That's what you think. But if I'd told what I knew, old Redfield woulda changed his plans and made it self-defense. And I didn't want Nate to squirm out of it." He hesitated, mouthed a curse before he spoke to Girard.

"Joe came here to get you. The cops found his gun here, so I know damn well he came. And he never got a chance to use that gun. Now you're gonna see just how it feels."

Murdock's face went stiff. He knew exactly what Cusick meant; he knew that regardless of the eventual outcome, Cusick intended to stick to his plan. Murdock's brain grabbed at the only available way to distract the gunman.

"And you had to knock off Spike Tripp too, huh?"

Cusick's blazing eyes shifted quickly to Murdock. Murdock met them steadily, but he felt a tingling of his nerve ends as he saw the sudden change of Cusick's interest. Somewhere in the room the ticking of a clock broke the silence with a monotonous regularity. Then Cusick spoke in a soft, ominous voice.

"I hadn't figured much on you, Murdock. But why not? Now that you're here it might not be a bad idea. See how it looks. I'm hot on this Redfield job. The cops would've framed me for it just as sure as hell. All they had was this: you saw me; Tripp saw me. But with my record that's about all they'd need to get me the chair.

"I was gonna pay a call on Redfield that night. I'd heard he'd got twenty-five grand of Girard's fee in cash. I was gonna go up there and get it. Because I was up against it, and I didn't have much to lose, and I knew Redfield was yellow. With twenty-five G's I could've skipped, and if I'd got in, I'd've got it, too. That's why you saw me on the stairs. How the hell did I know there was a party on? I had to run out. But I came back and— but to hell with all this crap!" Cusick shifted the automatic in his hand, and his eyes were at once wary, as though conscious of some new thought.

Grunting softly, he moved over behind the motionless Hymie and locked the apartment door. Murdock felt a despair that clogged his brain and got in his throat. His face gave some little clue to his thoughts. Cusick must have noticed this, because he grinned at Murdock briefly, said: "That's better."

Hymie said: "Well, what're we waiting for?"

Cusick snapped: "Nothing," and moved over to

Girard. Girard watched him silently, and if he knew any fear—as he must have—he did not show it. Murdock saw this and marveled at the man's self-control. The eyes were a gambler's, brooding but otherwise inscrutable; his face held a grayish tinge, but in no other way did he reveal his thoughts.

He said: "So you're going to gun us out, huh? Murdock and me?" He hesitated and his brows lifted. "You don't think you can get away with it, do you?"

"I can try," Cusick rasped. "And here's something maybe you've forgotten, Girard. They can only burn me once."

"Once is generally enough," Girard said insolently. "I understand it's permanent."

"Always a wise guy, huh?"

Girard appeared not to hear. "I've got a couple thousand here. If you've got any sense, which I doubt like hell, you'll take it and take a run out while you've got the chance."

"I'll take a run out anyway," Cusick said. He shifted the automatic slightly so that it was trained directly on Girard's chest. "But I've waited a long time for this and you nor anybody else is gonna talk me out of it. Do you want it like you are, or can you take it standing up."

Murdock's gaze was fixed on Girard's face. Judging by himself, he knew how the man must feel, yet Girard smiled. Murdock saw it and could not believe it. But the smile was there, somehow.

Girard said: "I don't suppose it makes any difference, but—" He started to get up and Murdock sensed the brittleness of his voice, and something in the hidden menace of the words decided him.

He knew what to expect. Cusick was a killer, had always been a killer. Not insane, as one thinks of an insane man, he apparently had jumped the borderline in one direction. His prison term, at Girard's hand; the shooting of his brother, the subsequent hounding of the police; Spike Tripp—all of these had nourished and built up the present state of mind until it was a complex, a phobia. It was fantastic somehow. Here in this lighted room—and happening to him. Yet—

That Cusick would shoot, deliberately and in cold blood, Murdock had not the slightest doubt. And with this conviction his racing brain quieted, his thoughts became cold, steady, and ran along with machine-like precision. What difference did it make *how* he was shot? A slug in the chest was a slug in the chest. Better to take it fighting than standing against the wall with his hands in the air.

A sidewise glance told him that Hymie, now held by the drama and suspense of the death scene, was more intent upon Cusick than himself. And Murdock put his right hand, which was already behind him, into the plate-case. He could reach just two things without shifting his position: a flash-bulb and his tripod.

Picking up the bulb with thumb and forefinger, he clamped the other three fingers about the top of the tripod. Tensed there, holding his breath, he waited and felt the sweat come out on his forehead. His lips were dry and stiff; his tongue came out to wet them. It would take him one long step to reach Hymie's side and—

The faint sound that met his ears, a faint clicking sound

like the closing of a distant door, sent an icy finger along
his spine. To him that sound was loud, shockingly so.
His glance shot to Hymie, who turned to look at him,
giving no sign that he had heard. But Cusick had. His
trigger finger was already tense and he took a backward
step, glanced towards the inner hall, jerked his eyes back
to Girard.

Then it happened.

Murdock's hand whipped out from behind his back
in a lightning-like movement. Pivoting, he swung the
tripod, let go of the flash-bulb. All this before Hymie
moved. Cusick's gun wrist stiffened, Murdock saw that
much; then he concentrated on the revolver in Hymie's
hand.

The flash-bulb struck the edge of the table, exploded
with a pop that, while not as loud as a gunshot, sounded
peculiarly like one. Hymie swung the gun towards him.
He heard Cusick curse. Then he completed his sweeping
swing and smashed the tripod down on Hymie's gun
wrist as he lunged forward.

The gun struck the floor as though Hymie had thrown
it and skidded a few feet. Murdock kept right on moving.
His lowered shoulder smacked squarely into the gun-
man's stomach and they went down, arms and legs flying,
Murdock on top.

From then on, Murdock ignored Hymie. He felt himself being thrown off by the man's brute strength. He did
not struggle. His eyes were on that gun, and as he rolled
clear his clawing fingers snatched it up. Then the roar
of a gun shook the room.

Murdock's back was to Cusick, and as he struggled to

spin around on his knees and bring his gun into play, he thought: "There goes Girard! And I'm next!"

Time stood still. The fraction of a second as he lurched round was interminable. Every muscle in his body was tensed for the shock of the next bullet. When no following shot rang out he could not understand the delay until he swung his gun around and saw the reason.

Girard was on the floor on his face. Cusick was on his knees. But—he no longer pointed that heavy automatic. It was still in his hand, but the muzzle was down, the gun dangling from one finger. His pinched face was white, slack-jawed; the eyes were staring. But there was a different look in them now, a hollow, vacant expression; the face hung loose. Murdock tore his gaze from the picture, jerked it up.

Bacon and Keogh seemed wedged in the doorway to the inner hall. Both held right arms stiffly extended, and each hand ended in a service revolver. They moved out of the doorway with short, slow steps, separating on the threshold. Behind them were two other plain-clothesmen with guns drawn; behind this second pair was the slack-jawed figure of Phil Doane.

Murdock blew out his breath, lowered the gun that trembled in his hand. Tense, aching muscles relaxed slowly. He turned his head, glancing over his shoulder. Hymie was sitting on the floor, both hands stretched high above his head. Then, as the sweat poured out on Murdock's forehead and oozed down into his straight brows, he saw Cusick fall.

The man wavered back and forth in a limp, rocking movement until he lost his balance. He went over on his face then, pitching forward slowly, easily, and settled there motionless on top of his gun.

Nate Girard dropped into the cushion-back chair, touched a bluish lump in the gray-streaked hair over one ear with one hand, mopped his glistening, sweat-covered face with the other.

"It's the first time," he said thickly, "the first time I was ever glad to see a cop. Who was the sharpshooter?"

Keogh, who had bent forward, both hands on his knees gazing down at Cusick, straightened up and growled: "Me."

"I thought so," Girard said, stuffing the now sodden handkerchief into his breast pocket.

"What d'ya mean?" challenged Keogh suspiciously.

"I mean"—Girard shook his head and grinned—"I mean it was nice shooting."

"Oh." Keogh scowled, apparently undecided whether there had been a hidden meaning in Girard's words or not.

Bacon stepped to the telephone and began to bark instructions. Murdock had already opened his camera. His fingers were still a bit shaky and the palms of his hands were damp, but he fought his shakiness with activity. Doane was at his side, pop-eyed, vociferous.

"Was it okay?" he wheezed. "I mean you told me to stay out there, but—"

"Okay?" growled Murdock. "It was perfect, only"—he looked up and scowled—"why the hell did you wait so long?"

"I saw Cusick coming down the street," Doane said

hurriedly. "I saw him talking with this other guy and then the guy came in here and Cusick went down the street and into a little alley. So I followed him. And when I saw where he was going I—well—" Doane's manner became apologetic. "I threw a bluff once—down to your place—and got away with it. But with two of 'em I thought I oughta call Bacon. I told him he oughta come up the back way and—"

Doane broke off again, hesitated. "Was it all right? I mean the way I did it?"

"All right?" exploded Murdock. He looked up from his camera and grinned. "Listen, I take it all back. I was wrong, like most wise guys are. You're not a pest, you're a miracle man. And I'm just a mug with luck enough to have a guy like you following me around and looking after me. If Van Husan don't give you a raise on this—"

"Jeeze!" gasped Doane, his face brightening. "I almost forgot. Where's the phone?"

"Wait!" Murdock grabbed Doane's arm. "Give him a flash, tell him you'll call back. Wait till you get the rest of the story. And"—he put down the camera and beat Doane to the telephone on the opposite side of the room, just as Bacon hung up. A half-minute later he was talking to MacShane.

He said: "It broke, Mac. And on time. Put Van Husan on here and get the dope from him." He turned, handed the telephone to Doane.

Bacon was rubbing his chin and staring thoughtfully at Girard. Hymie, a sullen, glowering figure, sat on the davenport nursing a bruised eye and acting very subdued between the two plain-clothesmen who flanked him.

Keogh had taken a cigar from the silver humidor, nodding in satisfaction as he smelled it.

"All right." Bacon pushed back his hat. "Speak your piece, Girard! All of it."

Girard sat back in the chair and told his story in simple, direct sentences. "That's all there is to it," he finished three minutes later. "He came here to gun me out, that's all. He'd worked himself up to it and he was going through with it. Murdock happened to be here and"—he glanced at Murdock and grinned—"he must've pulled something out of a hat, but don't ask me what."

Murdock had already taken one picture and was, at the moment, reversing his plate-holder and changing flash-bulbs. He continued with his work as he talked.

"I thought it was worth a chance, so I took it. Cusick meant business. The only thing I could reach was the tripod and flash-bulb and—" He continued, explaining what he had done.

Girard took a deep breath. "And what a break for me —all the way around! I didn't know it was a flash-bulb, I thought it was a gun. After that I didn't wait. I made a pass at Cusick. I hit the gun, but I couldn't knock it out of his hand. All I did was stop him from pulling the trigger. And then he crowned me and I guess I went down—and out."

Murdock said: "And what a break for me you slapped that gun!"

For a few seconds Bacon looked satisfied. Then he turned around and saw Hymie. Instantly a scowl knotted his lean face, and the eyes got hard and bright with interest. He walked to the davenport in slow, measured strides, his head lowered, his eyes studying the gunman.

The look told Hymie what to expect and he said: "Wait a minute, you got nothin' on me except havin' the gun. I didn't do no shooting."

"That's right," Bacon said. "And a nice break for you you didn't. I had the trigger half pulled when you got those hands up." He hesitated, put his hands on his hips, and continued in an easy tone that could have been no more ominous if he had shouted:

"But I think you might know a few things. I'm kinda interested."

"All I know is—"

"Maybe you can't remember," Bacon said. "Well, maybe we can help you out."

"I'm not gonna talk till I get a lawyer."

"It'll be a long time, then," Bacon said. He smiled so that his thin lips drew back against his teeth. "But you'll talk, punk. And you don't have to talk here. I'd rather get you down where I've got more equipment."

"Lissen," Hymie pleaded.

"You listen!" lipped Bacon. "I've got two chances and I ought to be able to hang one of them on you. If I can't make the Redfield—"

"I wasn't even here," Hymie protested. "This is just a sort of job. I was in New York the night Redfield got rubbed out and I can prove it. I didn't get here till the next afternoon."

"Why?" pressed Bacon.

And then Hymie forgot all about his determination to keep silent, forgot about it or had the background of necessary experience which told him it would be better to talk voluntarily than to take his licking and talk anyway.

"Cusick called me up Saturday morning and said he had a job for me. I came by plane—I can prove it—and I got here around noon. I didn't know what it was all about until Cusick told me there was a couple guys that needed attention. He said a lawyer had got knocked off the night before and that he had been around the place and you cops were tryin' to pin the job on him."

"He knocked him off, didn't he?" Keogh cut in as he drew up beside Bacon and sucked contentedly on his cigar.

"I don't know," Hymie said, and sounded as if he meant it. "He says he didn't, but—"

"He'd be a sap to admit it, wouldn't he?" Bacon said. He turned to scowl at Keogh's interruption, then continued to Hymie: "Go on, let's have the rest of it!"

"Anyway," Hymie went on, "Cusick had to hide out and he wanted me to find out things for him. We stopped around to see that guy"—Hymie jerked his head towards Murdock, who had already filled six plates and was bringing his camera towards the group on the davenport—"and we damn near gummed things."

Bacon nodded. "I know that part. How about Tripp?"

"Well—" Hymie hesitated and his glance was shifty.

"Go on!" rapped Keogh.

"Well, this guy Tripp had seen Cusick on the night the mouthpiece got ironed out. And he got in touch with Cusick and told him to lay it on the line or he'd squeal."

"Did Cusick pay?" asked Bacon sharply.

"I don't know if he did or not. I stayed outside the

place to see that we didn't get cornered and the two of
'em talked it over. All I know is that when Tripp went
out Cusick told me this Tripp had too many ideas and
that he'd made a little date with him."

"In the alley," Bacon said.

Hymie nodded; then he seemed to recognize his own
danger. He sat up stiffly, spoke jerkily. "But it wasn't me!
Honest to God! Cusick let him have it. It's the same gun
he brought here. You can check it—the slug. I was there,
but I never even made a move."

Bacon sucked at his lips. He was smiling now, not
broadly, but there was undisguised satisfaction in his
face as he turned, went back to Cusick's sprawled figure,
and glanced at the forty-five automatic, the muzzle of
which was barely visible under his coat. Girard still sat
in the chair, his eyes half-closed. Bacon looked at him
wonderingly a moment, then came back to the davenport.

"It's gonna be a break for you," he told Hymie, "if
that story of yours checks."

"It'll check," Hymie panted.

"Just an innocent bystander," Keogh grunted. He had
his hands clasped behind his back and was teetering up
and down on his toes, the cigar jutting upward at a satisfied angle. He shook his head. "Ain't that too bad?"

Murdock set up his tripod, focused the camera upon
Hymie, and shot two close-ups. Then he took out a new
plate, another flash-bulb, and said: "All right," to Bacon
and Keogh.

Bacon scowled a moment uncertainly, finally grinned.
Keogh's Irish face was all grin. Murdock said: "How
about the cigar?"

"That gives it the right touch," Keogh said.

Murdock opened the shutter, said: "Hold it!" and the flash-bulb exploded light into the smiling faces of the two detectives. Murdock picked up the camera and began to unscrew the tripod, and Doane pushed up to Bacon.

"Well, how about it?" he plagued eagerly. "Do I have to wait all night after tipping you off to a set-up like this?"

"Shoot it in," Bacon said. "Say—"

"That this thing solves the murders of Redfield and Tripp," Doane broke in. "Cusick went to Redfield's place to get the twenty-five thousand, shot him when Redfield held out. Tripp saw Cusick, blackmailed him, and got rubbed out to make sure he wouldn't talk. Then this thing tonight when Cusick and his hood came to get Girard. That close enough to be official?"

"Well," Bacon temporized, "there's some loose ends, but—"

Murdock, who had not finished unscrewing the tripod, tightened it up again. He set it on the floor, stepped to his case, and took out another flash-bulb. "Hell," he grunted. "I nearly forgot the most important shot. Hold it."

"Who?" Doane was goggle-eyed, incredulous. "Me?"

"Yes, you," said Murdock grinning. "Cub Reporter Balks Gangster Killing. Write your own head. Now hold it!"

Doane was still wide-eyed when the flash-bulb went off, but he recovered quickly. He crossed to the telephone, scooped it up, and barked a number. Bacon drew Murdock to one side.

"There's a reward," he said hesitantly. "Arrest and conviction stuff. May not be anything to it. I was thinking—"

"Don't look at me," Murdock said, closing his camera. "I just happened to be here when the trouble started." He glanced across at Doane, who had his discolored felt pushed back and was saying: "Don't give me any argument. You just hold on and get an earful of this." Murdock grinned and continued to Bacon: "If there's any money coming, you ought to split it. Only don't forget, Doane's got a share coming."

"That's all right then," Bacon said, looking relieved. He turned to Keogh, growled: "Now where the hell's that examiner?"

As if in answer to the question, the door opened. A uniformed policeman stood aside and the examiner's physician bustled in with his habitual "Hello, boys, what's all this?"

Murdock packed his paraphernalia, then stepped over to one of the front windows and looked out. The sidewalk below was a milling knot of reporters and camera men who were kept at bay by two uniformed policemen. Murdock recognized one of the camera men as Wixon of the *Herald*. He went over to Doane then, waited until he had finished talking, and gave him the exposed plates.

"Take these in. Wixon's downstairs. Give him half of them and you take the rest so—"

"Hell," Doane said confidently, "I'll get 'em all right. Van Husan wants me to come in and write an eyewitness story. You don't need to worry about—"

"Suppose you get run over by a taxi," Murdock said.

"You split 'em with Wixon. I'm going to be sure some of these get printed."

During the next half-hour Hymie was hustled off to headquarters. The examiner completed his inspection of the body and had it removed. Bacon and Keogh were the last to leave. Girard still sat lazily in his chair, and Bacon, who had been walking around in circles and looking extremely pleased and calm, stopped in front of his chair, spoke curiously.

"What's the matter with you?"

"I'm taking it easy," Girard said. "That was a healthy crack I got."

"Oh." Bacon nodded. "Sure. Well."—he buttoned his coat—"I'm damn glad the mess is cleared up. No hard feeling for that questioning the other day?"

Girard shook his head. "No. But I'm damn glad it was Keogh and not me that shot Cusick or you'd probably try to railroad me again."

"Heh, heh," Bacon laughed, "don't be like that."

Keogh, who had been standing near by, still sucking on his cigar butt and glancing longingly at the silver humidor, finally succumbed to temptation. He opened the lid, took two, one of which he thrust into his mouth, the other in his breast pocket.

"Not bad, these," he said patronizingly. "I'll have to get me some."

Bacon stopped at the door and looked at Murdock. With the look something akin to suspicion filmed his alert eyes. "Say," he drawled, "just how the hell did you happen to be here right when things busted wide open? I guess I forgot to ask you."

Murdock felt his muscles tighten. He did not answer until he was sure he could make his voice bored, indifferent.

"You really have to know, huh?"

"Yeah," said Bacon, his suspicion becoming more apparent. "Why?"

"Well, it was a personal matter."

"You had the camera."

"I generally do, don't I?"

"All right, what's the personal matter?"

"You've got to know that too, huh?" Murdock said, his voice now a bit scornful.

"Yeah," challenged Bacon.

"My pal, huh?" Murdock said. He shrugged. "All right. You know my wife?" And when Bacon said he knew who she was, "Well, she's been running around with Nate—and you can check that if you want to—and I wanted to find out just what the pay-off was going to be."

"Oh," Bacon said, and sounded embarrassed. "I thought it was something else."

Again Murdock felt his muscles tense, the dampness at his palms. He shot Bacon a quick, covert glance, but the Lieutenant had his eyes fixed on some remote object.

"I thought," Bacon went on casually, "maybe you were sore because I closed down on the information. I thought you'd got hold of a lead and was holding out, trying to crack something all by yourself."

"Oh," Murdock said, and let his breath out slowly.

"Yeah," Bacon said. He opened the door, grunted to Keogh, who filed out ahead of him. Then, as he went through the doorway, Bacon turned, spoke over his shoulder with a grin.

"Anyway, I was right about one thing, right in the first place. You come in here to talk about your wife and leave that kid in the taxi; he sees Cusick and tips us off. If it hadn't been for that kid—"

Bacon sighed. "Boy! With your kind of luck I'd be a millionaire. No matter what you do, bingo! Smack into the breaks every time."

22

*N*ATE GIRARD STOOD UP, felt gingerly of the lump over his ear, and made a slow, complete circuit of the room. Murdock sat down in the chair by the magazine stand. He lit a cigarette and puffed thoughtfully at it until Girard came back and sat down opposite him.

"I'm just beginning to get back to normal." Girard reached for the silver humidor and took a cigar. "And for once my luck was in." He bit off the end of the cigar, rolled it gently between his lips. "If you hadn't stopped in here to talk about Hestor—" He broke off, lit the cigar, and puffed silently, his eyes on the ceiling.

Murdock said: "Yeah." His voice was neutral and his narrowed, searching gaze never left Girard's face. He sat that way for perhaps a minute without shifting his eyes and when he leaned forward in his chair his mind was made up. "You said you had a couple thousand here."

Girard's eyes jerked from the ceiling, narrowed. "Oh."

He started to smile, but the effort faded into a puzzled expression and he finally added: "You need some. Is that it?"

"I could use all of it," Murdock said, keeping his voice flat.

"A loan?"

"Call it that if you like."

Girard's cigar twisted around in an impatient arc. For a moment Murdock thought he was going to refuse. Instead he shrugged, put his palms on the chair arm, and pulled himself erect. He went through the doorway to the inner hall and was gone nearly a minute. When he returned he had a neat stack of new bills which he handed to Murdock without speaking.

Murdock glanced at them, fanned them out slightly. He looked back at Girard, tapped the bills against an open palm, and finally laid them on the top of the magazine-rack. The tension he felt was within himself, but it was an effort to break the grip and speak normally. Perhaps he overdid it; his voice was casual, nonchalant.

He said: "I suppose you read about Tripp?"

Girard nodded, took out his cigar, and looked at it; he thrust it back in one corner of his mouth without speaking.

"I was there when they found him," Murdock went on. "And I was down to headquarters the next day. Tripp had about twelve hundred dollars on him—I don't know if the papers told about that or not—and a thousand of this was in new fifties—like these."

Girard crossed his legs and watched Murdock with a steady-eyed gaze that was fathomless, waiting.

"Bacon was pretty well satisfied that Cusick was the one who got Redfield, especially when I told how Cusick tried to scare me out of talking. I saw him, you know, earlier the night Redfield was murdered." Murdock ground out his cigarette, blew out his final inhalation in a thin blue cone. "And Bacon had the idea that Tripp knew more than he told. When they found him, Bacon felt sure about it. He doped it right—part of it. We found that out tonight. Tripp tried to blackmail Cusick, and Cusick put him away for good."

"What do you mean, part of it?" Girard asked softly.

"His hunch was that Cusick paid the thousand to silence Tripp and get him off guard, then made another date and shot him."

"You don't think so?"

"Cusick was hard up. I don't think he'd be the kind to leave a thousand around on a dead man. The only way I could figure it was that he did not know the money was there. So I wondered—just wondered, you understand—if maybe Tripp had seen somebody else that night, and that that somebody had paid."

Girard's eyes flicked to the stack of bills on the magazine-rack, and he jerked them back. Murdock saw the shift. Girard must have sensed this, because he looked away and had trouble clearing his throat before he spoke.

"Just how far have you got this theory worked out?"

"That one," Murdock said, "is all worked out." His smile was a searching stare. "The numbers on those bills Tripp had were consecutive. I made a point to memorize the first and last numbers. *These bills continue to run consecutively with Tripp's thousand!*"

"I see." Girard's voice was bitter, disgusted. "This is more blackmail, after all?"

"I guess it is," Murdock said, flushing, but controlling his voice. "A form of blackmail, anyway."

"And that's the kind of a heel you are?"

"That's the kind of a heel I can be when I have to."

"Just a chiseling bast—"

"Wait!" rapped Murdock, sitting erect. "This is more than you think."

Girard broke off as Murdock reached into his coat pocket and pulled out his tiny camera. He watched fascinated as Murdock snapped off the case, pulled out the lens, and began to adjust the shutter. When Murdock reached for the bills, Girard's face went gray and he leaned forward in his chair as though ready to spring.

Murdock dropped the bills and his hand shot to his coat pocket. His fingers found the gun there which had been returned to him by Keogh. He took it out. He did not point it at Girard, he just placed it on the table within easy reach.

"Let's not get melodramatic about it," he said, and there was an ominous thinness to his tone. "I'm playing my hand face-up. Don't forget I could have taken this money and photographed it some place else—say at police headquarters."

Girard held his position for a few seconds and his angry scowl was constant. Then he seemed to relax. He took his hands from the chair arms, leaned back.

Murdock spread the new bills out on a newspaper and, still watching Girard, leaned down and unstrapped his plate-case. Taking out the single photo-flood bulb which he carried for emergencies, he unscrewed the regular light-bulb from the floor lamp, substituting the five-hundred-watt affair. He directed this cone of blue-white light down on the bills. He stopped his lens down to get more depth of focus and took six pictures from different angles and distances.

Girard's cigar had gone out. He was slouched down in the chair again; his lids were lowered so that his eyes looked sleepy. When Murdock finished and put the automatic back in his pocket, Girard said:

"You've got more than that. This was luck. You didn't know if I had the money—couldn't know it would check. It was luck."

"Yeah," Murdock said.

"But you came here with some other idea," Girard said slowly. "You stayed behind to see about these bills. What else?"

Murdock lit another cigarette, then leaned forward so that the upper half of his body was supported on elbows propped on the chair arm. "The bills helped. Cusick's coming here helped. If you want some other guesses, I'll give them to you.

"I wasn't interested in the Redfield murder—at first. But even then there were a couple little things that didn't fit; not to my mind. Redfield was killed with a small-caliber gun, probably his own. He was killed after some little struggle; the broken finger showed that. It looked as if he pulled a gun on somebody and this somebody was quick enough to grab it. The contact wound bore this out—as though the gun was turned on him, possibly with it still in his hand.

"But any kind of murder would point towards Sam Cusick, if it could be proved he was around. And he was. He had it in for Redfield and you; and he was a killer. That part was okay. I think he was Bacon's choice from the first."

"He wasn't yours, huh?" Girard prompted lazily.

"No." Murdock's grin was centered entirely on his lips, an outward movement only. "And anybody can guess. Redfield must have weighed two hundred and thirty or so, and he was better than six feet tall; Cusick couldn't weigh a hundred twenty-five with a machine-gun under his arm."

Murdock shook his head, his smile fixed. "It didn't fit. Cusick could never have put up a fight against Mark Redfield, much less broken his finger. And Cusick was not the kind to get in a spot where he'd have to put up a fight. That kill was not his kind of a job. He was a gun-man from the word go, remember that. He carried a forty-five and he knew how to use it. If he had gone after Redfield, he would never have given Redfield a chance to get his own gun; certainly he would never have got close enough to risk a fight. A high-school boy could have taken Cusick with one hand. What made him so danger-ous was that he was well aware of the fact. Assuming that Redfield was alive when Cusick went back to get that twenty-five thousand, Cusick would have been in the driver's seat all the time he was in the room. He had technique; he was an expert."

Girard said: "It sounds all right."

"And by eliminating him," Murdock continued levelly, "only you and Archer were left. Either of you were physically able to do that kind of a job. Neither of you carries a gun. It looked to me as if someone came to Redfield's place and threatened him. He was drunk, and he might have been yellow. My guess is he pulled his gun and was too slow to use it.

"A little while after that I began to get interested in the case. Not to be the fair-haired boy and outsmart the police, but because I finally found the sort of girl I've wanted all my life, and I could not get rid of Hestor. I told you about putting Fenner on you that night. For a while I had no reason to doubt him, and I could find no motive why you should have killed Redfield. But I couldn't figure Archer either. He was hot-headed, he was in love with Redfield's wife; they'd had a fight. But I could not see him coming to kill Redfield deliberately. Yet if he had killed him at all, it had to be figured that way. Here's what I mean."

Murdock crushed out his cigarette and leaned forward again.

"He was seen coming back fifteen minutes or so after Redfield was killed. Now, if he had originally come to kill him, had killed him, he might have come earlier—come and gone out the back way—and come in again to make a better case for an alibi. But if he killed as Redfield *was* killed, probably on impulse and with no premeditation, he would not have bothered to sneak in the back way in the first place."

Girard's cigar ash dropped to his vest unnoticed and he said, grudgingly: "You think of things."

Murdock hesitated. He felt a certain stiffness to his body, as though he had been holding the same position for hours. He pulled his shoulders back, finally settled comfortably down in the chair.

Girard said: "You going to guess some more?"

"I might as well."

"Then"—Girard pulled himself out of the chair—"maybe we'd better have a drink." He stopped at the door. "This is one of the times when I wish I had a man; but I've never got used to having one around. I tried it once—a Jap. He got in my way."

He came back a few minutes later pushing a mahogany cellaret. "Name it," he said as he stopped beside his chair.

"I'll stick to Scotch," Murdock said.

"Soda?"

"Please."

Girard mixed Murdock's drink, poured out a whisky glass full of rye. "To crime!" he said sardonically, and took the whisky straight before he sat down.

Murdock realized his throat was dry, that he was genuinely thirsty, when he took his first swallow. He drank two-thirds of the highball quickly, then put the glass aside and lit another cigarette. Over the match-flame he watched Girard, and he began to see why the man had been so successful. He was calm, at ease, with an almost detached manner that was tolerant, polite. But for the alertness of his eyes, he might have been listening to a friendly account of a personal experience.

Murdock tossed the match into an ash-tray and settled himself in the chair again. "I didn't begin to get really hot about the thing until yesterday. I had just one good idea—that telephone call the killer made to Redfield's apartment. I'm not clear as to why he made it, although it might have been done with some idea of making it fit with an alibi. But it doesn't matter. ʃ '—Murdock moved the hand holding the cigarette in a careless arc— "it was interesting, and the police had not followed it up, as far as I knew. And I had a hunch on how I might run it down."

He explained his work with MacShane, and Girard's eyes widened. He said: "Neat," and Murdock continued:

"I didn't find out about it until this evening. In the meantime I'd talked to Hestor—last night. I was after a divorce and I told her about Fenner. There was something in her manner, in her reaction to my statement that you were there from three-thirty until five-thirty that morning, that really made me think I was wrong. I can't explain it, but I believe that little reaction did as much as anything to show me you were *not there*. And then this evening I found out for sure. You made a call from a lunch-room on Charles Street at around four-thirty the morning Redfield was murdered."

Murdock sucked on his cigarette, hesitated a moment, and when he continued he did not raise his voice or attempt to give any added emphasis. Actually the emphasis came from the very matter-of-factness of his tone.

"You knew you were going back to Redfield's when you left. And while you couldn't know about Fenner—although you might have seen him—you did not want anyone to see you leave Hestor's building. You went out the back way, went back to Redfield's place by the back way. You had a fight and he pulled the gun on you—the telephone was probably knocked off as he fell." Murdock shrugged. "You saw what you'd done. And then the phone rang when the operator called back." Murdock took a breath and shook his head. "That must have been a bad moment."

"It was," Girard said grimly.

"And then you got out as fast as you could—by the back way. As I said, I'm not quite sure why you called back, but it would not have been hard—at that hour—to get to this place unseen. There's no desk clerk or anything here, so this part was made to order. When Bacon got you down at headquarters, you told him you'd tell where you were only if charged with murder. And you were big enough to get away with it."

Murdock smiled wryly. "I suppose if they'd actually booked you, you'd got to Hestor and paid her to tell your story."

"I never got that far with the idea," Girard said.

"Tripp must have worried you," Murdock added dryly. "He saw you, huh? And you paid to stall him. And Cusick couldn't, or wouldn't, pay except with the gun."

"Tripp," Girard said, his voice angry for the first time, "was a fool! And yet"—he hesitated, his voice calming—"it's a nice break for me he was."

Girard smiled then, and pushed erect in his chair. "The way you tell it," he said, pouring another drink of rye, "it doesn't sound so bad. But you've overlooked the most important factor—from the standpoint of the police. There's no motive. Why should I want to—"

Murdock said: "It must have taken a lot of practice to get your kind of control." He grunted softly. "I don't think you went back to kill Redfield—but I can think of a reason why you might have had some idea. And as long as it doesn't cost anything to guess, I'll try it once more."

Murdock's voice was clipped, sharp. "*Redfield was so hard up he tipped off the police about Joe Cusick's murder so he could defend you and earn a fat fee.* You must have told him something about it."

Girard did not speak for fully a minute, and again from somewhere in the room came the rhythmic ticking of the clock. Murdock picked up his glass and finished his drink. Girard tossed off the rye and sucked at his lips. Then he said, flatly:

"Why didn't you tip off the police?"

"There's one reason," Murdock said. "And that one leads to another. Right now this second seems the more important. But"—Murdock's brows knitted in a scowl, and his eyes were brooding, troubled—"well, I'm just a button-pusher. It's not my job to condemn or acquit. You've always seemed like a decent sort to me. I rather like you, not that you give a damn; but like you or not, no matter how morally justifiable your motives might appear, I'd turn you in in a minute if I thought it would do any good!"

"I know you would," Girard said simply.

Murdock said: "Thanks. Believe it or not, it helps some to know that."

His lips tightened and he continued doggedly: "But I've been around long enough to recognize certain facts, and in this case—" He broke off, pushed out his lower lip. "I'd like to hear your story before I start the hard part. That is, if you want to tell it."

Girard stood up immediately, moved to the door. Opening this, he looked into the hall, closed the door, locked it. He came back to his chair, said: "I don't know why not. Nothing that's said here, with no witnesses, can do me any harm."

His lips, framed above by the clipped mustache, fashioned an enigmatic grin. He lit a fresh cigar, spoke in quick, low tones.

"It starts with Joe Cusick. And it's like I told you and everyone else. Strange as it may seem, I didn't kill him. You came the closest the night of the party when you said: 'But you know who did.' I do. Ever since I started bootlegging, I had a man with me. A bodyguard if you want to call him that, but he was more than that. A friend, and a damn good one."

"Nick Peters?" Murdock asked.

Girard nodded. "My man Friday. Well, he was here the night I got the call from Joe Cusick. Before I opened the door, I chased Nick into the bedroom. I didn't know who the caller was and sometimes it was better to seem to be alone. Anyway, Cusick came in with the gun in his hand. He came to the point immediately. He wanted money, but I knew that wasn't all. He was the same type as Sam, and I had an idea that once he got the money— But to hell with all that. I argued and when he lost his head and set himself with the gun, Nick let him have it from the doorway." Girard nodded his head towards the inner hall.

"And there we were. And that's where I made my first mistake. We might have made out all right with a self-defense plea. But I knew my reputation was against me;

I had never been mixed up in a killing, and I didn't want to stand trial—or have Nick take the rap for me. So I called Redfield. He came right over and we doped it out. To protect Nick, we decided to ship him to New York and get him out of the way. We carted Cusick's body down the back stairs, put it in a car which we found unlocked, and Nick drove it off. He was to take his own roadster and skip. I came back here, cleaned the rug, and went to bed. That's how the police found me."

Girard took the cigar from his mouth. It was out, but it did not seem to matter, because he put it back between his teeth and chewed on it as he apparently marshaled his thoughts.

"It didn't take me long to find out my mistake. There were plenty of breaks—all bad. The police found Cusick's unfired gun. That was bad enough. But the worst—" Girard shook his head, spoke bitterly. "Nick Peters was killed in an automobile accident early the next morning, near Rye. If you check you'll find a little paragraph in the papers. I had no witness at all then, and it was up to Redfield. The self-defense was out, unsubstantiated. They cut me off from newspapers," Girard continued slowly, "or I might have tumbled sooner. You see, I didn't know how the police got to my place, how they knew anything about the killing. I didn't find out until the trial was half over. But when I found out about the anonymous tip, I knew. I knew it had to be Peters or Redfield, and I was sure of Nick; he was that kind."

Girard laughed softly.

"So I was stuck. Redfield double-crossed me and I had to have him. I couldn't let on. Staying in jail didn't improve my mind. Fifty thousand to Redfield, another thirty for costs, experts, all that stuff. Two months in jail, and a harrowing sort of experience which pulled me right next to that electric chair.

"But I played along, and when I got the verdict, I threw the party at Redfield's—still playing along. Then, that night, I was going back there"—Girard's voice thinned out and took on a metallic hardness—"to even up in some way. I wanted to throw the fear of God into him; I wanted to get back that fifty thousand. Not because I was broke without it, but just—" He hesitated.

Murdock said: "I know."

Girard shrugged: "I went out the back way at Hestor's because I expected trouble. What, exactly, I didn't know. I had no gun; had no thought of murder; but I did want to see the dirty bastard squirm.

"You know the rest. When I told him what I thought, he denied it, naturally. But I kept after him, told him I'd get the money—the whole fifty thousand—or twist his filthy neck. Well, he went all to pieces. When he snatched the gun from the desk drawer, I grabbed him. I think that broken finger of his pulled the trigger."

Murdock blew out his breath and sat up in the chair. "Peters saved your life and you got him out of the way to give him a break. And Redfield double-crossed you into holding the bag. What a pay-off!"

"That isn't all," Girard said bitterly. "Cusick—Sam—came in Redfield's place before I could get out. I hid behind the living-room davenport." Girard grunted savagely. "He didn't stay long. But that's why he went after

you and Tripp. He thought, and he was probably right,
that the police—"

The telephone rang, interrupting him, and Girard
looked at it, startled. When he finally lifted the receiver
he said: "Hello—yes. Sure, just a minute." He turned
to Murdock. "For you."

The woman who answered was the *Courier-Herald*
operator. She said: "Mr. Wyman. Just a minute." There
was a pause, then Wyman's voice boomed across the wire.

"Hey, when you coming in?"

"Pretty soon," Murdock said. "A half-hour maybe."

"I'll wait. I want to see you."

"How did the shots come out?" Murdock's voice took
on new interest instinctively.

"Terrific! Terrific! Every God-damn one of 'em! The
hottest thing we've— But never mind. You hurry it up!"

Murdock felt the grin tug at his mouth. He went back
to his chair and sat down. He reached over and poured
another drink without bothering about ice.

Girard said: "That's about everything except the
phone call that you were smart enough to pin on me. But
for once you were wrong. I know why I did it at the time.
It may not sound convincing now, but I was rattled. I
never killed a man in my life until then and I couldn't
think quite as logically as I can now. And the hell of it
was I didn't know if he was dead or not.

"I never touched him after he dropped. I wasn't sure,
couldn't be sure. And I was panicky. If he was still alive,
it would make no difference to me and I wanted him to
have his chance. If he was dead I had to know, wanted

to hurry up the discovery. I waited here for the police."
Girard lifted one hand, let it drop to the chair arm.
"Looking at it now, it was just one of those dumb ideas.
But I was fogged, and I did it and—"

He broke off, shrugged as though dismissing an unpleasant subject. "That's the story. But you haven't yet
explained why you didn't turn me in—not all of the
answer."

Murdock put aside the drink untouched.

"I'll tell it to you another way," he said slowly. "I said
it was blackmail. This is it." His skin seemed to stretch
taut across his cheek-bones, like a banjo-head, and he
made an effort to speak deliberately.

"You're going to Europe. *Take Hestor!*"

Girard flushed. He shook his head negatively, but he
did not speak.

"Take her with you," Murdock said, his voice omi-
nously slow, "and get her to write me a note. I want her
to say she's tired of our arrangement, that she's going
with you and that I can have a divorce if I want it."

"Suppose she won't?" Girard said caustically.

"She will!" Murdock argued. "I know her. She will. It
will cost you something, but it will cost you more the
other way. And when you go I'll manage to be on hand
to get a couple pictures of you on board. That, and the
note, and Fenner's story will get me a divorce in a hurry."

"What if I don't?" Girard wanted to know.

"Then"—Murdock spread his hands and reached for
his drink—"I'll have to turn this stuff, this information,
over to Bacon."

"You couldn't convict—"

"Not in a million years," Murdock broke in brusquely. "And there you have the reason why I didn't turn you in. They can't convict. Tripp's dead. I've got a chance to prove you made the phone call; this picture of the money should prove you paid Tripp a thousand dollars. Against this, for the right sort of treatment—financial and other-wise—you can probably get Hestor to say you never left her apartment. You could probably persuade the lunch-counterman to change his mind—because you have dough. I'm not damn fool enough to kid myself about that. And if the D.A. tried you, and he might take a chance, Howard Archer and his sister and Rita Redfield would have to be dragged through the mess. There's no use in it, because if you get wise to yourself we can get round it. That's why I'm here.

"So make up your mind. Play ball with me or you'll play ball in the District Attorney's office." Murdock's voice was sharp now and there were beads of moisture on his forehead. "Because I'm going to crowd you. I'm in love with Joyce Archer and I want the chance to live a normal life with her. I'm going to get that chance. You do as I say or I'll talk to Bacon."

"You'd be a damn fool," Girard argued, "to raise the stink when they can't hang it on me. What good would it do to—"

"I guess I haven't made myself clear," Murdock cut in. "Maybe I should have expressed the idea in another way—or maybe you're too thick-headed or stubborn to see what I mean. I'll try it once more."

Murdock looked at the glass in his hand, seemed to be studying the sparkling amber liquid for a moment. His face was still white and tense, and when he looked back at Girard his eyes were hot and narrowed.

"You take Hestor so I can get a divorce," he said grimly, measuring his words and keeping his voice low, "or I'll turn you over to the District Attorney. And if I do, the only way you can stall off a prosecution is to prove your alibi. I've got just about enough half-baked evidence to make the D.A. curious. You'll have to prove—and Hestor will have to swear to it—that you were in her apartment. *And when you do that—and you will if he corners you—I'll have what I need to get a divorce.*

"There you have it." Murdock took a long drink and stood up. He shouldered his plate-case, retrieved his hat. A tight, mirthless smile stretched his lips flat, and his voice continued low, the emphasis in the meaning behind it rather than in any accented delivery.

"And that's the kind of a heel I can be. I'm going to crowd you. I can't convict you of anything, but by God I can get free of Hestor and I'm going to, one way or another. You've got your choice, but make up your mind."

Girard sat motionless until Murdock reached the door. Then he said: "Well," and stood up. The little smile that lifted the corners of his mouth and tugged at his mustache was passive and bitter and resigned.

Murdock said: "You might even marry her."

"No." Girard shook his head and continued to smile. "But like I said before, you think of things. I guess there's a break in it for both of us. You're entitled to yours; you sort of made it for yourself. And you offer me one and I

argue with you, huh?" He shook his head. "Just a chump
—always out of my class.

"The way you've got it figured out"—his tailored
shoulders moved in a suggestion of a shrug—"it's the sort
of an idea that grows on me. The south of France might
be a good place for both of us—for a while anyway.
Hestor may be expensive, but there are some compensa-
tions."

Murdock's lips curved, relieving the set look of his
mouth. Color began to ooze into his face. As he opened
the door and backed from the room he said: "And don't
forget the note, either."

23

C. A. WYMAN WAS smoking furiously and chewing the
end of his cigar as though he genuinely enjoyed the taste.
His thick, muscular face was flushed; his eyes were bright
with interest.

"And you're the guy," he said disgustedly, "that wants
to get out of the newspaper business."

Murdock stretched out his legs and surveyed the tips
of his shoes. His lean face was tired-looking now, but
there was something about the set of the mouth, the relaxed expression of his eyes, that lent an air of satisfaction
and contentment to his pose.

Wyman fidgeted in his chair, took out the cigar and
spat savagely at the cuspidor beside the desk. "You're

nuts!" he grunted. "Just like I told you. The way you and Doane turned this thing in tonight just proves what I—"

"Luck," Murdock grumbled.

"Luck? Sure. Everybody's got luck."

"I just happened to be there when it happened."

"Sure. But that isn't all." Wyman jabbed the cigar back in his teeth and swiveled it to its accustomed corner of his mouth. "You kept plugging. If you'd been sitting here in the office wearing out the seat of your pants like most of my trained seals, where'd you've been?

"The point is you get pictures. You've got brains and you use 'em to think with. When you get a chance, you know what to do. You know people, you get around, you—damn it! You get pictures and that's what interests me. Who cares how you get 'em."

Wyman pulled open a drawer of his desk and Murdock looked up. Wyman had a check in his hand. He scowled at it, growled: "You made a liar out of me. I didn't think you could do it, and I don't know yet how or why you put it over. But you did it. I'm giving Doane a raise for the story and his part, but it was you that had the idea and took him with you. Here, damn it!"

Murdock took the check, looked at it. He was conscious of a definite warmth to his blood, an inner glow of some kind that he could not analyze. It may have been his reaction to Wyman's praise; it may have been the knowledge that Girard would play his part; perhaps it was the thought that Joyce Archer was waiting for him. In any case he cast from his mind all doubt about the ethics, the moral responsibility of what he had done.

He still believed he was right. It was better for Howard and Rita, for Joyce, immeasurably so for himself. Even Hestor might get what she wanted. Girard would pay, but in a different way. But, and his eyes were at once morose with the thought, right or wrong, he was glad he'd worked it as he had.

He said: "No," and handed the check back to Wyman.

"No?" exploded Wyman. "No, hell! Take it, you earned it!"

Murdock grinned as Wyman pushed the check back. He picked it up, folded it neatly, and tore it in small pieces.

Wyman opened his mouth to speak, closed it with a snap, and seemed to collapse back in the chair. Murdock kept grinning.

"It wasn't a very good idea. I sort of forced you into meeting the *News* offer. Besides, the pay-off was on arrest and conviction and—"

"Cusick's dead," Wyman protested. "That's arrest and conviction enough. When the police are satisfied—"

"I don't like the idea of taking money under false pretenses," Murdock said enigmatically.

"What?" Wyman's face cracked in a puzzled scowl.

"Never mind," Murdock said hurriedly, and straightened up in his chair. "I've changed my mind about several things. Is that proposition of yours still open, about heading up the photograph department?"

This sort of conversation Wyman could understand. He recovered quickly and spoke naturally once more.

"Will you take it over?"

"On a contract?"

"I told you, write your own."

Murdock's grin broadened. "Suppose," he said slowly, "suppose I tell you what I want in it. If it's not too tough you can have it drawn up."

Wyman said: "Shoot!"

"Three years," Murdock began.

"Five," pressed Wyman.

"Well—"

"Check."

"And," Murdock seemed to be taking special pains with his words, "I think the ninety bucks a week you're paying me is probably more than I'm worth so let it ride for the first year. Make it a hundred for the next two and let it slide up to one fifty for the last two."

"Okay." Wyman was still grinning.

"Two weeks' vacation each year."

"Check."

"And don't forget it, either," Murdock said. "I've never been able to get two weeks at one time since I've been here."

"We'll take care of it from now on," Wyman said. "That's all?"

"One thing more." Murdock hesitated. "My spare time is to be my own to do all the experimenting I want on advertising work or portraits or anything else that isn't newspaper stuff. Because some day I might change my mind after all."

"You won't," Wyman said, and put out his hand.

The clasp was firm, hard. Murdock stood up and put on his hat. "I've got two more unofficial requests," he said.

"I'd like a two weeks' bonus for signing the contract. A two weeks' vacation." His lip lifted and the corners of his eyes wrinkled with a smile. "I want to make it a honeymoon."

"A—" Wyman was speechless.

"Yeah," Murdock said. "Which hinges on the other request. I'm getting evidence—divorce evidence—together. I'll have all I need within a week. When I get it, I want you to pull every string you can think of to put through a decree for me in a hurry."

"Can do," Wyman said, and, taking out a fresh cigar from a partly opened desk drawer, sank back in his chair with a sigh and the satisfied air of a man well pleased with himself and temporarily content to rest on his laurels.

Joyce Archer was sitting bolt upright in the wing chair. She did not move when Murdock opened the door, nor when he closed it. She did not move when he moved towards her and stopped in front of her chair. The concentrated rays of the floor lamp put her face, her eyes, in shadows and he did not sense her mood until he bent down and put his hands on the chair arms.

He saw then that her face was somber, tight-lipped; that there was a sullen, hostile look in the smoky-blue eyes. The intensity of her gaze made him forget his own elation. He felt a certain helplessness before her, all the more poignant because he did not understand it. He said:

"What's the matter?"

"You said you'd let me know just as soon as—"

"Oh." Murdock breathed a sigh of relief and laughed

lightly. That was rather a mistake; he realized it when the hostile expression remained unchanged. He said: "I came as soon as I could," defensively. "I had to go to the paper and—"

"You could have called me."

"Yes, I—"

"You didn't think of it," she challenged.

Murdock straightened up then, and his mood reacted to hers as it had done the first time he ever saw her. Anticipation had fired his imagination; the let-down was all the more severe and he found a stiffness in his voice when he spoke.

"I wanted to tell you myself," he said. "I knew you would be here and I loved you for deciding to wait. The news I had was good, too good, I thought, to tell over the telephone. I wanted to get my arms around you before I—"

Joyce Archer forgot her grudge, her complaint, or whatever it was. Instantly she dropped the sullen, hostile mask; her tanned face was alive, her eyes bright, sparkling.

"Good news? You mean about Hestor?"

Murdock could not shake off his own resentment so quickly. He backed up, sat down on the davenport.

"They got Cusick tonight," he said finally. "He came to kill Girard. I happened to be there, but the police—"

"Oh!" Joyce Archer's cheeks whitened and a hand flew to her throat. "That's why you had the gun. You didn't use it? You didn't have to—"

Murdock shook his head, and his resentment vanished with the appreciation of her concern. "No, I didn't use it. Some day I'll tell you the whole story. It's too long now. The police shot Cusick, arrested a witness to prove he killed Tripp. It sort of cleans up the Redfield job. You won't have to worry about Howard—"

Joyce Archer came out of the chair with a single lithe movement. She ran to the davenport and gave a little jump which landed her on her knees at Murdock's side and facing opposite him.

"Oh, Kent," she wailed, "I'm such a little beast! But it seemed so long, and I worried so. I called the office twice and they said you hadn't come back and—"

She put her head down with a little sob. Murdock reached out and her arm went around his neck as he crushed her to him. For five minutes there was no need for talk; they just clung together until she let her arm slip from his neck. Murdock lifted his head and slackened his hold while they caught their breath; then Joyce Archer snuggled down with her head and shoulders in his lap.

"Then it's all right—about Hestor?" she asked him finally.

Murdock nodded. "I've got what I wanted—what I needed. And I don't think I'll have to be bothered with alimony."

"How long will—"

"Two weeks—a month, maybe. No longer."

It seemed impossible that Joyce Archer's blue eyes could brighten any more, but they did. "Then you're not going to New York. You won't have to give up your job?"

Murdock kept smiling.

"Why do you say it that way?"

"You like it, don't you? Your work?"

"I like it now. And I've got sort of a raise. I mean there'll be enough to keep us alive anyway, and I'll have some time to keep on with my experiments. But"—Murdock broke off, then continued bluntly: "There's no social prestige in being married to a fellow with my kind of job."

Joyce Archer's eyes clouded, fastened on Murdock's lapel. "All my life," she said, with just a shade of bitterness, "I've had social prestige; some little bit at least. It never brought me happiness or love or very much kindness. If I have the chance to have all three with you—"

Murdock bent down and kissed the moist warm lips lightly, as though kissing a little girl.

She would not be denied. She smiled at him, but she kept talking the moment he let her.

"Your work is yours alone. It doesn't make any difference what it is, does it, so long as it's your job? If you like it, and you are good at it—and you are—you'll come home happy. That's what matters. Be happy in your work and save the rest of yourself for me."

They were silent then, for a minute or so, content with their individual thoughts. Joyce broke the mood first. Struggling, helped by Murdock's arms, she got turned around and sat down beside him.

"A month seems long."

Murdock grinned. "To me, yes. But you"—the grin broadened—"it'll be short enough when you start to get your clothes together. And we'll have two weeks—a poor man's vacation. And I've got a ring." He looked away.

"I hope you'll like it. It's in a safe-deposit box. It was

my mother's. Just a thin gold band with a solitaire. Maybe it's a little old-fashioned, but the diamond is quite good and—"

"Did Hestor—" Joyce Archer began, her voice troubled.

"No," Murdock said. "It was in the same box then. We were married Saturday night. By Monday I didn't think—I wasn't so sure I wanted her to have it. I bought her another."

"I'd love it," she said, and kissed him. He held her tightly and she said: "I don't want to go."

Murdock said: "I don't want you to, but—"

She said: "But," and got quickly to her feet, snatching up her camel's-hair coat from the arm of the davenport as she moved. "But—" she smiled until he smiled back at her and stood up.

"But what?" he demanded.

"But you've done such a good job of keeping me respectable, it's time you had a little co-operation, don't you think?"

"Now that you mention it," Murdock said, grinning until his teeth flashed in the reflected light, "I do. I may not be entitled to a respectable wife, but it sounds like a good idea. If we start respectable and you spend enough time on me, maybe you can fix it so I can keep respectable and still be a button-pusher."

THE PERENNIAL LIBRARY MYSTERY SERIES

E. C. Bentley

TRENT'S LAST CASE
"One of the three best detective stories ever written."
—Agatha Christie

TRENT'S OWN CASE
"I won't waste time saying that the plot is sound and the detection satisfying. Trent has not altered a scrap and reappears with all his old humor and charm."
—Dorothy L. Sayers

Gavin Black

A DRAGON FOR CHRISTMAS
"Potent excitement!"
—New York Herald Tribune

THE EYES AROUND ME
"I stayed up until all hours last night reading *The Eyes Around Me*, which is something I do not do very often, but I was so intrigued by the ingeniousness of Mr. Black's plotting and the witty way in which he spins his mystery. I can only say that I enjoyed the book enormously."
—F. van Wyck Mason

YOU WANT TO DIE, JOHNNY?
"Gavin Black doesn't just develop a pressure plot in suspense, he adds uninfected wit, character, charm, and sharp knowledge of the Far East to make rereading as keen as the first race-through." —Book Week

Nicholas Blake

THE BEAST MUST DIE
"It remains one more proof that in the hands of a really first-class writer the detective novel can safely challenge comparison with any other variety of fiction."
—The Manchester Guardian

THE CORPSE IN THE SNOWMAN
"If there is a distinction between the novel and the detective story (which we do not admit), then this book deserves a high place in both categories."
—The New York Times

THE DREADFUL HOLLOW
"Pace unhurried, characters excellent, reasoning solid."
—San Francisco Chronicle

END OF CHAPTER
". . . admirably solid . . . an adroit formal detective puzzle backed up by firm characterization and a knowing picture of London publishing."
—*The New York Times*

HEAD OF A TRAVELER
"Another grade A detective story of the right old jigsaw persuasion."
—*New York Herald Tribune Book Review*

MINUTE FOR MURDER
"An outstanding mystery novel. Mr. Blake's writing is a delight in itself."
—*The New York Times*

THE MORNING AFTER DEATH
"One of Blake's best."
—Rex Warner

A PENKNIFE IN MY HEART
"Style brilliant . . . and suspenseful."
—*San Francisco Chronicle*

A QUESTION OF PROOF
"The characters in this story are unusually well drawn, and the suspense is well sustained."
—*The New York Times*

THE SAD VARIETY
"It is a stunner. I read it instead of eating, instead of sleeping."
—Dorothy Salisbury Davis

THE SMILER WITH THE KNIFE
"An extraordinarily well written and entertaining thriller."
—*Saturday Review of Literature*

THOU SHELL OF DEATH
"It has all the virtues of culture, intelligence and sensibility that the most exacting connoisseur could ask of detective fiction."
—*The Times* [London] *Literary Supplement*

THE WHISPER IN THE GLOOM
"One of the most entertaining suspense-pursuit novels in many seasons."
—*The New York Times*

THE WIDOW'S CRUISE
"A stirring suspense. . . . The thrilling tale leaves nothing to be desired."
—*Springfield Republican*

THE WORM OF DEATH
"It [The Worm of Death] is one of Blake's very best—and his best is better than almost anyone's."
—Louis Untermeyer

George Harmon Coxe

MURDER WITH PICTURES

"[Coxe] has hit the bull's-eye with his first shot."

— *The New York Times*

Edmund Crispin

BURIED FOR PLEASURE

"Absolute and unalloyed delight."—Anthony Boucher, *The New York Times*

Kenneth Fearing

THE BIG CLOCK

"It will be some time before chill-hungry clients meet again so rare a compound of irony, satire, and icy-fingered narrative. *The Big Clock* is . . . a psychothriller you won't put down." —*Weekly Book Review*

Andrew Garve

A HERO FOR LEANDA

"One can trust Mr. Garve to put a fresh twist to any situation, and the ending is really a lovely surprise." —*The Manchester Guardian*

THE ASHES OF LODA

"Garve . . . embellishes a fine fast adventure story with a more credible picture of the U.S.S.R. than is offered in most thrillers."

—*The New York Times Book Review*

THE CUCKOO LINE AFFAIR

". . . an agreeable and ingenious piece of work." —*The New Yorker*

MURDER THROUGH THE LOOKING GLASS

". . . refreshingly out-of-the-way and enjoyable . . . highly recommended to all comers." —*Saturday Review*

NO TEARS FOR HILDA

"It starts fine and finishes finer. I got behind on breathing watching Max get not only his man but his woman, too." —Rex Stout

THE RIDDLE OF SAMSON

"The story is an excellent one, the people are quite likable, and the writing is superior." —*Springfield Republican*

BLOOD AND JUDGMENT

"Gilbert readers need scarcely be told that the characters all come alive at first sight, and that his surpassing talent for narration enhances any plot. . . . Don't miss."   —*San Francisco Chronicle*

THE BODY OF A GIRL

"Does what a good mystery should do: open up into all kinds of ramifications, with untold menace behind the action. At the end, there is a bang-up climax, and it is a pleasure to see how skilfully Gilbert wraps everything up."   —*The New York Times Book Review*

THE DANGER WITHIN

"Michael Gilbert has nicely combined some elements of the straight detective story with plenty of action, suspense, and adventure, to produce a superior thriller."   —*Saturday Review*

DEATH HAS DEEP ROOTS

"Trial scenes superb; prowl along Loire vivid chase stuff; funny in right places; a fine performance throughout."   —*Saturday Review*

FEAR TO TREAD

"Merits serious consideration as a work of art."
                                                    —*The New York Times*

C. W. Grafton

BEYOND A REASONABLE DOUBT

"A very ingenious tale of murder . . . a brilliant and gripping narrative."
                    —Jacques Barzun and Wendell Hertig Taylor

Edward Grierson

THE SECOND MAN

"One of the best trial-testimony books to have come along in quite a while."   —*The New Yorker*

Cyril Hare

AN ENGLISH MURDER

"By a long shot, the best crime story I have read for a long time. Everything is traditional, but originality does not suffer. The setting is perfect. Full marks to Mr. Hare."   —*Irish Press*

(Cyril Hare continued)

TRAGEDY AT LAW
"An extremely urbane and well-written detective story."
—*The New York Times*

UNTIMELY DEATH
"The English detective story at its quiet best, meticulously underplayed, rich in perceivings of the droll human animal and ready at the last with a neat surprise which has been there all the while had we but wits to see it." —*New York Herald Tribune Book Review*

WHEN THE WIND BLOWS
"The best, unquestionably, of all the Hare stories, and a masterpiece by any standards."
—Jacques Barzun and Wendell Hertig Taylor, *A Catalogue of Crime*

WITH A BARE BODKIN
"One of the best detective stories published for a long time."
—*The Spectator*

James Hilton

WAS IT MURDER?
"The story is well planned and well written."
—*The New York Times*

Francis Iles

BEFORE THE FACT
"Not many 'serious' novelists have produced character studies to compare with Iles's internally terrifying portrait of the murderer in *Before the Fact*, his masterpiece and a work truly deserving the appellation of unique and beyond price." —Howard Haycraft

MALICE AFORETHOUGHT
"It is a long time since I have read anything so good as *Malice Aforethought*, with its cynical humour, acute criminology, plausible detail and rapid movement. It makes you hug yourself with pleasure."
—H. C. Harwood, *Saturday Review*

Lange Lewis

THE BIRTHDAY MURDER
"Almost perfect in its playlike purity and delightful prose."
—Jacques Barzun and Wendell Hertig Taylor

LUCKY DEVIL
"The plot unravels at a fast clip, the writing is breezy and Maling's approach is as fresh as today's stockmarket quotes."
—*Louisville Courier Journal*

RIPOFF
"A swiftly paced story of today's big business is larded with intrigue as a Ralph Nader-type investigates an insurance scandal and is soon on the run from a hired gun and his brother. . . . Engrossing and credible."
—*Booklist*

SCHROEDER'S GAME
"As the title indicates, this Schroeder is up to something, and the unravelling of his game is a diverting and sufficiently blood-soaked entertainment."
—*The New Yorker*

Julian Symons

THE BELTING INHERITANCE
"A superb whodunit in the best tradition of the detective story."
—August Derleth, *Madison Capital Times*

BLAND BEGINNING
"Mr. Symons displays a deft storytelling skill, a quiet and literate wit, a nice feeling for character, and detectival ingenuity of a high order."
—Anthony Boucher, *The New York Times*

BOGUE'S FORTUNE
"There's a touch of the old sardonic humour, and more than a touch of style."
—*The Spectator*

THE BROKEN PENNY
"The most exciting, astonishing and believable spy story to appear in years.
—Anthony Boucher, *The New York Times Book Review*

THE COLOR OF MURDER
"A singularly unostentatious and memorably brilliant detective story."
—*New York Herald Tribune Book Review*

THE 31ST OF FEBRUARY
"Nobody has painted a more gruesome picture of the advertising business since Dorothy Sayers wrote 'Murder Must Advertise', and very few people have written a more entertaining or dramatic mystery story."
—*The New Yorker*